THE KILLING PIT

A JAKE PETTMAN THRILLER BY

WES MARKIN

ABOUT THE AUTHOR

Wes Markin is the bestselling author of the DCI Yorke crime novels set in Salisbury. His latest series, The Yorkshire Murders, stars the compassionate and relentless DCI Emma Gardner. He is also the author of the Jake Pettman thrillers set in New England. Wes lives in Harrogate with his wife and two children, close to the crime scenes in The Yorkshire Murders.

You can find out more at:

www.wesmarkinauthor.com

facebook.com/wesmarkinauthor

PRAISE FOR WES MARKIN

"An explosive and visceral debut with the most terrifying of killers. Wes Markin is a new name to watch out for in crime fiction, and I can't wait to see more of DCI Yorke." – **Stephen Booth, Bestselling Crime Author**

"A pool of blood, an abduction, swirling blizzards, a haunting mystery, yes, Wes Markin's One Last Prayer has all the makings of an absorbing thriller. I recommend that you give it a go." – **Alan Gibbons, Bestselling Author**

"Cracking start to an exciting new series. Twist and turns, thrills and kills. I loved it." – **Ross Greenwood, Bestselling Author**

"Markin stuns with his latest offering... Mind-bendingly dark and deep, you know it's not for the faint hearted from page one. Intricate plotting, devious twists and excellent characterisation take this tale to a whole new level. Any

serious crime fan will love it!" – **Owen Mullen, Bestselling Author**

BY WES MARKIN

DCI Yorke Thrillers

One Last Prayer

The Repenting Serpent

The Silence of Severance

Rise of the Rays

Dance with the Reaper

Christmas with the Conduit

Better the Devil

A Lesson in Crime

Jake Pettman Thrillers

The Killing Pit

Fire in Bone

Blue Falls

The Rotten Core

Rock and a Hard Place

The Yorkshire Murders

The Viaduct Killings

The Lonely Lake Killings

The Cave Killings

Details of how to claim your **FREE** DCI Michael Yorke quick read, **A lesson in Crime**, can be found at the end of this book.

Text copyright © 2021 Wes Markin

First published: 2021

ISBN: 9798721034015

Imprint: Dark Heart Publishing

Edited by Brian Paone

Cover design by Cherie Foxley

For Carly and Warren

1

B LAKE THOMPSON DIDN'T want his family to die, but he knew there was very little he could do about it. They were already at the killing pit. He stared at his kidnapper.

Just like his father, Ayden MacLeoid had eyes which gave nothing away—hunter's eyes.

"Please," Blake said. "Whatever you think—"

One of the MacLeoid soldiers swung his Remington 700, and the butt stock set Blake's world on fire.

He fell to his knees and tried to focus through the flames. He heard the yapping of dogs far in the distance, one of his sons weeping next to him, the snigger of one of the thugs, and God-knows-what shuffling in the pit behind him.

When the fire dissipated, Blake spat out a tooth. It wasn't the first this evening. If anyone saw fit to look for him, they could follow his teeth like breadcrumbs to this dark hollow in the woods.

He glanced at his two trembling sons, Devin and Sean, on either side of him. On this cold April night, the wind blustered over the vast MacLeoid land before being slivered into spears by the branches of the twisted trees and their foliage. To say it was these spears that made his children quiver would be a falsehood. It was the yawning hole behind them and the armed thugs blocking their escape route that made them shake.

The kidnappers wore charcoal foam nose plugs. He recognized them because he'd used them before to dispose of animal carcasses in his own farmyard. Blake couldn't smell the stench coming from the fifteen-foot circular pit behind him, because a Remington butt had smashed his nose back at his home. Beside him, Devin winced, while Sean had already vomited down his front.

One of the three soldiers—all mid-twenties, same as his sons—checked his watch. "It's almost ten—"

"Shut up, Cole," Ayden said, fixating on Blake.

Blake, a religious man, broke eye contact with the younger MacLeoid and looked for support from beyond the clear skies. He found none, and instead watched a flurry of birds draw dark veins on the full moon before lowering his eyes to earth and the present moment.

Jotham Quimby MacLeoid stepped from the woodland, wearing a deerstalker and a fur hunting jacket. A rifle was slung over one shoulder. He clutched the rifle strap with one hand to stop it from bouncing. The ends of his shoulder-length gray hair rose on the spears of wind and across his heavily bearded face. This farmer, like Blake, was also in his sixties. They'd been in the same class at school. Blake was aware this would entitle him to nothing.

Jotham's son, Ayden, and his three soldiers shuffled backward to allow the property owner to walk between them and the three captives like a guard of honor. He kept his head down. After passing Devin, he stopped beside

2

Blake, who was still on his knees, and turned to look down at him.

Blake looked up into eyes framed by rough, knotty skin. *Familiar eyes. Hunter's eyes.*

Jotham had not opted for nose plugs.

Because his hands were lashed behind his back, Blake tried to use his shoulder to rub away the blood and spit running down his chin but failed. He wasn't flexible enough. "Jo, I think there's been a misunderstanding."

Jotham removed a hand from the strap of his rifle, ran the palm of it down the front of his hunting jacket to dry it of sweat and placed it on Blake's right shoulder. It was a strong grip but not one intended to cause pain and so seemed to carry the same meaning as a firm handshake. "Agreed." Jotham squeezed Blake's shoulder. "And we're here to put it right. But first, I'm sorry. I didn't expect them to treat you so badly." He took his hand off Blake's shoulder and eyed Ayden, who immediately looked away. "Seems it's an evening of many misunderstandings." When he turned back, he was smiling. His eyes narrowed, and his flesh wrinkled and swelled around them, but they continued to pierce. He opened his mouth to speak—

"We haven't done anything," Devin said, weeping. "We wouldn't be that stupid."

Blake glared at his son. "Devin, mind your manners." Blake focused on Jotham. "I'm sorry, Jo. Youngsters these days, you know."

Jotham shrugged. "It's fine. I'm sure we spoke our minds back when, eh?"

Blake smiled. It was excruciating; they'd made a mess of his face. He nodded, forcing back the pain, sensing some hope in the rapport he was building with Jotham.

"Do you know why I chose to dig the pit here?" Jotham pointed down.

A shiver ran down Blake's spine. *No, not that infernal hole. Let's discuss anything but that.* He shook his head.

"I've a lot of land. Too much, I wonder. It's hard to keep control of it all. There's so much *energy* in nature." He raised a finger, commanding their silence. He kept it there for a short time. "Can you hear it? Crackling?"

All Blake heard was the wind in the trees and the shuffling in the pit behind him, but he nodded, desperate to humor Jotham.

"Here is where it is strongest, Blake. The energy. Right here, where you kneel. Something about these trees." He pointed at the branches reaching like long, gnarled fingers, beckoning to them. "So, this is where I came to take control. Have I chosen right, Blake?"

"Of course, Jo. No one questions your authority."

Jotham brushed long hair from his eyes. One of his eyebrows was raised.

"No one," Blake said.

Jotham smiled again. He took a long, deep breath through his nose. He looked as if he was enjoying the stench that was repulsing Devin and Sean. He stepped alongside Blake so he was on the edge of his pit.

Blake realized he could throw his weight against the old bastard and send him sprawling into his own hellhole. But then what? Face down four rifles? He felt Jotham's hand on his shoulder again—firm and tight.

"If you answer this question now, Blake, only one of your beloved family has to go into the pit this evening."

Blake felt as if an invisible hand had reached in and clutched his heart. "Jo, I ... I—"

Jotham shushed him. *"Only one, Blake.* My gift to you.

Remember the importance of control? Please take the amount of control I'm offering you."

Blake opened his mouth to reply, but nothing came out, and before he knew it, Jotham was speaking again. "Your sons' contributions have been light. Maybe it was only one of your little bastards, maybe it was both, but it's up to you to set the record straight." His hand remained clamped to Blake's shoulder.

The farmer still had his mouth open. "I don't know anything about this. Jo ... please. This is the first I've heard of it!"

"Again, that maybe so ... maybe, maybe. Look, Blake. Sometimes the actual truth can be irrelevant. But what is relevant is we have something to maintain the illusion. Without it, I could lose control. I could lose everything."

"Jo, they're good boys ..." Tears formed in the corners of his eyes.

"Blake. If you give one of your sons to the pit and we restore equilibrium, you and your other son get to go home."

"Dad," Sean said, crying harder now and struggling to speak, "*I didn't do anything.*"

My most gentle boy, Sean, always so sensitive. Your mother's favourite.

"I didn't skim either, Dad. He's wrong. He's got it so fucking wrong."

And then there was Devin. Headstrong. A man always on fire. He looked between his two sons.

"I must press you for a choice, Blake. I have to get back. My dogs are expecting their supper."

Blake glared up at Jotham. Gone was any attempt to build rapport, to humor him. The rumours were true. The bastard reserved whatever compassion he did possess for his dogs. "It was me," Blake said, crying as hard as Sean now. "I forced them to do it. I told them to keep some back for us. These last couple years have been awful. The farm is—"

Jotham took his hand from Blake's shoulder and stepped backward. "Make a choice."

"*It was me!*" Blake's voice rose as he spit a mixture of saliva, tears, and blood.

Jotham sighed. "That's not an illusion I can sell."

Blake looked between the long, pale faces of his two boys again. He wished he could embrace both, draw them tight against him. He loved his children so very much. "You can't make me choose between my boys. You just can't."

"I respect that. I genuinely do." Jotham nodded and raised his hand. "I also anticipated it."

Two people emerged from the same patch of trees where Jotham had.

Blake recognized the taller of the two —Anthony Rogers. His dad owned the general store on Main Street. Anthony had helped on the Thompson farm a few years back before he'd taken up work with Jotham—a fate that now befell most of the youth in Blue Falls.

Anthony held the arm of a much smaller person. A burlap sack was over their head.

A child? Blake thought. *Surely not a child?* As they neared, Blake saw her familiar dirty gray jumper and muddy white Converse sneakers, and he felt his world turning in on itself. "No ... no ... It can't ..."

Then, her cries—the final confirmation it was Maddie, even before Anthony brought her close and removed the sack. Her mouth was taped, and her cheeks were streaked with black eyeliner. Her eyes met Blake's, and she broke away from Anthony. She managed to make it all the way to her father before one of the other soldiers seized her arm and dragged her back again.

"Let go of my daughter!" Blake lurched forward on his knees. "She's *fifteen*!"

Cole, another of the MacLeoid army, stepped forward and kicked Blake in the side, knocking all the air from his body.

He folded over, pressed his face to the cold soil and gasped for air.

"It may seem cruel, Blake, but smaller empires than this one were built on crueller acts," Jotham said.

Taking another gulp of air, Blake sat upright. "Please ... not my daughter ... not my daughter, not my Maddie. She never hurt anyone! Please, Jo! I'll give you anything!"

Jotham pushed back Blake's damp, thinning hair. "There is nothing you can give me, Blake. I gave you the opportunity. I told you one of your family would go into the pit. You could have chosen."

"I'll choose then. Take one of my sons if you must! It's their fault! But not her ... *Anyone* but her!"

"But this suits me now, Blake. Don't you see? It makes no sense to rewind the clock and change the outcome. The punishment is just, and I get to retain both of my mules." Jotham turned to his son. "Ayden, the blade."

Ayden shook his head.

"What?" Jotham said.

"Cole wants to this time."

"I didn't ask Cole."

"I don't mind, sir," Cole said.

Jotham held up a finger in Cole's direction without looking at him. He kept his eyes firmly on Ayden's.

"Please, Father, let Cole. I don't feel so—"

"Cole," Jotham said without breaking eye contact. "Give my boy the blade."

"Yes, sir." Cole handed the hunting knife to Ayden.

"Now, Ayden ..." Jotham paused to take a deep breath. "I want you to cut her."

"Dad, I—"

"Cut. Her."

Blake screamed from the ground and tried to get to his feet.

Another of Jotham's men pressed him to the ground by his shoulders.

"Get your fucking hands off me!"

"Isaac, keep the rifles on the two brothers," Jotham said.

"Yes, sir," Isaac said, readying his rifle.

"Do something Devin! Sean! This is your sister!" Blake shouted.

"They'll shoot us," Devin said.

"Fucking cowards," Blake said and writhed when he felt the soldier's knee in his back, then he was pinned face down. He managed to raise his eyes to see Anthony still holding his trembling daughter, and Ayden was on his knees, holding her foot, with the serrated edge of the knife next to her heel.

Jotham said, "Slightly higher than last time. Less mess."

When Ayden looked up at Jotham, Blake noticed Ayden's hunter's eyes were no more. They must have been for show. He was as scared as he was.

"Do it!"

Ayden sliced. Blood bubbled from her heel.

Maddie threw back her head. The wail rumbled deep inside her but never found the air because of the tape across her mouth. Her leg buckled, but Anthony held her upright.

"No! Stop ... *please!*" Blake shouted.

Jotham looked at Anthony. "Throw her in."

Anthony's eyes widened. He looked down at Ayden kneeling.

"What are you looking at him for?" Jotham asked. "Throw her in."

Blake pleaded. "Anthony ... remember, you used to play with Maddie on the farm. You used to chase her around the barn—"

"*Throw her in!*" Jotham shouted.

Anthony swallowed. His Adam's apple bobbed up and down. He threw her. There was a moment of silence and then a thump.

"Maddie ..." Blake said, wanting to reach toward the pit but unable to because his hands were bound. "Maddie." Tears streamed down his face. He pinned his face to the soil and squeezed his eyes shut. He heard his daughter's loud moaning from the pit. He heard the shuffling noises from earlier intensifying. He didn't want to hear. He rocked his head from side to side, rubbing dirt into his face. But he could still hear.

Rustling, movement, moaning ...

"*No! God, no! My Maddie! What have you done?*"

He could hear the bastard's voice. The hot breath on the back of his neck was the only evidence that it wasn't coming from within himself. "And now, Blake, we will take you home. But remember. The killing pit is always hungry. To anyone who asks, your daughter is out of town, now living with relatives. Should the story change, then we might just find ourselves back here ... feeding the earth all over again."

When the acoustic band started to ruin a Bryan Adams classic, Jake Pettman decided enough was enough. He finished his drink and winced. It was one of the worst IPAs he'd ever tasted.

"I'll get that," the barmaid who'd served him earlier said.

He put down the glass and kept his hand over the rim. "It's fine. You've got your hands full."

She smiled. "Wow. Have I stumbled upon a British gentleman?"

Jake nodded at the stack of glasses in her hand. "No. I just don't want to end up in hospital."

"Go on," she said with another smile. "Let me impress you."

He shrugged and took his hand off the glass.

She picked it up and added it to the stack.

He smiled. "Impressed. Now, can you juggle them on the way back?"

"If you want a show, there's a band over there."

"Is that what they are? I thought they were here to repair the instruments."

"Don't let old George hear you talking like that. He's been playing here for as long as anyone can remember."

"I guess if the customers could remember, they wouldn't be here?"

She raised an eyebrow.

"Sorry, just being an idiot."

"Well, most out-of-towners are. Where do you come from?"

"Wiltshire. South of England."

"I'd love to say I've heard of it."

"Stonehenge?"

She nodded. "Impressive. It's on my bucket list."

"Take it off. They fenced it off years ago. They won't let you up close any more."

"Well, we can't offer you history like that, but you could

10

take a look at the River Skweda. The main reason tourists come is to fish. Is that why you're here?"

"No, never heard of it."

She pointed at an oil painting of the serious-looking elderly man in a red military uniform on the wall behind Jake. "Captain William Ross. He was awarded Rosstown Plantation in 1765 for services in the Battle of Quebec. River Skweda ran through the heart of it. This painting is from 1801, the year our town, Blue Falls, was established on the Skweda. The first of three towns."

"Well, he doesn't look too happy about the establishment of Blue Falls. Maybe that's why he set up two more?"

"No, not him. Blue Falls was his swansong. He died this same year. He drank a lot. As many did." She scanned the Taps. "As many do. History books say he was lucky to have made it as long as he did. The next two towns, Sharon Edge and New Lincoln, came much later. The Skweda divides them."

In the background, George and his acoustic band had broken into "American Pie." The locals had responded in kind and taken to the dancefloor.

"A bit easier on the ear, I admit," Jake said.

"Wait for the second verse when the crowd joins in. So, who are you, and why're you here?"

Jake laughed. "Straight to the point. My name is Jake. I'm descended from a family who used to live in Blue Falls."

"Who?"

"Way back when, in the times you've just been talking about. They're long gone now."

"Try me. The suspense is killing me."

"Heard of the Bickfords?"

"The family who founded here? The Taps?"

"Yes. You know a lot." He pointed at the swelling crowd. "Unfortunately, it didn't stay in the family. It looks as if it's quite profitable."

"Yes. It weathered the downturn well and, despite declining tourism and being practically isolated from the rest of Maine, it does good business."

Jake had noticed the dancefloor was covered in peanut shells on the way in. "Why the shells?"

"A custom since your ancestors opened the bar. Barrels of peanuts. No need to use a bin."

"Don't they slip over?"

"Some do, but that is more likely down to the drinking than the shells."

Jake nodded. "Well, I was about to head off. Thanks for the conversation. It's the only decent one I've had this week. You really know your history."

"You sound surprised."

"Why would I be?"

"Maybe you just see a barmaid."

He laughed. "Look, I come from a liberal place. I see an educated woman doing a job to pay bills, like the rest of us."

"Good." She smiled. "Actually, my knowledge of history isn't that great. I know the Bickfords founded Blue Falls Tap, but I've no idea why they left."

"Don't think anyone really does. There're lots of rumors. None of them pretty, so we'll leave them alone for now. The good thing is ... sorry, I haven't asked your name."

"Piper."

"The good thing is, Piper, that some of the Bickfords stayed dotted around Maine and Vermont, right down to my mother's parents. So, I have a passport."

"So, you're here to stay?" She raised an eyebrow.

"I'll let you in on a secret, Piper." He leaned in. "I've no idea what I'm doing."

Here came the second verse. The guitarists hit their acoustics hard, and the crowd soared into song.

Jake said loudly, "Well, there goes the conversation!"

"I have to get back and serve anyway. You see my grumpy colleague?"

"Would that be the one staring right at us with the forehead like a freshly plowed field?"

"The very one."

"I'll walk with you. All this talking has made me thirsty. I think I'll give the IPA a miss though."

———

PIPER GOODWIN PULLED a glass of Stinson IPA, placed it on the bar for old Isaiah, took a handful of dollars from his worn-out laboring hands and stared at Jake. Until this point, Chief of Police Gabriel Jewell was one of the tallest men she'd ever come across, but this man right here had just stolen the accolade. He was broad, strong-looking, and attractive.

She refocused on her customer. "Thanks, Isaiah."

"You keep the change now."

Piper smiled. "I was planning on doing so."

"Feisty as ever," Isaiah, who was deep into a retirement filled with late nights and strong drinks, winked and shimmied toward his friends congregating in front of George and the band as they prepared to deliver their trademark final set—acoustic rock ballads from Bon Jovi and Aerosmith to wind down the crowd.

Piper stole a glance at her cellphone—10:15 p.m. and still no sign of Maddie. She texted her for the fifth time and tried to ring her mother again. Still no answer. She hoped all was well at the Thompsons' and set off from behind the bar to collect the glasses Maddie would normally be swooping for.

As she neared the dancefloor, she felt peanut shells crush under her sneakers and thanked her lucky stars, as she always did, that she wasn't the cleaner who'd be sweeping up this mess come Saturday morning. After she'd circled the Taps and greeted a few locals who were still sober enough to greet her back coherently, she eyed Jake again. She noticed that his long, chiselled face was not unlike Captain William Ross's face depicted in an oil painting from 1801 on the wall beside him.

He caught her staring, and she looked away, embarrassed.

Piper reminded Jake of his ex-wife, Sheila—slight, long black hair, green eyes with a feisty, no-holds-barred temperament. She was also very attractive.

After making eye contact with Piper, he looked away. He was supposed to be keeping his head down, but, as had so often been the case in his thirty-five years, he was failing miserably. He kept his eyes down while he drank his Jack Daniels and Coke until raucous laughter and loud voices drew his attention to the bar.

Three drunken men. At this distance, they looked to be around mid-twenties, the same age as Piper. One of the men made a beeline for Piper at the opposite end of the bar. He announced his approach to not only her but most of the patrons in the Taps. "Pipes!"

Jake watched Piper shake her head, making it clear she had no time for him. *So like Sheila!*

Even though the band had finished, Jake couldn't hear the conversation at this distance. It wasn't hard to pick up on the unpleasantness though when Piper regularly scowled at him and shook her head. When the idiot grabbed hold of her hand, Jake stood.

From the corner of his eye, Jake saw the two drunken friends had focused on him, and he felt his adrenaline levels rising.

Piper snatched away her hand and shoved three drinks toward him. Her eyes flitted to Jake, and she shook her head to warn him off. But it was too late; her antagonist followed her gaze to look at Jake too.

The cocky fool strolled toward the table, grinning. He had a rather patchy goatee, making Jake wonder why he'd even attempted to grow it.

His two friends tracked behind him.

When he reached Jake, he looked up at him. "You like her?"

"Who are you?"

"Do I need to repeat my question?"

"Do I need to repeat mine?"

His forehead creased as if stunned. He held this expression for a moment before bursting into laughter. He turned his head to look at his friends, who looked uncomfortable at first but obliged him by forcing some laughter. He pointed at Jake's chest. "I'm Justin Stone, tall boy. You're from out of town, so you probably don't recognize the name. It would be better for you if you did."

"And why's that?" Jake leaned over, grabbed his glass and took a mouthful.

"My dad's first selectman."

Jake swallowed and put down the glass. He creased his brow. "Is that like a mayor?"

"Yeah."

"Oh. Good for you."

"That's a big deal. This is *his* town."

"Like I said"—Jake reached for his drink again—"Oh."

"I've not met many British before. I can't say you're impressing me much."

Jake finished his drink in one large mouthful. He swallowed, put his glass on the table and shrugged.

Justin's face reddened. He prodded Jake in the chest. "Listen, tall boy, me and Piper go way back."

Jake nodded then looked down at Justin's finger.

"So you stay away from her."

Jake enveloped the finger in his large hand.

"Get the fuck—"

Jake forced his finger backward.

With Justin's face folding in pain, he reached with his other hand to pry away the hand.

"Listen," Jake said. "I don't care who you are, but seeing you getting forceful with that young lady, now that interested me."

"I can handle myself," Piper said from beside him.

Jake didn't look at Piper. He continued to stare down at Justin. "I don't doubt—"

"So cut the hero bullshit."

Jake released Justin's finger.

The prick staggered backward into his friends, gasping. His face glowed, and he clutched his sore finger with his other hand. "You won't get away with that."

Piper stepped in front of Jake and pointed at Justin. "You three need to leave."

"You are fucking joking—"

"No, or I'll call your father myself so he can come to your rescue."

Justin released his finger, stood up straight and narrowed his eyes.

"Yes," Piper said. "As I thought. You've called on him one too many times this month already. You don't want him stopping your allowance again, do you?" Piper glanced at Jake. "For your information, this happens every Friday night. Justin gets drunk then comes in here to declare his undying—"

"Fuck you."

Piper raised her eyebrows. "—love for me. He reminds me several times of how rich his family is."

"The richest."

Piper nodded. "Yes, the richest. And I remind him about the hashtag me-too movement and the fact I don't want a powerful man to sexually assault me."

"Powerful?" Justin asked, his expression lightening slightly.

"Yes, but that's kind of the point. That's why this makes you such a dickhead. But you're just not getting it, are you?"

"I can help with that," Jake said.

Piper raised her hands. "Right, fuck this. Testosterone overload. Justin, take your friends, leave, and when you return tomorrow night, sober, I'll repour the three drinks you paid for."

Justin pointed at Jake and narrowed his eyes. He turned to his friends. "Come on."

Jake and Piper watched them leave.

"Someone else who just sees me as a little barmaid."

Jake spied her stern profile and smiled. *You're anything but.*

On Piper's next break, she sat with Jake and tried to explain the dynamics of Blue Falls to him. "So even though Charles Stone is first selectman and is, as Justin loves to tell everyone, rolling in it, he's more of a figurehead these days. It's the chief administrative officer, Alex Whittmore, who runs things at a more detailed level."

"Police?"

"Among other things."

During their conversation, Jake noticed Piper regularly checking her cellphone.

"Is everything okay?"

"I hope so."

"What do you mean?"

"Our glass collector, Maddie, didn't show up tonight."

"How old is she?"

"Fifteen."

Jake shrugged. "She probably got a better offer."

Piper sat back, shaking her head. "No, she's not like that. She's conscientious. She also keeps to herself, more bothered about school than boys, which is a good thing. Wish I'd followed the same path."

"I'm sure she's just sick."

"She'd have called. Honestly, Jake, this girl is as straitlaced as they come. I kind of love her for it too."

"Have you spoken to her parents?"

"They're not answering, and I've sent countless texts."

"Anything I can do? I can head around to the parents."

Piper considered it then shook her head. "Thanks for offering, but no. There must have been a family emergency. I'll try again in a bit. I'm sure there's an explanation." She checked her watch. "That's almost my break. You sticking around?"

"I think I'll call it a night. I should be in town for a while longer though," Jake said, realizing he had no idea if that was actually the case.

Piper stood. "You know, the only time I see tourists out of tourist season is when they are looking to get away from their partners and get laid. And that can be male or female."

"I'm divorced." He almost added that he had a little boy named Frank but left that out for now.

"Okay." Piper smiled. "But that doesn't mean you're getting laid."

2

JOTHAM KNELT TO ALLOW Bo Peep to lick his face. Then he eased his favorite American pit bull terrier into her cage by her flanks. Bo paused to regard him with close-set eyes before she turned, padded to her bowl and sank her teeth into a chicken breast.

Jotham's other dogs whined from the adjacent cages.

"Wait your fucking turn," he said, and they quietened. While locking Bo's cage door, he sensed Ayden behind him. "Not when I'm with my bitches, you know that."

"I'm sorry, Dad. It's important."

Jotham stood but faced away from his boy. "Speak."

"It's Kayla."

"What about her?"

"She's not in her room."

Jotham turned. "What do you mean?"

"She's not there. I searched the whole house. She must have gone somewhere."

When the dogs whined again, Jotham kicked Bo's cage with his heel. "I said, *wait your fucking turn!*"

His son's top lip quivered.

Pathetic. He checked his watch. "It's past eleven. Where would she have gone?"

"I've no idea."

Jotham pushed back his long, thick hair. "She's thirteen."

"I can check the house again."

"And if she's not there?"

"I'll search the land."

"All two thousand acres of it?" Jotham scratched his beard. "Why do you think she would leave the house?"

"She's needy. Trying for attention."

Jotham rubbed his beard. "Do we not give her that?"

"We've been busy recently. Too distracted—"

Jotham slammed his fist hard into Ayden's stomach.

His boy slipped to his knees and vomited at his feet.

Bo barked.

"For fuck's sake." Jotham hopped to the side and lifted his steel-toed boot to check for any sick on it. When he was happy there wasn't, he kicked his son hard in the face.

Ayden collapsed onto his side, and the other dogs barked.

"Mr. MacLeoid?" Jenna Hanson came through the back door wearing a blue paper oversuit. She had her four colleagues with her. They weren't too far away and could see what was going on. Not that it mattered. They wouldn't say anything. They valued their work too much.

Jotham again kicked Bo's cage with his heel. "Shut the fuck up, *all* of you." He brushed hair from his eyes, raised his hand and called back to Jenna. "Done?"

"Yes."

"And all locked up?"

21

"Yes, Mr. MacLeoid."

His son moaned on the floor.

"If you wait by the van, I'll let Oliver know you're ready."

Jenna, the oldest of his workers at forty-two, led the girls in the opposite direction from where he was currently trouncing his only son.

He knelt beside Ayden. "Jesus, are you fucking crying?"

"No. You just kicked me in the eye."

"You lost your sister. Get up. Let Oliver know that Jenna and the girls are ready then get a team together." He rose. "Cover every inch, you moronic fuck. What're you waiting for?"

Ayden sat upright.

"Pathetic. Stand up! You know my daddy beat me a lot harder and for a lot less. Your sister! Jesus! What the hell is wrong with you?"

Ayden stood in front of him, one eye swelling.

Jotham prodded him in the chest. "Every inch. Do you hear? And if she went over the fence and drowned in the Stinson, you'll sleep with my bitches tomorrow night."

As JAKE WALKED to the motel, it became clear that Blue Falls had seen better days. On Main Street, most storefronts were boarded up, several of the streetlamps had blown, and hazardous cracks in the sidewalk could send inattentive pedestrians to the ground. Jake wasn't surprised. With a population of barely three thousand and following a rather steep recession, extreme wear and tear was to be expected. Piper had also mentioned tourism was at an all-time low. *"For years, it has mainly attracted older tourists, but that number is shrinking, and what is there here for the younger traveler?"*

Jake had almost quipped, *"Fishing in the Skweda?"* but had held back in time. It wasn't his home to criticize.

Compared to the poverty-stricken areas he'd policed in Wiltshire, Blue Falls was remarkably peaceful. At first, he'd kept his eyes on the side alleys and the darkened storefronts, but relatively few suspicious characters were about. Attached to the Rogers general store was a gun shop.

A weapon wasn't something he'd considered until now, but it would probably be a good idea. Justin Stone had just introduced him to the edgier side of Blue Falls, and he could be leaving himself vulnerable. Unfortunately, he couldn't get one at the moment, not without a Maine state ID. He'd have to organize that, preferably when he'd found some employment and a decent residency.

The clatter of a pickup hitting a pothole made him flinch. The driver weaved from one side of the road to another. Getting hit by a drunk driver was more plausible than getting mugged around here.

Jake strolled into the creatively titled Blue Falls Motel, and its abundance of blue neon lights momentarily blinded him. If the rooms didn't come with blackout curtains, Jake doubted they would get any customers. It was two months until the tourist season began, so it was very quiet. He had room fifteen on the first floor, but he doubted anyone occupied many, if any, of the other fourteen rooms. The parking lot only contained two cars, including his own.

He approached the door to his room, key in hand.

"Hey, Tallboy."

Jake sighed. He was too tired for this. He turned and saw Justin and his two friends standing in the empty car parking space reserved for number fourteen.

Justin rubbed the back of his hand. A knuckle duster glowed blue under the neon shower. "You hurt my finger."

"Sorry to piss on your bonfire." Jake pointed at a camera protruding from the second-floor roof. "We're on camera."

Justin smiled. "Did you not listen to anything I said back in the Taps? Rules don't apply to me."

"So, Daddy will approve of you mugging a tourist then?"

"Unless you're a tourist here to spend money, which we know you're not, then he really wouldn't give a shit."

"Okay. How do we do this then? Three of you and a knuckle duster against me. Doesn't sound like the fairest fight."

"You're a big guy. I'm sure you've had this kind of attention before."

Jake shrugged. He was fond of his Barbour jacket, so he peeled it off, turned and hung it on his door handle. When he turned back, he saw Justin working his knuckleduster down the side of his rental car. The grating sound made him wince. "You're going to pay for that."

Justin ignored him and continued.

Justin's small friends hovered several feet behind him, and Jake figured he could take a pop at the lead dickhead before they got too close. If he floored Justin, he fancied his chances against them. He went in fast, but before he reached the bastard, he felt a blow to the side of the head. Everything flashed, but he managed to steady himself against the car's trunk and reply with a swift elbow. There was a satisfying crunch, and when he turned, he saw his ambusher staggering backward, clutching his nose.

Jake glared at Justin. "Four against one now, is it?"

"Well, I wasn't going to take any chances, Tallboy."

Jake pounced and drove Justin's head into the side of his

car. The damage to the car had already been done; what was one more dent? He released Justin's head, expecting him to fall. He didn't. He just stared up at Jake with blood streaming from a gash in his forehead.

Jake felt the victim of his right elbow diving in for another go. The bastard was rather handy and managed to get off two body blows, the second of which sucked the air from him.

Jake folded over, winded. He recovered just in time to see Justin delivering a blow with his knuckleduster. He lost a couple seconds before realizing he'd gone down and landed awkwardly on his left arm.

Their boots pummelled him.

Justin's other two lackies, who had spent most of the confrontation hanging back, were clearly now in on the act.

"When you wake up tomorrow and you can barely move, I want to be the first thing you think about, Tallboy," Justin said.

It was dangerous rolling onto his back, exposing his face, chest, and ribs, but it had been a very long time since Jake had avoided risk, and he wasn't about to start now. In his new position, he could throw one hand above him to catch the ankle of a falling foot while simultaneously kicking forward at one of the bastard's knees. He heard a crack, followed by a squeal, and then completed his comeback by yanking on the ankle. The assailant came down on top of him. This had been his intention all along because it prevented the remaining two bruisers from landing more blows. He also could wriggle underneath the fallen man and apply a headlock. "Back off, or I'll break his neck."

Jake noticed Justin was one of the two men still standing. Lucky for him. Jake was so furious with the little shit that, if he'd been in this headlock, he probably would have gone and finished him off.

A gunshot sounded.

Justin and his friend backpedaled with their hands raised. The handy fighter who had ambushed him rose to his feet and limped backward.

Another gunshot rang out, followed by a deep male voice. "You too, big boy."

Jake released Justin's friend.

He rolled away, clutching his neck and gasping for air.

Jake sat upright and saw a slim, Native American older man wearing a black leather jacket and scruffy jeans.

His damaged assailants had now clustered several feet behind Jake—too far to challenge the man with the rifle but not too far as to get shot.

"Dogman," Justin said. "All washed up with a gun. A dangerous combination. You're about the only person in this town who I'd walk away from."

"It's past your bedtime," the man said.

Jake dusted off his jeans and eased himself against the car. He winced but stifled a groan. He didn't want to give Justin the pleasure of seeing him injured. "You heard him, Justin. Time for you to go home and tuck in your sheep."

"This isn't finished, Tallboy," Justin said.

Jake stretched out but didn't turn. "Lucky for you, it is." He passed the man with the rifle toward the door. "And my name isn't Tallboy. It's Jake. Or Mr. Pettman to you."

"Last chance, Justin," the man said.

"Fuck this. You can wait, Tallboy. You too, Dogman. Come on, let's leave these lovers to it."

Jake listened to them leave. He unlocked the door and turned to the man. "You coming in?"

AFTER PETER SHEENAN had introduced himself, he offered to clean Jake's wounds, which he declined.

"Can't say I blame you," Peter said with a smile. "Traditionally, the hero gets tended to by the fairer sex."

"Hero?" Jake sat on the edge of the bed, dabbing his split eyebrow with a towel. "Is that how it looked?"

"You looked like you had it under control." Peter sat on a rickety chair by an end table.

"I certainly didn't feel in control!"

"You were."

"So, why step in then?"

"I couldn't risk you getting up and killing Justin Stone."

"Why? Because his daddy is first selectman?"

"Among other things."

"Is killing him definitely off limits?" Jake stood, stretched his side and winced over the flickers of pain throughout his body.

"If you want to make it to my age, it is."

"Which is?"

"Seventy-three."

"Impressive. I had you pegged at sixty-something."

"The blood of the Abenaki people is strong. I'm grateful for it. You too look like you are of good heritage."

Jake smiled. "I think I might just be about to disappoint you there, Peter. I'm probably descended from the same group of people as that wanker outside."

"With that accent?"

"My ancestors were part of establishing this town. Anyway, I'm hoping Justin and his crew are anomalies and the town isn't stocked full of wankers."

"I think it might be my turn to disappoint you."

Jake chortled. "Great."

"However, it's also full of good people too. But you'll hardly come across many of them late on a Friday night in a watering hole."

"Oh, I don't know. I did meet someone quite nice in there."

"Piper Goodwin?"

"You saw that?"

"The whole place saw, Jake. And there'd be nothing wrong with it if Justin Stone wasn't carrying a flaming torch for her. This whole evening has been predictable."

"And here's me just trying to find somewhere to mind my own business."

"A man like you can never mind his own business."

"What does that mean?"

"You know what it means, Jake, but it's not a criticism, so don't take it that way."

Jake went to the suitcase in the corner of his room and changed his shirt. He groaned and recalled Justin's words. *"When you wake up tomorrow and you can barely move, I want to be the first thing you think about, Tallboy."*

You won't be wrong on that one, Jake thought. "This won't be the last time I hear from Justin then?"

"Unfortunately, not."

"Won't he target you too? You did embarrass him out there."

"No. His father is keen to maintain good relations with our people. Do you think I would have pulled this on him otherwise?" He tapped his rifle leaning against the dresser. "If I was a white man, they'd find me floating face down in the Skweda come first light. No way they'll risk that with a Native."

"Why do they call you Dogman?"

"I served with the K9 corps in Vietnam."

"You took dogs with you? I don't know a great deal about that, but I don't know a great deal about the Vietnam War in general."

"When you arrive in the Vietnamese jungle, the element of surprise is with the indigenous people. Most Americans never even saw their killers. Rockets out of nowhere, snipers concealed at ridiculous distances. But when you had a well-trained dog, you stood a chance. And when you had thousands of them, you could turn that element of surprise all the way around." Peter paused, looking away from Jake at the far wall. His fingers ran up and down the rifle. "I had a few dogs in my time but none like my lab retriever Prince. Ninety-four pounds. A civilian family donated him. So clever. He knew when he was off service, because he was a big, stubborn bastard, but on duty, he was as efficient and obedient as they come. Two-four-three-three. That was his number. Tattooed in his left ear."

Jake sat on the edge of the bed. "Sounds like you were close."

Peter, still staring off into the distance, nodded. "So many lives are owed to those dogs. Over ten thousand to be sure. Our dogs had over two-hundred-and-twenty-five-million scent receptors in their noses. Us mere humans only have around five million! They can hear sounds four times farther away than us. They scouted the jungle for Vietcong ambushes and saved so many men from the traps. One time, me and Prince were on a routine patrol in Tay Ninh to protect an ammunition dump. Enemy fire erupted. I let my boy off his leash. It stunned them, and I managed to take a few of them out, but then I took a bullet." He pulled down his shirt collar and showed Jake some white scar tissue on his shoulder. "That was me on the floor, ready to be picked off. And I would have been if Prince hadn't been ripping into them. They even shot him in the head, just underneath the eye, but he was relentless. He kept on going, tearing into them. It gave me time to radio for backup, and then he threw himself on top of me to shield me. No human being, white or Abenaki, has ever shown me such dedication. He saved me, and fortunately, the veterinarian saved him." He looked back at Jake. "Sorry to give you the long version, but when someone pleads ignorance to dogs in war, something always comes over me."

"Not surprised with that story."

"With more Old Crow in me, it'd be a longer one."

"I'm glad your dog survived. He sounds like a real hero. Not like me floundering under the boots of several drunks outside. What happened to Prince?"

"For that part of the story, I do need the Old Crow."

"Sorry, but I've only just moved in, and these rooms don't come with a drinks cabinet."

Peter smiled. "We'll save that part of the story. It's nice to end it there tonight." He stood and stretched. "But now that you've told me there's no drink, I'm heading home for a nightcap."

Jake saw him to the door and shook his hand. "Thanks for the hand."

"You're welcome, Jake. But the problem hasn't gone away. I like you, so don't take this wrong, but it may be time for you to move on."

"Should I expect a brick through the window?"

"I doubt that. The owners here are old friends with Charles Stone. Justin wouldn't be stupid enough to piss off his father."

"Good, I shall sleep soundly on your suggestion then."

"Do that."

"And, if I'm still here tomorrow night, I'll see you in the Blue Falls and get you some ... what did you call it? Old Crow?"

Peter smiled again. "Goodnight, Jake."

"Goodnight, Peter."

3

GABRIEL JEWELL HAD always been houseproud. His father had beat it into him with a slipper from an early age. At the time, he'd resented it. Now, he was grateful for it. Tidying calmed him and took his mind away from the demons.

He checked his watch—almost twelve. As always, he'd spent the entirety of Friday night hoovering, dusting, and cleaning the windows of his old stone-built house. He was exhausted and took a hot bath. He tried reading the news on his cell, but, as was always the case, this time on a Friday, the demons returned.

Gabriel sighed, climbed from the bath, dried himself and inspected himself in the bathroom mirror. He needed a shave. Good. More distraction. After shaving, he rubbed moisturizer into his skin, working it up his face to his crow's feet by his eyes. Mid-forties. Officially an old man to any adolescent. He sighed.

Wearing a dressing gown, he descended the stairs, wishing he was tired enough to sleep but knowing he wasn't. He never was—not when the demons came knocking.

He stooped to enter his living room. His house dated back to the first English settlers. Doorframes didn't cater to the six-foot-five man back then. The room was decorated in a Victorian style. He crossed over a Persian rug and checked his lace curtains were straight and no one could peer in. Not that anyone could. When his demons were nearby, he could never be too careful.

Gabriel approached the mantlepiece over his burning log fire. He ran his fingers down the photograph of Collette in her blue school uniform—her first week at high school, fourteen years old.

How he longed to see what Collette looked like at fifteen. Sixteen. Seventeen ... *Now*.

No. Not possible. The day after that photograph was taken, his sister went to Rogers general store for some groceries and was never seen again.

He watched the burning wood in the fire spit sap. Noticing he was clenching his fists and his teeth, he took a deep breath and threw another log onto the flames. He stared until this new log spit too. It was no good. He too needed release. He dropped his dressing gown, sat on the sofa, opened his laptop on his coffee table and sought out one of his favourite videos.

He watched an older man, about his age, enter a whitewashed room, holding someone by the hand. Gabriel's teeth remained clenched, not from frustration anymore but from the onslaught of arousal. The older man was discussing sex with a young girl, barely into her teens. Nothing physical had happened yet, but Gabriel was already touching himself and moaning with pleasure—

"Shit!"

He'd forgotten. Collette's photograph. She was staring right at him.

He ran across the room, desperately trying to cover his erection. He turned her photograph facedown and sighed. He returned to the sofa.

The older man was now undressing the young girl.

Gabriel's demons had come out to play, and he hated and loved it at the same time.

JAKE OPENED the door to Piper. She was shielding her eyes from the glare of the blue neon.

"How did you know which room I was in?"

"Just three people are staying here, and only one with a rental car outside. That Ford looks like it's seen better days by the way."

"It was the cheapest option."

"Is that your excuse for the dressing gown too?"

"No, fortunately, this belongs to the motel, so it won't be going with me. Do you think I'd have chosen one that barely covers my thighs?"

"You wouldn't be the first crazy to wander through the town."

Jake smiled. "Come in."

Her eyes widened after she'd stepped inside and turned to face him. Away from the neon glare, she'd obviously noticed the cut above one eye and the swelling around the other. "What happened? Actually, don't bother. It was Justin, wasn't it?"

Jake closed the door and gestured toward the chair Peter

had sat in earlier. "Yes. Well, him and his small army. He seems hellbent on accelerating the demise of your tourist trade."

Piper shook her head. "I wish that was his reason. That man is so possessive of me. Even though we've never dated and I've made it very clear I don't like him very much, he practically stalks me. If the police department weren't in Charles Stone's pocket, as well as being a bunch of misogynistic bastards, I might have made a report. Instead, I've opted for the alternative—save enough money to get the hell out of here."

"And how's that going?"

"Slowly."

Jake winced as he sat on the edge of the bed.

"Are you okay?"

"Sore ribs. Nothing broken."

"You're a doctor?" She raised an eyebrow.

"No, just very tuned in to my own body. A man named Peter Sheenan helped me out."

"He's a nice guy. Although he does carry a lot of baggage."

"Don't we all? So, Piper, to what do I owe this pleasure? Being that you warned me off at the bar."

"Hardly warned off. I just warned you that you wouldn't be getting laid, and that still stands."

"I wasn't asking! But, if you've stopped by for a drink, I'll have to give you the same disappointing news I gave to Peter. I've nothing to offer you, I'm afraid."

Piper sighed. "I wish that's why I was here."

"It's about your friend, isn't it?"

Piper nodded. "Maddie."

"The offer still stands. We can head around together."

"No need. I've just spoken to her parents on the phone."

"And?"

"They said she's fine. Too sick to come to work."

"But you're not convinced?"

Piper shook her head. "Maddie's mother, Marissa, sounded drunk, then her father, Blake, snatched the phone from her and sounded irate. Something isn't right. Maddie is still not answering her phone or replying to my messages."

"You think it's worth calling the police?"

Piper raised an eyebrow. "Believe me, with the police service in this town, you want to make that a last resort."

"Why?"

"Well, they're useless, for a start."

"They're not about to ignore the disappearance of a fifteen-year-old girl though?"

"Jake, there're things you don't know about this town. It's like a spider's web—all tied up in itself."

"You're not making much sense."

"It doesn't make much sense to me either. It's like everyone is connected, and no one can be trusted. It's one of the reasons I am so desperate to get away."

"And you think Maddie is mixed up in this spider's web?"

"Not Maddie, no, but her family ... possibly."

"You're being very cryptic, Piper."

Piper sighed. "I've already put you in hot water, I'm not about to set it to boil."

Jake smiled. "You like your metaphors. Here's an idea. You tell me some of your secrets, and I'll tell you some of mine."

She didn't return his smile. "There's a farmer named Jotham Quimby MacLeoid. He's not a selectman, and I don't think he even sits in on board meetings, but he's been around as long as the rest of them. I've personally had nothing to do with him, but Maddie has spoken of him a few times. She told me he holds a lot of sway over the running of Blue Falls—I'm guessing because he owns a lot of land and provides employment to many families."

Jake nodded. "Including Maddie's family."

"Her brothers, Devin and Sean."

"Farming?"

"I guess." She looked away.

Jake could tell she wasn't being completely transparent, but he didn't push her. She was here for his help after all, and she'd surely get there eventually. "So, what concerns you about Jotham MacLeoid?"

Again, she looked away. "He's not a good person. People try and stay out of his way."

"Why?"

"As I said before, it's someone I have nothing to do with. But that phone call to Maddie's parents and the fact her brothers are involved with Jotham? This is not a good combination."

"What would you like me to do?"

"I don't know. Advise maybe?"

"In that case, I'm sticking with the police."

"I'm really not sure it's the best option. I'd like to keep it as a last resort."

"Okay. You could visit the family first thing and actually *see* Maddie firsthand?"

"If she's there."

"Well, if she isn't, you'll really need to jump to the last resort, as it's better than nothing."

Piper sighed. "I guess you're right. Will you come with me tomorrow morning?"

"Of course."

"I'm exhausted. Shall we lie down?"

Jake was speechless.

"Don't look so shocked. I just want to rest a little while you fulfill your end of the bargain."

"Ah, my secrets?"

Piper smiled for the first time since arriving at his room.

AFTER JAKE HAD TOLD Piper about his short career as a police officer, excluding the part where he'd become mixed up with the wrong people, he excused himself to shower.

When he returned, fully clothed now, he said, "Thought you'd be asleep by now. My showers are notoriously long."

"There's a lot of you to wash, I guess, but you couldn't expect me to fall asleep before finding out what happened next?"

"Sorry to disappoint, but I just quit the police and left the country." Like Piper had done earlier, he looked away as he said this. He'd not quit; he'd run.

"You don't have any family then?"

Jake shook his head and glanced over to the bedside drawer where he kept his five photographs of Frank—one for every year of his life. "So, there aren't any more secrets, I'm afraid. You're best getting some sleep." He climbed onto the bed and lay as close to the edge as he possibly could so as not to worry her.

She clearly wasn't worried. She rolled onto her side and shuffled closer to him. "Adopted by a god-fearing family when I was a baby, studious at school but results weren't the best, attended a Lutheran church throughout childhood but haven't been in over a year much to the displeasure of Mom and Dad, dead-end bar job, chronically bored in Blue Falls." She smiled.

"Wow."

"Well, two can play at the boring life story."

Jake rolled over so he was facing her. He propped up his head by his elbow and noticed her blouse's top buttons were undone, revealing a pink blemish on her collarbone.

"This?" She pulled the blouse to expose the whole of her collarbone and a large pear-shaped birthmark.

He thought briefly of the white scarring on Peter's shoulder. "I like it."

"Yes, me too." Piper smiled and closed her eyes.

Jake didn't speak again. He let her drift off, and when her breaths started to quietly whistle, he closed his own eyes and listened to them for a while.

JOTHAM SAT on his daughter's bed and surveyed her poster of boys in bands with perfectly cropped hair. He hated their air-brushed faces, hated their music, and hated what they stood for, but he loved Kayla, so he allowed it in his house. He noticed the toy monkey she still slept with on her pillow and picked it up—a gift from her mother, Iris Clark. A prostitute. Pretty woman. Calm temperament. She'd died young from breast cancer. The eye was hanging out of the monkey. He kept hold of it so he could repair it. A welcome home gift.

His cell rang. "Go on."

"No sign of her, Dad," Ayden said.

Jotham took a deep breath through his nose.

"Dad? What do you want me to do?"

Jotham stood and approached one of the boy band posters. This particular ponce irritated him. He'd spent most of his irrelevant life bouncing from sunbed to gym and went for the tightest sleeveless shirt he could find to prove it.

"I don't want you to call me again until you have her."

"But, Dad—"

He hung up, slipped his cell into his jeans pocket, secured the monkey into his jacket pocket and tore the poster from the wall. Then he started to shout and roar.

Outside, his dogs barked.

AFTER HIS ERECTION HAD WANED, Gabriel Jewell closed the laptop. He went to the kitchen, put the used tissue into the trash and scrubbed his hands. When he felt they were clean enough, he returned to the living room, put on his dressing gown and stood Collette's photograph back up. He sat and watched sap bubbling on a log while he appreciated the absence of his demons.

A frantic knocking sounded at the door.

He went to the front door, glanced at his Remington 700 propped against the wall beneath his jackets then looked through the peephole. His eyes widened.

Kayla MacLeoid.

As best he could, he tried to see around her through the peephole. No sign of her brother Ayden or her bastard father, Jotham. He opened the door. "Kayla, why're you here?"

She entered quickly.

He sidestepped so she'd brush against him, rather than

barging straight into him. He closed the door, and she turned to him.

Her long black hair was disheveled, and she was crying hard. She threw her arms around him. "Help me."

"Of course. Come in where it's warm." He led her into the living room and sat her on the sofa. Under the room's light, Gabriel saw how red and swollen her face was. He grabbed his laptop off the table. "Let me get you some milk."

Leaving his laptop in the kitchen, he returned with a mug of warm milk. He sat alongside her and eased her forward. He put the mug to her mouth, and she managed a sip.

"Thank you."

He put the mug on the coffee table and slipped an arm around her shoulders. He eased her against him and squeezed her tightly to offer her some reassurance. He allowed several minutes for the racking sobs to subside then scooted away from her so he could look her in the eyes. He put his palm against her hot cheek. "Tell me, child, what's happened?"

"The pit."

"The pit?"

"Maddie ... oh god, Maddie. Dad told Ayden to hurt her ... and he did ... and then Anthony pushed her in ..."

Gabriel's heart bashed against his ribcage, and he tasted bile climbing the back of his throat. He'd heard of the pit—many had, of course—but he'd never really believed in its existence. It was just a rumor, wasn't it? Another ingredient in the terrifying aura that surrounded Jotham MacLeoid and kept people in line. "Why were you there?"

"I followed Dad."

Sweet Jesus, what have you just involved me in, girl? "Why did you come to me?" He tried his best to not allow his rising irritation and anxiety to creep into his voice, but he couldn't stop his eyes narrowing slightly.

She noticed and recoiled. She would also be disturbed by his question because the answer was all too obvious. Her bottom lip trembled as she spoke. "Because you're the chief of police."

4

JAKE RAN HIS finger down the deep scratch on the side of his Ford. "Once the rental company has finished gouging me for this, I may be applying for the cleaning job at the Taps to help take on those peanut shells."

"I know someone who'll do a fair price," Piper said. "I'll see what I can do."

"Thanks." He patted his back pocket. "I've forgotten my wallet. Just hop in the car; I'll be back in a moment."

Piper nodded and climbed in.

Jake ensured the motel room's door was closed behind him before he removed a large bundle of British notes from the back of the closet. He peeled off about two hundred pounds. He doubted he'd find anywhere to exchange it on a Saturday around here, but he was running significantly short on dollars, so it was best to stay prepared in case there were any options. When he eyed the money in his hand, his mind flew back to the burning car and the eyes of the broken boy, Paul Conway. Lowering his head, he sucked in a deep breath and tried to stifle the memory—

A pounding at the door knocked him out of his own world.

"Are you all right in there?" Piper asked.

"Yes, coming." He pushed the bundle to the back of the closet, folded the four fifty-pound notes and slipped them into the inside pocket of his Barbour then joined Piper outside. Because he was stiff from last night's conflict and hated driving, he was glad when Piper offered.

She looked surprised when he nodded.

"Sorry, am I challenging gender roles?" Jake said.

"Yes, I'm glad to say. You'll be surprised how deep-rooted those gender roles are around here."

"I probably wouldn't be, to be honest."

She drove at a steady pace to the Thompson farmyard, and he was glad. He was a nervous driver.

Being from Wiltshire, Jake was no stranger to farmyards, but the size of the Thompson one surprised him. The narrow dirt road that speared into the heart of it seemed to go on forever. "How much land does this family own?"

Piper shrugged. "Does it matter?"

"I guess not. But, if a man owned this much land in Wiltshire, he wouldn't need to send his sons to work for a man like Jotham."

"They've had a couple of bad years, according to Maddie. It's been too hot, and we've had below-average rainfall. Crops have suffered."

They pulled alongside a Cape Cod-styled farmhouse—a large white-washed, single-story building with a steep roof and a large central chimney.

"Do you think we should have warned them that we were coming?" Piper said.

"Too late now," Jake said, climbing out of the car.

They headed down the path and climbed the steps onto the covered front porch. While Piper rang the doorbell, Jake stood back against the railing, admiring the wicker furniture —a far cry from the rustic rocking chairs he'd always assumed sat on every farmhouse porch in America.

A young man answered the door.

"Hello, Sean," Piper said.

Sean edged backward. "You shouldn't be here."

Jake stepped forward and noticed a black eye.

"I just came to check on Maddie—"

"She's fine." His tone of voice suggested otherwise.

Jake stepped alongside Piper. "You wouldn't mind us saying hello then?"

"Sorry, who are you?" Sean asked, his top lip trembling.

"That's a good question," a younger man said with a calmer, more confident tone. He stepped alongside Sean, displaying his swollen lips and bruised cheeks.

"Good morning, Devin," Piper said. "Sorry to stop by unannounced, but we're worried about your sister."

"No need to worry. She's fine."

"Yes, your parents said so last night, but we'd like to come in and wish her well, if that's okay?"

"It isn't," Devin said.

Jake glanced at Piper and saw her eyebrows were raised. He refocused on Devin and watched it dawn on him that he'd been far too abrasive.

"Sorry," Devin said. "On any other day, you'd be welcomed in, Piper, but not with this stranger, I'm afraid."

"My name's Jake Pettman. I don't mind waiting in the car—"

"No," Sean said. "We don't want you left alone on the property. No offense."

"None taken," Jake lied.

45

"There isn't much point," Devin said. "Maddie has gone to Vermont."

"Why?" Piper asked.

"She needed some time away."

"Okay ... strange she didn't let me know. When will she be back?"

Devin shrugged. "I don't know. Look, we're quite busy here."

"How did you split that lip?" Jake asked.

Devin turned his gaze from Piper and stared up at Jake. "Fell over a buckled rug in the living room."

Jake nodded. "I see." Keeping his focus on Devin, he pointed at Sean. "Did you not think to straighten the rug before he fell over it too?"

Devin's eyes narrowed. "You maybe want to watch your mouth—"

"Who is it?" a woman's voice asked.

"It's okay, Mom. Just a delivery," Devin said and elbowed Sean to gesture at his mother with a nod. He went back to get her.

"Mrs. Thompson, it's Piper Goodwin—"

"Shut up!" Devin said.

Jake inched forward. "I respect this is your house, but I don't respect that tone."

Mrs. Thompson joined Devin at the door.

Sean was floundering around behind her.

"Piper, so good to see you." She reaching out and took her hands. Her face was pale and withered, her eyes glazed, and her hair hung drably over her face. She was still in a nightgown.

"You too, Mrs. Thompson."

"Please, you have been ever so good to my Maddie. Call me Marissa." Her voice was frayed.

"Of course, Marissa."

"She always talks about you. Would you like to come in?"

"Mom," Devin said. "Do you think that's a good idea?"

Marissa ignored her son and pulled Piper into the house.

Devin thrust out his hand to stop Jake from following her in.

Piper turned back. "May I bring in my boyfriend please, Marissa?"

"Of course."

Devin kept his hand where it was.

Jake stared down at him. "Don't make this difficult. Our intentions are good."

Devin dropped his hand and turned away. "Shit!"

Marissa led Jake and Piper into the kitchen which, again, was far less rustic than Jake expected—stainless-steel appliances, spotlights, and a granite tabletop in the center with stools around it. "Please sit," Marissa said, "while I make some coffee."

Jake and Piper took a seat.

While Marissa filled the carafe, Devin entered the kitchen and leaned against a cabinet with his arms crossed, glaring at their two guests.

"Marissa, I wondered—"

"Just a moment, my dear," Marissa said, measuring the ground coffee into the carafe. "There's an art to this. Blake is forever at me to get this just right."

Piper and Jake waited in a silence that stretched and stretched to the point where the tension was palpable. Jake rolled his shoulders, and Piper flashed him a look when his back cracked.

Eventually, Marissa approached the table with four

cups of coffee rattling on a tray and a small dish of sugar cubes. Piper had told Jake that Maddie's mother was in her early fifties. Right now, she looked much older than that.

"Here, let me help you." Jake rose and circled the tabletop. He gave Devin an angry look for not making any effort to help his mother.

Devin's expression remained unchanged, and his arms stayed folded.

Jake took the tray from the frail lady and placed it on the granite surface.

"Marissa, where's Maddie?" Piper asked.

Marissa looked up at Piper and smiled. "My daughter. She's a beautiful girl, isn't she?"

"Yes, she is."

"Such a good girl too. Always does as she's told." She pointed backward in Devin's direction. "Girls are always so much easier than the boys."

"Well, I'm not sure my parents would agree with you there," Piper said.

Marissa reached to take Piper's hand. "Maddie talks about you all the time, you know."

"That's nice. We've been working together a long time. With all that drinking and male bravado going on in the Taps, it's good to have another like-minded individual to stick to."

"You make sure you never take grief from any man, girl," Marissa said.

"I don't intend to."

"Blake used to treat me like a princess, you know."

"I'm sure he still does, Marissa."

"No, dear, those days are long gone."

"Marissa, where's Maddie?"

Ring-ring.

48

"Do you hear that, dear? The old bastard ringing a little bell?"

"Why is he doing that?" Piper asked.

"Hunger, no doubt. He smashed some teeth, and he hasn't eaten since last night."

Jake took a deep breath. "How did that happen, Mrs. Thompson?"

Ring-ring.

"I was thinking of soup," Marissa said. "Chicken is his favorite. Do you think he could eat that?"

"Yes, Mrs. Thompson," Jake said. "How did he damage his teeth?"

"Went over an old fencepost in the dark last night."

Accident prone, your family, aren't they? Jake thought, eyeing the young man with the split lip.

Ring-ring. Ring-ring.

Marissa smiled and faced her son. "Don't just stand there. Get your father some *goddamn* soup!"

Jake and Piper both flinched. The sudden rise in volume from a seemingly frail old woman was surprising.

Devin walked across the kitchen and opened the refrigerator.

Marissa turned back, smiling. "They never fall far from the tree, do they?" She looked down and took a deep breath. "But my daughter ... my Maddie ... now she's different."

"Where is she?" Piper asked, for possibly the third time.

Marissa looked up. "She's gone, dear. Didn't you know?"

"I didn't, no. You told me on the phone last night that she was sick."

"Did I? No, she's not sick. No. A mother would know that, wouldn't she?"

Devin stepped up and put his hand on his mother's shoulder. "Mom."

Ring-ring. Ring-ring.

Marissa placed her hand on Devin's. She closed her eyes and sighed. "She's in Vermont with family. Didn't my son tell you that at the door?"

"He did, Marissa. But not why she's there."

"The plague of all families, dear—arguments. She'll come back when the tension has gone."

"Arguments about what?" Jake said.

"That's none of your fucking business," Devin said.

Jake was about to reply, but he felt Piper's hand on his arm.

"Can I do anything to help with these arguments?" Piper asked. "I know she listens to me."

"No, dear, it's fine. My sister will handle it just fine."

Ring-ring. Ring-ring. Ring-ring.

"Old bastard," Marissa said and pushed her son's hand off her shoulder. "He'll wear that bell out. I'll do it. No one else seems capable of soup around here."

"Please, Marissa," Piper said, "can I just have your sister's number? I'd love to talk to Maddie, see how she is doing."

Marissa smiled and took Piper's hands again from across the table. "Aren't you a sweetheart? My beautiful girl is so lucky to have friends like you. I'll be sure to tell her you were asking after her."

Ring-ring. Ring-ring. Ring-ring.

"Goddamned *bastard*. Will he not shut the hell up?" She raised her voice again and turned from her two guests.

Jake looked down at the four untouched coffees.

Piper drove away from the farmhouse.

"Well, I've had some bloody strange experiences in my time, but nothing quite like that," Jake said.

"That bell. Jesus, Jake, that bell. I can still hear it ringing. What the hell have they done with Maddie? Vermont? How did she even get there? Did they throw her on a plane last night? Surely Marissa's sister didn't spend most of last night driving here and back again?"

"I don't think she's in Vermont."

"What have they done with her?"

"I can't answer that. But I can tell you they're terrified."

Piper nodded. "Sean looked like he was going to collapse from a heart attack when he saw me at the door."

"Yes. And that aggressive little shit, Devin, was ready to wrestle us off the property. Marissa, the mother, is in a complete state of shock. And the father? God knows ... I wasn't in any mood to find out what was behind that little bell. There's only one place we can go with all this, Piper. I know you don't like it, but we really have no choice."

Piper sighed. "You're right."

"But just because we're going to the police doesn't mean I'm trusting them. Especially if the town is as corrupt as you say it is. But a young girl missing is a young girl missing, and someone has got to give a shit about that."

"I hope so."

"Also, I'll go. I want you to stay out of it as best you can."

She glared at him. "So, the big man is speaking for the little lady now, is he?"

"No, the sensible person is speaking for the concerned friend."

"I can take care of myself, Jake."

Jake smiled. "Nothing I've seen so far has suggested otherwise. But, if I wind up the wrong person, I can disappear from this town. In other words, I've got far less to lose than you have. Drop me off at the station, please."

"I don't know ... I think it's best if—"

"You want my help, don't you?"

"Yes."

"So, trust me."

She thought about it and sighed. "Yes, boss."

THE STINK of death had never bothered Jotham. Growing up on a farmyard with all that slaughter and decay had desensitised him. But his lab stank like cat piss, and that was one animal he simply could not abide, so he forced the charcoal nose plugs in deep before summoning out Jenna Hanson.

As she came to the door in a powder-blue oversuit, he regarded his lab with some degree of pride. Before having his built, he'd visited an array of them. Many were unkempt, unsanitary, and stank far worse than this one. Supplies were often piled high in obscure places—a mountain of Sudafed in one corner, a mound of lithium batteries in the other, used coffee filters scattered on the floor, and smashed beakers kicked to the side of the room. His lab was clean and orderly. He wanted it to resemble a kitchen in a five-star restaurant, and the people he'd employed to build it had not let him down. No expense had been spared—air-conditioning, stainless-steel surfaces which were disinfected every day, clearly labeled equipment and storage bins. He also spared his staff the paranoia he'd seen in some of the other labs. They worked in a calm environment with no need to fear law enforcement. He provided them with fresh sanitary equipment daily, including masks, gloves, hairnets, overshoes, and oversuits. He also paid them well above average and gave them leave and sick pay. And all they had to do was get in the van driven by Oliver every morning at ten a.m., Monday to Saturday, cook meth, and return home, and when anyone asked—although most were not foolish enough to do so—they were simply cleaners working for Mr. MacLeoid.

"Mr. MacLeoid?" Jenna said with her facemask hanging from one ear. "Are you okay?"

Jotham closed the lab door and put his hand on her shoulder. "Been a long time since anyone asked me that."

"I'm sorry. You just look tired."

"Don't apologize." He smiled. "I like it, Jenna. I need your help."

"What can I do, sir?"

He withdrew his hand and took a deep breath. "You're going to think me a bad father." He looked away. "I seem to have lost my daughter."

"Kayla ... I don't understand. How?"

Jotham looked back at her. "Try not to worry, Jenna, not just yet. I suspect she's had a teenage moment and is staying with a friend somewhere."

"Cody?"

"Yes, that was my hope. I know they're close. If I get Oliver to drive you home now, can you see if your son knows anything?"

"Yes, of course."

"Thank you, Jenna. I'll have Ayden wait in the van so you can report back to him. Then you can have the rest of the day off."

"That won't be necessary, Mr. MacLeoid."

"I insist." He put his hand on her shoulder again, smiled and walked away.

Jotham held Bo's leash. It wasn't necessary; his dog was obedient and simply sat at her master's heel, but every now and again, Jotham liked to remind his bitches who was in charge.

He surveyed his twenty soldiers. Some were young and just starting out on their careers; others were much older, and like any other profession, they would be coming up to retirement. Yet, there was no retirement in this game. They couldn't complain; they'd been fully aware of this when they'd started out.

Jotham liked the younger soldiers more—Anthony, Cole, Isaac, and Lucas. He recalled their effectiveness the previous night in rounding up the Thompsons. An eagerness and energy existed in youth that quickly disappeared in middle-age.

He'd sent Ayden with Oliver to drive Jenna. He didn't want his son here. He was angry with him for his hesitance last night at the pit. It wasn't behavior befitting of a MacLeoid. If necessary, Jotham would beat him daily to remind him of that. He also held his son responsible for Kayla; he was supposed to have kept an eye on her. Also missing from the crowd were the Thompson boys. After watching their younger sister disappear into his pit last night, making them search for a younger girl might inspire thoughts of mutiny. It was best not to test them when their feelings were still raw. Besides, he still needed some of his mules in the other towns. He couldn't have them all out of action today. This was costing him money as it was.

"You all know about Kayla, and most of you have tired faces, so I thank those who tried throughout the night." Jotham pulled the monkey with the broken eye from his pocket. "But to those of you with sleep in the corners of your eyes and coffee on your breath from breakfast with your families, I want you to hear what I have to say." He kneeled, unclipped Bo's leash and stroked her muscular head. "A missing MacLeoid is not just a MacLeoid problem. It's everybody's problem." He gripped Bo's collar and held the monkey under her nose. "I assumed you would all know that. So, it got me thinking." Bo strained against Jotham's grip. She had Kayla's scent. "Maybe someone here knows more than they're letting on." He released Bo.

She moved quickly toward the crowd of men.

The men exchanged glances as the terrier approached, and some backed away.

"If anybody moves, I will feed Bo their fucking balls. If you haven't touched my daughter, you've nothing to worry about." Jotham scanned his frozen soldiers. It was impossible to spot guilt amongst them because every single one had grown pale and clenched their teeth.

Bo weaved around them, sniffing. She paused at Anthony, intrigued by his work boots.

Anthony's eyes widened, and he shook his head.

This worried Jotham. Anthony had been his most promising soldier for some time now. Still, Jotham narrowed his eyes and prepared himself to do what was necessary if the boy was in any way connected to his missing daughter.

He wasn't. Bo continued her hunt. When Bo had circled the men and had failed to find Kayla's scent on any, she returned to her master's side.

He heard several sighs of relief. Jotham kneeled, clicked on the leash, stroked her head and handed her beef jerky.

"Good girl." He stood. "Next time, if any of you disappear when I need you, I will just assume responsibility and give one of my bitches a real treat."

Everyone nodded vigorously, even the many who had toiled throughout the night.

"But I understand what I expect of you, so I'm offering five thousand dollars to anyone who can bring my daughter home safely."

The crowd exchanged glances again, but this time with less anxiety and even a few smiles.

5

THE POLICE DEPARTMENT was more welcoming than Jake had expected. The desk sergeant heard his concerns with a raised eyebrow and showed him through to a small room with a sofa and some magazines. The sergeant gave him coffee, which he received gratefully following his previous night of over-indulgence, and he took a seat.

Many photographs of Blue Falls decorated the wall. He stood and wandered toward a grainy black and white one of Main Street. He recognised the Rogers general store. The storefront looked identical. Only the clothing of the passers-by betrayed its era which, according to the handwriting below the image, was 1883. Jake's eyes moved along to another old photograph, this one of the Blue Falls Taps, the watering hole responsible for his growing headache and, in a way, his existence. If the owners, the Bickfords, had not been run out of town and back to the UK all that time ago, Jake may have never come into being.

The door opened, and a man not much shorter than

Jake entered. "Gabriel Jewell, Chief of Police," he said, shaking Jake's hand.

"Jake Pettman."

"Ro from the front desk told me." Gabriel smiled. "Where have you been all my life, Mr. Pettman? I was the tall kid who everyone wanted to prove themselves with. I'm surprised I made it this far. If you'd have turned up thirty years ago, my life would have been easier."

Jake returned the smile. "Well, if it makes you feel any better, I had similar issues growing up in Wiltshire."

"If you come through with me, Mr. Pettman, we'll go to my office to discuss the concerns."

Jake counted five officers in total as Gabriel led him through his department. Four male officers clustered around a desk, chatting and laughing. He recalled his days in Wiltshire HQ. He didn't remember many moments like this one.

One short female officer sat alone at her desk with blond hair tied back so tightly it glowed. She smiled a welcome at Jake. He returned her smile, and she refocused on a report she was filling out.

Gabriel opened his office door for Jake at the precise moment when someone shouted, "You fucking pricks!"

Jake turned to see the female officer's calm demeanor was no more. She was red-faced and on her feet, holding a G-string in the air. The drawer beside her was open. The unimaginative chauvinists had obviously planted it there.

"Get a fucking life."

One of the male officers called over, "We can order in the pole for you to dance around if you'd like, Lil."

"I'd skewer you with it," she shouted back.

Gabriel was red-faced. "Please, Mr. Pettman, wait in there."

Jake sat in the chair in the front of Gabriel's desk and let him rage at his staff.

Following a stream of incomprehensible expletives, he told them to do some work, and came into the office. "Sorry about that."

"Seems like you've got an issue with workplace bullying," Jake said.

"What? That?" Gabriel waved his hand. "They're all friends. They just like to joke sometimes."

"There's banter, and then there's misogyny. That looked like the dark ages to me."

Gabriel narrowed his eyes and took a deep breath. After exhaling, he took a seat. "Well, how can I help you, Mr. Pettman?"

Jake told him about meeting Piper in the Taps, her concerns over Madeline, and his visit to the Thompson farmhouse this morning.

"And you went alone?" Gabriel asked.

Jake nodded.

"And how did they respond to a complete stranger on their doorstep?"

"Graciously," Jake said, continuing the lie.

Gabriel made a few notes while Jake surveyed the photographs on his desk. All of them were of an elderly couple, presumably his parents. No wife or children. Jake was about to ask him if he was married or in a relationship when he quickly remembered what side of the table he was on and not to push his luck.

"Okay," Gabriel said. "Before I look into this, I'd like to ask you a few questions, Mr. Pettman."

Jake nodded, knowing this was inevitable.

"It always helps if an out-of-towner brings a passport to the station when they make reports, Mr. Pettman."

"I understand." Jake removed his passport from his pocket and slid it across the table.

"American ... Except you're not American, are you?"

Jake nodded. "You have the passport that says I am."

"But the British accent?"

Jake explained his history as he'd done with Piper the precious day.

When he mentioned the Bickfords, Gabriel's eyes widened, and he sat back in his chair. "Do you know what happened with the Bickfords?"

"Not in its entirety, no. Is it relevant to the reason I've come to see you?"

"I don't know," Gabriel said. "There's relevance in a lot of things. You don't always know until you look."

"Well, let me assure you then, Chief, that my ancestry will have little to do with the whereabouts of Maddie Thompson."

Gabriel leaned forward in his chair again, reviewing his notes. "Well, thank you, Mr. Pettman. I believe I have all I need for the time being. I'll —"

"So, what're you going to do about it?"

Gabriel looked up from his notes with narrowed eyes. "I'll be in touch if we need anything else. You can leave your contact details with Ro out front."

Jake shook his head. "That's not good enough."

Gabriel sat back again with a raised eyebrow. "Excuse me?"

"I'm reporting a fifteen-year-old girl missing."

"And I said we'll look into it."

"You"—Jake thumbed toward the unruly staff—"or them?"

"We, Mr. Pettman."

"You could start by trying to phone the relatives in Vermont to see if she got there okay."

Gabriel smirked. "Are you still a policeman, Mr. Pettman?"

Technically, yes. "No. It just seemed the most obvious course of action."

"And the reason it seems so obvious to you, Mr. Pettman, is because you're not from around here. And an ancestry of that nature really doesn't count. To be honest, you really wouldn't want it to count for much."

"There's a missing girl, Chief—"

"And there's an ecosystem. In this town, as well as any other. And it's our ecosystem. If I start calling up the relatives of some of our most respected residents, how does that make us look?"

Capable? Jake thought. *Proactive?*

"Look, I'm not a betting man, but, if I was, I would put my money on her being where her parents say she is. And until I suspect otherwise, I have an ecosystem to think of."

"But the bruises? Devin and Sean had been scrapping, and the father too, it sounds like."

"People fight, Mr. Pettman. Especially in towns like this. Looking at your face, I'm guessing you're no stranger to it either."

Jake gripped the underside of the desk as a need to stand up and shout grew. He heard more raucous laughter and another shout from the female officer. He stared at Gabriel, who fidgeted over the disarray on his shop floor. Sensing weakness, Jake nodded at a photograph of an older officer with a handlebar moustache, looking proud and capable, on the wall behind Gabriel. *Earl Jewell. Chief of Police. 1980.*

"Your father?" Jake asked.

"Yes, if it's any business of yours, Mr. Pettman."

"Would he be responding to my concerns in the same way?"

"I don't know. Things change. I earned my stripes on my own time."

"I don't doubt it, Chief. I just hope that, deep down, you care about a missing fifteen-year-old girl, because I do. Very much."

"Sounds almost threatening."

Jake leaned back in his chair. "Just a concerned citizen."

"You can be assured that if there's a need to care, I'll care."

"And what about this Jotham MacLeoid? Is he part of this delicate ecosystem you mentioned?"

Gabriel drummed his fingers on the table. "Well, our Piper really has been talking."

"You leave her out of this. This is down to me. I ask a lot of questions."

"Well, keep asking questions, but you won't get the answers you want. Mr. MacLeoid has brought nothing but good to this town. You'll struggle to find a bad word spoken against him. I think we're done here, Mr. Pettman."

I think we were done here a long time ago, Jake thought.

Gabriel stood and offered his hand.

Jake pretended he hadn't noticed. "Same way out?"

"I'll take you so you can leave your details with Ro. And, Mr. Pettman, I will look into it, and, if there's anything to it, I'll raise the alarm. But, if there isn't, I thank you for being a good American citizen and showing concern. But can I offer one piece of advice?"

Jake nodded. *I can guess what's coming.*

Gabriel leaned in. "Don't hang around too long, Mr.

Pettman. This is not a place for outsiders. I'd hate any harm to come to you."

Jake sighed. "Thank you for the cliché, Chief. I'll be sure to call later to find out if you've made any headway."

———

Outside, the victimised officer was smoking.

Jake went to stand beside her.

"Want one?" she asked.

Jake shook his head. "No thanks."

"I work with dickheads."

"I noticed. I also noticed that your boss is the biggest one."

She laughed and showed a fist. "Maybe I should just go in swinging?"

"I'm sure you will one day. I'll be happy to pick up ringside seats when you do."

She stood up straight and threw her cigarette on the ground. "You're funny." She faced him and brushed fluff off his Barbour jacket. "Scruffy, but funny. You also must be about a foot taller than me."

"More, I reckon."

"Fine. I like being down here. Although it doesn't help keep me inconspicuous. Especially up there." She nodded toward the station.

"You don't want to be inconspicuous. You're better than that."

"You mean, show them my worth?" She raised her eyebrows and laughed. "How do you think that will go?"

"Don't know. But don't let them grind you down."

She pointed at the station. "Is it that bad in England?"

63

"I've seen some things, but overall, no. I've never seen anything quite as bad as that."

"It wasn't mine you know."

"What?"

"The G-string."

Jake smiled. "I gathered that."

"I'm Lillian Sanborn. Lil for short." She proffered her hand, like Gabriel had done before.

He was happy to shake hers. "And I'm Jake Pettman. I'm descended from the Bickfords. Thought I best get that out in the open right away. It seems to be a source of great anxiety to anyone who finds out."

"Never heard of them."

"Great. Now how did you end up working with them?" He pointed at the station.

"My mom worked as a cleaner her whole life. Was spoken to like shit on a daily basis. Mainly by men, including my father. A few years ago, I decided to change the record and join the police. Put some steel into the Sanborn women."

"Bet she was proud."

"Graduation was the proudest day of her life. She's in a nursing home with Alzheimer's now. She can't remember much, but she can remember that. I'm glad she doesn't know what a circus I walked into."

"You walked into that, and you're surviving. Hats off to you."

"Yeah. Great. I spend most of my time either in that building, issuing traffic citations, or rescuing cats from trees. Every time anything even remotely exciting happens, I'm relegated to the coffee station."

Jake smiled. "I'm still stuck at *exciting*. Here, really?"

64

"It's been known to happen ... I'm going nuts. And I'm bored. What would you do?"

Jake considered his most recent behaviours. Those that made him flee the UK. "I'm probably not the best person to ask."

"Go on."

"Well, I'd probably look for something to do. Maybe put some things right."

"Easier said than done. Have you seen any problems worth solving?"

Jake smiled. "As a matter of fact, I have."

HAVING BEEN WOUND up by Jake Pettman, Gabriel struggled to control his demons on his journey to see Jotham. At the bottom of Main Street, he slowed as he drove past a couple of fourteen-year-old girls enjoying their weekend.

They smiled at him out of respect for his status.

He smiled back at them because his demons told him to. He circled back on himself so he could cruise past them a second time.

Again, they saw him, and again, they smiled. They wouldn't think anything of him circling—just a concerned man of law patroling his streets ...

Except wasn't that a glint in one of those young smiles? And wasn't that curiosity in that young lady's raised eyebrows?

His demons seemed to think so.

Then, throughout the rest of the journey, he couldn't still his beating heart and his baser instincts until his demons cackled so loudly and so violently he eventually found himself in a small rest stop, relieving himself into a tissue.

When he arrived at Jotham's house, he warned the old drug dealer that the conversation was serious. "They always are with you, Gabriel."

So, together, they went for a walk around the property. Jotham carried his rifle, which Gabriel wasn't best pleased about, but he let it go. Jotham could handle a lot of heat, but shooting the chief of police may be one step too far even for him.

Every time Gabriel tried to start the conversation, Jotham would shake his head. "Not yet. Let's just enjoy the quiet a moment longer."

Gabriel bit his lip. He really couldn't be bothered with the old bastard, but arguing, as they so often did, always ended unproductively.

Eventually, Jotham stopped and faced him. His long white hair rose in a gust of wind that raced over the empty field. "How can I help you, Gabriel?"

"Maddie Thompson."

Jotham raised an eyebrow. A ghost of a smile crossed his face. "The Thompson kid? What about her? Did you fuck her?"

Gabriel flinched. He supressed the urge to lunge for Jotham. He instead focused on a bouquet of colourful warblers swirling low over the fields. It did little to calm him. He turned back. "I don't appreciate you speaking to me like that."

"Maybe I'm out of line, Gabriel, but you don't get to come here to interrogate me like I'm some drunken bum in one of your fucking jail cells."

"I simply mentioned a name to you Jo—"

"You mentioned a young girl's name to me to provoke a

response."

Gabriel took a deep breath. "Okay, let's try this again. Someone came to the station to report Maddie Thompson missing. Your name came up."

"Who?"

"A man named Jake Pettman." He paused to see if Jotham would exhibit a response. He didn't. "A tall British man. He's only been in town a couple days."

"Why would a tourist be interested in Maddie Thompson?"

"He's not a tourist. He's got an American passport. He's also descended from the Bickfords."

"The Bickfords! You're shitting me!"

"That's what he said."

Jotham laughed. "The Bickfords! Jesus. Thought that line would have long since burned out. Probably best for all if it had."

"Do we need to be worried, Jo?"

"Well, if the man really is a Bickford, it's certainly something to worry about! Blood is blood, Gabriel, you know that as well as me. You are your daddy, and I am mine." Jotham stared across the field. He'd clearly caught sight of the warblers too. "Who has he been talking to?"

"Piper Goodwin. When Maddie didn't turn up for work, she got worried and spoke to Pettman."

"Uh-huh." Jotham nodded.

"They've both been round to see the family."

Jotham stared at Gabriel.

"The Thompsons told them Maddie is staying with relatives in Vermont."

"Sounds reasonable."

"So, if I call these relatives, Jo, will she be there?"

Jotham laughed. He lifted his rifle and fired into the

warblers. They dispersed. "Sounds like another interrogation to me."

"Look, Jo," Gabriel said, shrugging, "if you don't want my help, that's fine—"

Jotham lowered his rifle, turned back to Gabriel, narrowed his eyes and stepped toward him. "Oh, I want your help, alright. You tell this Bickford sonofabitch that Maddie is with her relatives, and then you tell him to leave town by the same road his ancestors did."

"You don't tell me what to do, Jo."

"No? Okay, call it advice. And you must know by now, Gabriel, that my advice is worth a hell of a lot. Get him out of town."

"Jesus, Jo. Maddie Thompson? She's just a kid."

Jotham snorted. "If there's one person who shouldn't be passing judgement in that department, Gabriel, it's you."

"Those rumors again?"

Jotham chortled. "Was it a rumor when you asked me personally for the youngest-looking whore up at the Edge?"

"Fuck you, Jo."

Jotham smiled. "I like your bile, Gabriel. Now spit some of it in the direction of this Bickford kid."

"I'll consider it."

"Stick to what we do best, like our daddies did, and we'll die old and fat in our beds."

"I don't want to get fat, Jo."

Jotham waved him away. "I've got other things on my mind right now, Gabriel. Big things. *Sensitive* things."

"Care to share?"

Jotham took a moment, clearly considering it, then shook his head. "No. I'll handle it. Safer that way."

"Thanks for the vote of confidence."

"I'm going this way." Jotham pointed toward the warblers. "I'm sure you can find your way back."

As he walked away, Gabriel thought of Kayla in his spare room and smiled to himself. *And there she will stay, far away from you, you sick fuck.*

6

STINSON LAKE WAS a long and narrow body of water.

"Took its name from a family of early settlers who lost a small child in the water here," Lillian said.

A strong wind cut into the lake, and Jake watched the ripple spread.

"Used to be a popular summer spot a long time back."

"Until that?" Jake pointed at the twenty-foot-high wooden wall which spread across the entire other side of the long lake.

"Yes," Lillian said and sighed.

To reach the lake, Jake and Lillian had walked a long muddy track and cut through a woodland. The scenery had been jaw dropping and had reminded him of home. Now, faced with the monstrous wall, Jake could see the significance of their draconian planning permission laws back in England. This most perfect spot had been desecrated.

Jake sat on a small mound of grass at the water's edge. He felt the moisture seep through into his pants but wasn't bothered. This wet and muddy world was the one he'd been raised in.

Lillian decided to remain standing.

His question outside the station to Lillian had been, *"So who the bloody hell is this Jotham MacLeoid?"*

Her response was to bring him here.

"So, this is the kind of man Jotham is," Lillian said. "He builds a wall to shut out the world."

"Secretive."

"Maybe. Except people already know nothing good is happening in there. He doesn't need a wall. No one in their right mind would step onto that property unless invited—or *told to*, anyway! I think it's about intimidation. A symbol. A look-at-the-size-of-my-dick symbol."

Jake smiled and nodded. "So, how did his dick get so big?"

"By giving the town exactly what it needed."

"No offence, but judging by how rundown your town looks, I'm not sure he's giving out that much."

"A deception. There are people in this town with a lot of money, and there are also people in the town given enough so they toe the line while thanking their lucky stars. Don't be fooled by some boarded-up shops on the main street. People are living well. He's got most people eating out of his hand."

Jake gestured at the wooden fence. "So, these are his palace walls?"

"Something like that."

"Who are the MacLeoids?"

"Traditionally, the MacLeoids were dog breeders. During prohibition, they ran a liquor racket. Over time, Jotham's father, Boyd MacLeoid, continued the family name by being a local bully who shook down businessowners for protection and kept the town supplied with recreational drugs during the swinging sixties. Nothing could prepare Blue Falls for Jotham though. He's the worst of the lot."

He sighed. "You're about to tell me he's more than just a farmer, aren't you?" Inside, he felt disappointed that Piper had held back on him last night.

"Well, depends how you define a farmer. He definitely farms goods. Although, I think the more correct definition would be *cooks*."

His eyes widened.

Lillian nodded. "I think I may have signed some kind of death warrant for myself telling you that." She shrugged. "Ah well, fuck it. Maybe they'll stop looking at me like some pathetic little girl."

Jake had stopped listening. "He makes drugs"—he pointed at the wall—"in there?"

"Yep. He has a meth lab beneath his property."

"And everybody in town knows about it?"

Lillian nodded again. "He has many people in the town working for him. Some in the lab itself, others distributing in other areas."

Piper's spiderweb. Gabriel's ecosystem. They all amounted the same thing. "This is corruption. Why is no one contacting the Maine State Police? The FBI? Someone?"

"Are you not listening? Everyone is terrified of him."

"He's one man."

"He's one man with a lot of power and a lot of allies. If he knew I was telling you this now, you'd struggle to find me tomorrow."

"Still, if he's taken out with one fell swoop ..."

"Except it doesn't work like that, does it? You know that

as well as me. You're police. You have the little matter of suspicion, evidence, and bureaucracy. The state police won't swoop in and arrest on a phone call from you, Jake. They turn up to investigate, the town will close ranks. He'll probably torch his lab before they acquire a search warrant. Then, after they leave, people will die. And he'll start all over again."

Jake noticed movement at the top of the wooden wall directly opposite them. Someone was accessing a small pedestal with a chair on it, almost like a lookout tower, presumably from a ladder on the other side.

"You've got to be fucking kidding me," Lillian said. "No one has ever seen him on that."

The lake was so narrow that Jake could clearly see the older man with the long white hair looking out from his pedestal. He had a hand up in greeting. In the other hand, he held a can of some kind.

"Is this his fucking throne?" Jake said.

"Hello!" Jotham called across the lake.

Jake nodded in response.

"Nothing like drinking the beer from your own lake," Jotham called.

And then Jake recalled the awful beer he'd been drinking the night before—Stinson IPA. Jake eyed Lillian. "His lake?" he asked quietly, although he wouldn't be heard unless he shouted.

"No. The lake isn't his, but he probably does feel like he owns everything."

"Come and join me," Jotham called. "I have a cooler full of beer."

"No, thank you," Jake called back.

"I understand. No drinking on duty, eh Lillian?" Jotham called.

Lillian sighed at Jake still perched on the mound. "We should go."

"Why? This is just getting interesting."

"Haven't you been listening to a word I've been saying?"

"Of course, I have, but when you run from a dog, it chases. And being descended from dog breeders, he'll know that. So the best thing you can do right now, Lillian, is carry on telling me about him."

Jotham sat in his chair and watched Jake and Lillian continue their conversation.

"Okay, but, if he gets out his binoculars and starts lipreading, you're on your own."

Jake spied Jotham and smiled. "Who does he live with?"

"His son Ayden and his daughter Kayla. Ayden is in his twenties. Kayla is quite young and still at school."

"Their mother?"

"Different mothers. Ex sex workers. Kayla's mother died a few years back. Ayden's mother lives in Sharon's Edge. You sure you want the most interesting part of Jotham's tale?"

"Of course."

"It's horrible."

"To be expected."

"He had three children before Kayla and Ayden ... triplets—"

"You two really are chewing the fat!" Jotham called. He'd not taken his eyes from them yet. "Must be an interesting place where you come from, Mr. Bickford."

"Pettman," Jake called back. He wasn't surprised. How could news not travel fast in a town with a population of three thousand?

Jotham cupped his ear. "Sorry? I didn't catch that."

"Pettman. My name is Jake Pettman."

Jotham held up the palm of his hand. "Sorry! Seems I've been misinformed. Please carry on with your picnic."

"Wanker," Jake muttered.

"Be safer to keep those opinions to yourself."

"Like everybody else in this town? Change must start somewhere. Anyway, you were saying, triplets?"

"A while ago, when he was in his thirties, he married someone named Amber Colson. She was the daughter of the chief selectman at the time."

"Another shrewd move," Jake said, recalling yesterday evening's exploits with the current chief selectman's son. "No wonder he's found it easy to build his empire, with the town council on his side."

"Well ... it hasn't all been easy."

"Good," Jake said, staring into Jotham's smug eyes. "Enlighten me."

"He came home one day to find his three baby daughters dead. Amber had fed them disinfectant."

Jake felt his eyes twitching, but he kept them on Jotham's.

"Postnatal depression."

"Jesus," Jake said, watching Jotham take another mouthful of beer.

"The story is that he stood by her, tried to help her, but one night, she locked herself in an old barn and burnt it down."

Jotham smiled.

"Awful way to die," Jake said.

"She blew her head off with a shotgun before the flames got to her."

Jake flinched.

Jotham stood and walked to the edge of the pedestal. "Been good catching up!" He crushed his can and threw it.

Jake followed its descent into the lake. Ripples spread far and wide. The can bobbed up and down—a pollutant that didn't sink. He looked back up to see Jotham walking to his ladder. *An angry, bitter man who has lost everything but wants to keep on taking.*

Jotham descended the ladder. Just before his head disappeared, Jake gritted his teeth.

I don't care how powerful and how dangerous you are, if you've hurt Maddie Thompson, I'll kill you.

———

WHEN PIPER VISITED his motel room early evening, Jake didn't want her to realize that he felt betrayed that she hadn't told him about Jotham MacLeoid and his hold over the town. However, as was always the case when he was with the opposite sex, he struggled to hide his true feelings.

"What're you pissed about?"

After he told her, she sat on the edge of his bed. "I'm sorry."

"If you need my help, you must tell me everything."

"I know, but I cannot help feeling ashamed of Blue Falls. I'd quite like you to stick around, and telling you my town is a cesspit wouldn't be the most convincing approach."

Jake sighed and sat beside her. "It does have some things going for it. Stinson Lake was nice. The walk to it reminded me of home."

"Until you get to the lake and actually see that wall."

"Yep. That was quite an eyesore."

"Who was the cop who took you to Stinson Lake?"

Jake smiled. "Now, you want *me* to be open and be transparent?"

Piper looked down. "Fair enough."

Jake told her about Lillian Sanborn and their afternoon together.

"She's nice, Lillian," Piper said, still looking down. "I'm glad she wants to help."

"Yes, she's definitely one of the nicest people I've met in town."

Piper regarded Jake with a sad expression.

"I did say *one of*."

Piper smiled. "I'm sorry for holding back."

They seemed to be moving closer. Jake hadn't adjusted his position on the edge or noticed Piper shuffling, so he guessed their faces were edging toward one another's.

His cell rang. Jake reached behind himself to grab it up from his bed. "I hope this is Jewell. I've been leaving messages for him every five minutes for the last two hours." He answered, "Jake Pettman."

"It's Gabriel Jewell."

"You're a busy man."

"Well, I am the chief of police."

Yeah right! Chief of police in a small town where the only thing happening right now is something you've no inclination to investigate!

"I've contacted the relatives," Gabriel said. "Maddie's fine and dandy. In fact, they're enrolling her in a school on Monday. They are keen to stay law abiding in this difficult situation."

"I see. Who did you speak to?"

"Not really my place to share names with you, Mr. Pettman. In fact, it's not really my place to share any of this with you. I just figured that with all the concern you've shown, you deserve something. So, there it is; she's safe. Case closed."

"Why have the family fallen out?"

"Look. Where you come from, it may be part of the deal to pry and pry until the relationship between you and the community rots to shit, but here, we try and maintain a certain degree of respect for one another."

Jesus, not your fucking ecosystem again!

"But, if you *really* must know, and this is the final thing I'm saying on this matter, the argument was to do with the brothers. Bad news them two, if you ask me. Mother wanted her away from them. Clean break."

"Bad news? How?"

"I've done as you asked. Now, do me a favor and consider what I said to you before you left the office. The cliché, remember? Think on it long and hard. Good evening, Mr. Pettman." The phone went dead.

Jake sighed.

Piper patted his upper arm. "What?"

"He claims to have contacted the relatives, and everything is fine. In other words, the police won't do anything."

"Hate to say I told you so."

"Let's find out if the idiot actually rang the relatives." Jake phoned Lillian. He greeted her, thanked her for the day and the information then led straight into a request. "So, thank Marissa again for providing the phone number of her relatives in Vermont to the police then apologize and say you think the number was written down wrong."

"So, she either gives me the number or wonders what the hell we're talking about and drops the chief in it for talking bullshit?"

"Precisely," Jake said.

After the call, Piper put her hand on his knee. "Thank you so much for all this."

Jake eyed her. "You don't have to thank me."

"I know I don't, but I am."

Jake shrugged. "Something's wrong here. It's never been in my nature to look the other way. It sounds noble, but it's a curse. It's taken me down some bad paths in my time." *And it killed my last marriage.*

She leaned over and kissed him.

He allowed it to linger but didn't press back.

When she saw it was going nowhere, she pulled away. "Sorry. I thought …"

"You didn't think wrong."

"Doesn't seem that way."

"I don't expect any kind of repayment."

Her eyes widened. "*Really?* Is that what you think this is? Some kind of service—"

"No … no." Jake waved his palms at her. "Bad choice of words. I don't mean that. I just don't want to take advantage of someone who feels grateful to me. This help. It's just part of who I am—probably a lingering hangover from the job I used to do. I like you, I do, but getting involved with me would be a mistake."

"You make it sound like I just proposed to you."

Jake's cell rang. "Lillian?"

"Okay. Get ready for this! It totally threw Marissa. She asked her sons which one had given out the number. They all denied it."

"Because it never happened," Jake said.

"I pressed her for it again. The husband, Blake, snatched the phone and said his sister-in-law's phone was out of order and then hung up on me. Something really is going on here."

"Something involving your boss."

"Shit."

"Lillian, could you phone in sick tomorrow and meet me at the Blue Falls motel at eight a.m.?"

"Shit ... is this real policework, Jake?"

"If you class fumbling around in the dark with no fucking idea what is going on, then yes, I guess it is."

"Sounds exciting. See you at eight."

He eyed Piper.

She didn't look convinced. "You really have got yourself a new sidekick, haven't you?"

"No, *we've* got ourselves a dose of good luck. She's a police officer. How far do you think we'd get without one?"

"Still, I'd rather I tagged along."

"I know, but after meeting Jotham and hearing all about the insidious monster, I'm not about to parade you around in the investigation."

She kicked off her shoes, hoisted up her legs and leaned in so her head was on his shoulder.

He considered slipping his arm around her but hesitated and tilted his head toward hers instead. He almost sighed when he felt the contact but forced it back; he didn't want to give her too many clues that he was enjoying it as much as she was.

A mistake ... a mistake ... a mistake ... The words ran through his head. Maybe she was turned on that he'd come to help, that he was like some knight in shining armor, but was that such a bad thing? He looked down as her hand moved over him.

Her multi-colored nails slid down over his chest. "You've got a good body. Strong." Her hand moved lower.

Both were breathing faster now.

She slipped her hands underneath his T-shirt and moved them over his stomach.

A mistake ... a mistake ... a mistake ... He couldn't shake his warning, and it did little to stop him. If anything, it turned him on even more.

She slipped away.

He leaned into her, not wanting her to go.

She raised a finger to still him then removed her own shirt, unhooked her bra, lifted his shirt and pressed her breasts against his skin. She nuzzled his chin, his cheek, the corner of his mouth, before kissing him.

This time, he kissed back.

A mistake ... a mistake ... a mistake...

The kiss became firmer. Her hand fell below, and she began to touch.

He grew hard quickly.

She climbed on top of him, pushing him back, then leaned over him so she could kiss him again.

A mistake ... a mistake ... a mistake ... The words tortured him, but his hands couldn't be stopped. He yanked at the belt on her jeans as she forcefully kissed him.

She allowed him some air to unpin her hair and let it fall all over him.

He popped the button on her jeans with one hand while, with the other, he massaged her breast.

She leaned down and kissed him for the longest time.

A mistake ... a mistake ... a mistake ...

A wise person once told Jake that you cannot learn without making mistakes. He turned her over onto the bed and slid down her jeans. *Tonight, then, was all about education.*

7

AFTER JOTHAM HAD spent the day working through the cooler of Stinson IPA, he paced Kayla's room. The boy band posters which he'd torn down earlier lay crumpled on the floor. He kicked them around then thumbed the patches on the wall where his tearing had damaged the yellow paint. *You will paint that, Ayden. You will paint this whole fucking room.*

He went to the full-sized mirror by her bed and stared at his reflection. He gripped each hanging white curtain of hair in a different hand, yanked them back over his ears and held them there. *I see you, Daddy.*

He panned up and down the weathered face, lingering for a time on the beady eyes drowning in pulpy sacs. *I see you, Boyd.* He slammed his forehead into the mirror. Keeping his head against the glass, he waited for the burning sensation to spread a dull ache over his nose and cheeks. He pulled his head away, smiling.

A spider's web had spread across the glass.

He felt blood running down the bridge of his nose.

I—

He thrust forward and heard the glass splinter some more.

See—

He drove in, keeping his eyes open so when he drew back he could see the wound splitting on his forehead.

You.

Blood filled his eyes. He stumbled backward, blind, ripped open his buttoned flannel shirt and removed it. He wiped the blood from his face and eyes and held it against his burning forehead to stem the flow. He approached the mirror again, his vision clearing. The spiderweb had grown in detail and glowed red, but he could still see himself. He traced his reflection, starting at his exposed stomach just above the buckle of his jeans and up his bloody chest— which, although not muscular, was slim and did not sag as was often the case in men his age. He touched his face, which was splintered by the heart of the cobweb.

"I lost her, Daddy—"

He narrowed his eyes.

"Don't you look at me, Boyd—"

He slammed the palm of his hand into the mirror, splintering it further.

"Don't you *fucking* look at me!"

He thrust his palm into the glass. It was useless. The mean old bastard stared back.

He turned from the reflection and leaned his naked back into the glass. He took a deep breath and, with his shirt still pressed to his leaky forehead, slid into a squat, the ruptured glass biting into his upper back. He pushed himself back into a standing position and felt the glass chew on him.

He screamed in agony.

I'm going to rub you out, Daddy.

He went down the glass again and listened to his back rip.

HALF-NAKED AND COLD, still gripping his shirt against his forehead, Jotham opened the cage door and crawled in with Bo.

The other dogs barked, jealous of the attention she was being shown and not knowing it was actually Jotham seeking out the attention on this occasion.

Jotham curled up on his side next to his dog and closed his eyes.

Bo excitedly padded around her owner, nuzzling his neck, but once she sensed he wasn't here to play, she hunkered next to him and swept her long tongue up and down his torn back.

At first, it stung, but Jotham no longer possessed the energy to move, and so allowed it. Eventually, it started to soothe. Jotham eventually found sleep, smiling over that final moment before, in Kayla's room, when he'd turned back to look at his daddy's face again but could see only the blood obscuring the reflection.

SLEEPING BEAUTY.

Kayla lay on her back with her long black hair fanned out on her pillow. She wore one of his T-shirts, which was far too large for her, but, as her chest rose and fell, her small but developing breasts pushed against the loose material.

One kiss to wake her.

Gabriel edged into the room, both excited and fearful of what he'd allowed into his house.

This was Jotham MacLeoid's daughter. If the old bastard knew she was here, he'd organize a lynching the likes of which hadn't been seen for generations. He stood over the bed. The duvet was over her waist. It was a simple matter to lift it and fold it away from her body without disturbing her. He sighed when he saw her shorts tight against her narrow hips but loose against the thighs of her slim legs. He reached down ...

Today, on his land, Gabriel's hatred for Jotham had intensified. To rise to the lofty heights of police chief only to bow down to an insidious drug dealer who corrupted the soul of the town he loved was a grueling weight to bare.

His fingers were an inch from the sleeping girl's thigh ...

So easy to corrupt the daughter of the tumorous Jotham. And so exciting. He chewed his bottom lip and took deep breaths. His hand trembled.

He closed his hand and stepped away.

DOWNSTAIRS, in front of his laptop, Gabriel struggled to find satisfaction. He hopped from video to video. He'd watched most before, many times, and with great pleasure; yet, tonight, none of them would help him sustain an erection.

Knowing where this journey may take him, he dug in, determined to fight it. No matter how far his demons tried to drag him down, there was one level he *must* avoid at all costs. He tried to look into his sister's eyes for support, forgetting, of course, he'd already turned down her photograph, and there was no friendly gaze for him to meet.

He tried one last video, but his erection then his willpower both ebbed away, and he found himself opening the video he'd been so desperate to avoid.

And then he was staring into the abyss.

A twelve-year-old girl begged a man in a mask to allow her to go home to her parents and her baby brother Samuel. The man shook his head and told her that if she ever wanted to see them again, she would need to undress. She removed her school uniform.

Gabriel cried as he masturbated.

WHILE PIPER SLEPT, Jake stared at the ceiling. He battled with insomnia most evenings anyway. But tonight, with the Thompsons lying about their missing daughter while the shadow of the infamous Jotham MacLeoid grew ever larger, he really was on the losing side. He leaned over and kissed the large birthmark on Piper's collarbone and turned to sit on the edge of the bed.

As he often did when wakefulness had the upper hand, he took the photographs of his son from the drawer. The first couple of weeks he'd been traveling around New England, they'd reduce him to tears, but he was getting more resilient now. The pain was hardening him.

The latest photograph showed Frank wearing a Southampton football shirt and celebrating a goal he'd just scored in an inflatable football net in his garden. Jake smiled. He'd allowed Frank's shot to slip between his legs, and once he was celebrating wildly, none-the-wiser to his father's assistance, Jake had quickly snapped a photo on his phone.

As he slipped the photographs into the drawer, Jake

considered what he would do if Frank ever needed help like Maddie Thompson needed help right now. His instincts, his desperation to help, would have him on the first plane home, but how long would he last after the plane landed? They would have eyes everywhere. He would be dead before he got anywhere near helping his son.

Jake sighed, stood and stretched. He turned and stared at the drawer. So, this was his reward for turning his back on them, for choosing honesty—exile. Never to return. Never to see his boy again.

He sat on the stool used last night by Peter Sheenan, the ex-soldier dubbed Dogman by some of the more incendiary locals. He turned away from Piper so as not to disturb her with the light on his phone. He set to work researching the more sinister residents of Blue Falls. Of which, unfortunately, there were many.

Blake Thompson opened his bruised eyes and gasped.

A cross-legged figure sat at the end of the bed, facing him.

He sat upright, gulping air, and after his eyes adjusted to wakefulness, sighed with relief. It was Marissa. He groaned and winced as he adjusted his sitting position. They'd made a mess of him out by that pit, psychologically and physically. And now the mere thought of that place and what had occurred there reminded him of the deep hollowness inside himself, and he wanted to cry out in anguish. But he suppressed it, for Marissa's sake, for his sons' sakes. That was to be his punishment, his purgatory— to rot in silent anguish.

"My dear, you must try to sleep."

She didn't reply and wore a vacant expression. Her eyes weren't even on him. They seemed to be staring elsewhere.

"Marissa?"

Still nothing.

"Keeping yourself awake will just make you ill."

Marissa smiled and lowered her eyes to him. "You know I won't sleep until Maddie's home, silly! But it's given me some thinking time. Do you know what I reckon we should do?"

Blake could feel tears in his eyes. "No."

"I think we should stay on Soft Rain Bay again, like we used to every year. Just a weekend, mind, I know you and the boys are busy."

"That sounds lovely, dear. Now please come and get some—"

"Is she coming home soon, Blake. *Is she?*"

Blake felt his heart melt. He wanted to scream at the heavens. "I hope so, dear."

Marissa smiled. "I'd like that so much."

"Me too."

"Maybe you could ask Mr. MacLeoid to let her come?"

Blake felt his blood run cold. He didn't want to have this conversation again, certainly not in the middle of the night. Every hour, he felt himself teetering closer to insanity, but he had to hold it together, just had to. If he lost control, as Marissa had clearly done, that monster would return to finish them off.

"We can't rush it. I told you that. He will allow her home when he's ready." Every time he lied to her, he felt another piece of himself break inside.

"Those stupid boys, I will never forgive them for this. They should know better than to break that man's rules."

Don't turn on your boys, dear, Blake thought, wiping tears from his cheeks. *They're all we have left.*

"If I come to bed now, will you think about Soft Rain Bay?"

"Soft Rain Bay? Ah yes, of course."

She crawled up beside him and put her arm around him. "I hope he's feeding her well."

"I'm sure he is." Blake turned away, worried his tears might fall on her head.

"Do you remember when you used to love me, Blake?"

Blake sighed. "I still do."

"It was such a wonderful time."

"Go to sleep, Marissa, please."

"One day, we'll all be together again."

God, how I wish that were true, Blake thought and cried as quietly as he could.

8

JAKE LEFT PIPER sleeping in his bed and joined Lillian in her car.

She offered him a plastic cup full of a light green sludge. "Juice? I made too much."

Out of politeness, he took it but immediately betrayed his real feelings by lifting the lid and sniffing it.

"Cucumber and kiwi," she said.

"I'm in America. I was expecting coffee and donuts."

"This isn't downtown New York."

"More's the pity." Jake took a mouthful and shrugged. "Not bad actually." He drained his cup. "Enough calories for me to tell you about something that caught my interest in the early hours of the morning, but after that, I'll need fueling up."

"What caught your attention?"

"Samantha Kelly."

"She's a selectwoman."

"Yes, I know that. That's why I looked into her. Your chief is big on his delicate ecosystem, so I've done my best to map it all out."

"All night?"

Jake shrugged. "That's why I was hoping for coffee."

"Now I feel bad! Well, at least my juice is good for your skin. What have you found out about Samantha Kelly?"

"She's very well-off. But that didn't surprise me. Anyone on this board is minted! What really interested me was she was a property developer. Often, in England, they're worth a closer look. Her biggest project was in Soft Rain Bay. What can you tell me about this place?"

"It's on the edge of another town on the River Skweda—New Lincoln. It used to be a popular vacation spot way back when, before flying became affordable and traveling became more ambitious. I used to go there as a kid, and I can tell you that the rain, when it comes, is anything but soft."

"Do people from around here still travel there?"

"Some. Not as many. Cheap motels don't exist around there anymore—just expensive summer homes and rich retirees. It looks totally different; most of the older properties have been bulldozed."

"Yes, I saw some of the destruction online. I also noticed something else online—or rather, a lack of something else. Usually, when a property developer swoops down on an older property that has been with families for generations, there's an uproar. I couldn't find anything in the news. No interviews with disgruntled elderly houseowners, no news reports on any residents taking legal action, not even a pissed-off blog from a local. Nothing. Does that happen? Does everyone just sell up? No complaints?"

"Maybe Kelly's company paid them well?"

"Doesn't matter how handsomely they were paid, there are still people out there not interested in money. Someone would have objected. I guarantee. Except, I'm guessing some powerful people stopped it making it to the press—or making it anywhere for that matter."

"Well, it does sound rather typical of Blue Falls. So, where now then? Samantha Kelly?"

"No, that will go down like a lead balloon, and you'll probably find me in the clink by sunset."

"Or worse."

Jake nodded. "Do you know anyone in the police department in New Lincoln?"

"No—"

"Shit."

She smiled.

"What?"

She raised an eyebrow. "There isn't a police department in New Lincoln. *Our* department has the contract for New Lincoln *and* Sharon's Edge."

Jake's eyes widened. "Bloody brilliant. Massive change of plan here then, Lil. Have you already phoned in sick?"

She shook her head and checked her watch. "Was going to do it at eight-thirty."

"Fantastic. I want you to go to work and access your department records."

"What am I looking for?"

"Complaints of harassment from ex-Soft Rain Bay residents."

"You think I'll find any?"

"Probably not. Jewell is part of the fucking ecosystem he loves to waffle about, and he'll keep clean files. However, there is something you'll definitely be able to find out ..."

"Go on?"

"The names and current addresses of the ten Soft Rain Bay residents who gave up their homes. Then, come back here and get me."

"Dad ... Dad ... Dad?"

Jotham woke shivering and in pain.

Ayden offered him a blanket through the open door of the dog cage.

The concerned expression on his son's face confirmed what he already knew; he'd done significant damage to himself. He rose on an elbow and pushed away the blanket.

Bo whined and nuzzled Jotham's neck from behind.

He reached around and brushed off his dog.

"What happened, Dad?"

"You know what happened, Ayden. You know because it's happened before. Why do you always have to act so dumb?"

Ayden's face sagged.

"Have you found her?"

Ayden shook his head.

"Why do I even bother asking?" Jotham tried to crawl from the cage. He squeezed his eyes closed, moaned and stopped half-way out. The cuts on his back would have started congealing during the night; the movement would be reopening the wounds.

"Dad, your back—"

"I *know!*"

"Let me help you ..."

Jotham batted away his son's hand. "Don't fucking touch me."

"You can hardly move."

Jotham took a deep breath, gritted his teeth and rose. He held back until he was fully upright, but, at that point, the pain could no longer be bottled. He released a guttural cry.

The dogs barked. For once, he didn't bother trying to silence them.

He limped past his son.

"You're bleeding."

"Send one of the girls to bandage me."

"Maybe you should get it looked at."

Jotham stopped and laughed, stopping when the vibrations from doing so burned like acid. "*Looked at? Where? At the hospital?*"

"Yes ... maybe."

"Jesus. You really are a funny little fucker."

"No, I just fucking care! What the hell is wrong with that?"

Insolent little shit. I wanted my father's approval too. Fought for it day in, day out. But I never raised my voice to him. Not once. Jotham turned slowly to face his son—not because of the pain but because he wanted to keep his adrenaline in check. He was in no fit state to beat his son, and so it was imperative he exercised restraint. Besides, there was more than one way to skin a cat. And he should know, he'd skinned his fair share of them.

"When I was a young boy, we had this one bitch on the farm, completely untrainable. We've had our share here, Ayden, but nothing like this. Almost took Boyd's hand clean off one day. Anybody else, you'd have laughed. But you didn't laugh when Boyd was involved. He commanded too much respect for that."

"I know the story, Dad. You command the same respect—"

"Interrupt me again, Ayden. *Go on.* I fucking dare you to."

Ayden went pale.

"Command respect? You don't even understand the

fucking concept. My father kept a chain which he never cleaned. It was stained with the blood of so many of his dogs. One day, he put it in my hand and dragged out his untrainable bitch. You've never beaten a dog, Ayden, not properly. It lunges for you, snapping and snarling. In that moment, you are fair game, and, if it catches you just right, it'll take you to pieces. I beat that dog. I had it down on its belly, shitting and pissing itself. It was *fucking* writhing in a cesspit of its own making. After, I gave the chain back to my father stained with the blood of yet another dog. Guess what? This dog was now as obedient as they come." Jotham blinked as blood ran into his eye. He touched his stinging forehead and inspected his stained red fingertips. "I was thirteen. When I was fourteen, barely a month later, I was fucking a farmgirl on our kitchen table." He pointed at their home. "My mother walked in. Later that night, Boyd beat me with that chain for soiling the dinner table. The next day, he beat me again for disrespecting my mother."

Ayden's mouth hung open.

"From that moment, I never stepped out of line." He sighed. "And yet, for all that, here I stand, having failed you." Jotham tapped his son's chest. "Raising your voice, interrupting me, unable to control your sister ... *I failed*. If only, if only I could just turn back time. Beat you harder. Train you better."

A tear ran down Ayden's face.

"If Kayla isn't back by this time tomorrow, I'm going to go into Boyd's things in the cellar, and I'm going to pull out that bloody chain, Ayden. Then I'm going to start beating you. And I warn you, if I feel half as disappointed as I do right now, I don't think I'll be able to stop."

GABRIEL'S ALARM found him in his sleep, and when he opened his eyes, he saw Kayla in bed with him. He bolted upright, and the duvet dropped from him. He looked down and saw he was in pajamas. He sighed and remembered. Nothing had happened. He'd gone to bed alone. She must have crawled in during the night.

"Sorry," she said.

"No, it's fine."

"I kept dreaming about the pit. I kept seeing Maddie ... her face ... and then ..."

Her hair hung over her face. Gabriel brushed it gently back and tucked it behind her ear. With the other hand, he pulled the duvet over himself to conceal his growing erection.

"I was scared."

"You're safe now."

"Have you arrested Daddy yet?"

"No ... soon." He wiped away a tear from under her eye.

"Why does it take so long?"

"Investigations do."

"Have you got Maddie from the pit?"

"It's best you don't talk about it, Kayla. Really. You've been through enough already."

"I can't go back until you arrest him. If he knows I've been talking to you, he'll kill me."

Gabriel shook his head. "You don't have to. But I don't believe that he'd hurt you."

"No, really. You don't know what he's like."

He nodded. *Yes, I do. The sonofabitch is capable of anything.*

"When he's gone, I can live with Ayden. He's different to Daddy. He'll take care of me."

"Sounds perfect."

She sat upright, wriggled over and put her head onto his shoulder.

His erection pushed painfully against his pajama bottoms.

"You're nice. Thank you for helping me."

He gritted his teeth and fought his demons. "You're welcome. Why don't you run down and watch some television?"

"Are you getting ready for work?"

"Not today. My team are handling your father. I've got some things that really need taking care of."

"I'll make you some coffee."

"That would be nice, but maybe get dressed first."

After she'd left the room, Gabriel listened for her bedroom door closing and headed to a door underneath the stairs. He forced back some stiff, heavy iron bolts. It had been ages since he'd last been down here. He opened the door and, covering his mouth against the dust, leaned in to pull on a light cord. The bare lightbulb glowed. Gabriel looked down the stairs into the dusty cellar.

He hated missing work, but it would take a day to clean up down here, and he so wanted Kayla's new room to be perfect for her.

9

JAKE'S MORNING WITH Piper couldn't be any
different from their frenetic evening together. Her
personal concern for the welfare of Maddie Thompson
had transitioned into a *shared* concern. With that came a
solid emotional connection and tenderness as they sought
and found solace in each other.

Lillian's trip to the station was quicker than he'd
anticipated though, and her knock at Jake's door interrupted
their lovemaking.

"Just wait in the car for me, please, Lil!" Jake called.
After dressing and kissing Piper farewell, Jake joined Lillian
in the car.

She handed him a handwritten list. "All ten addresses."

"Let's get cracking then."

While she was driving, Lillian said, "Did you have
someone in there with you?"

Jake flushed. "Blunt round here, aren't you?"

"So, yes, then?"

"A gentleman never tells."

"Piper Goodwin?"

Jake rose an eyebrow. "What makes you think that?"

"When you came into the department yesterday, I overheard the boys talking. One of them had seen you in the Taps the previous evening, putting the moves on."

"Putting the moves on?"

Lillian smiled, stopped at a junction and signaled left.

"Bloody hell, I've only known you five minutes, Lil, and we're already discussing my intimate affairs!"

"You come to a place like Blue Falls, then your intimate affairs are everyone's affairs. The sooner you learn that, the easier it'll be to fit in."

"Don't worry, I'm learning fast."

"Piper's a gem, by the way."

"Thanks for the seal of approval."

The first three ex-owners of Soft Rain Bay property were living well. They were all hospitable toward Jake and Lillian and offered them coffee. Jake accepted each time and listened to three stories of how Kelly Properties had changed their lives for the better. They'd been paid generously, and their lifestyles had benefitted massively.

Jake, who was now riding a caffeine high, panicked that he'd led them down a dead end.

"There's still seven to go," Lillian reassured him. "Maybe you should slow down on the coffee?"

Jake took her advice, and when they sat down in a pleasant little bungalow with Noah and Emma Watson, he refused their coffee.

"We've got tea," Emma said.

"That would be great, thanks," Jake said.

"Chilled or hot?"

"Definitely hot." Jake sank into a deep sofa which reminded him of his former home in Salisbury.

On the opposite sofa, Noah and Emma held hands as

they spoke. They had a warm glow about them, and Jake hoped he too was destined for such contentment in later life.

When Jake mentioned the reason for their visit though, the couple frowned, and the warmth glow disappeared. "I'm sorry."

"Don't be. We're happy to talk about it," Noah said, clutching his wife's hand, as if the experience they were about to relay had brought them a lot closer together. "Four generations of Watsons lived and died in that house. We won't forget about it, and no one will stop us telling the story. We owe our family that much."

"Thank you, sir," Jake said.

"It started off politely enough. Evan, one of my neighbors, chased them out with a broom, but we listened to them and were hospitable. They offered a lot of money, more than the place was worth. Three times they came back, and their offer grew ridiculously. The last time, Samantha Kelly herself, the company owner, offered us the most lavish retirement you could imagine. We told them it wasn't about us; it was about our family. This property belonged to the Watsons, and one day, our children would return to live here." The older couple turned to look at one another.

Jake allowed them a moment by taking a mouthful of tea. It wasn't Yorkshire tea, which he could drink by the gallon, but it wasn't bad.

Noah looked back. "We had three rabbits in the back garden."

Emma put her fist to her mouth.

"The day after we refused Samantha, we found some cats eating them at the back door. This was no accident. We hadn't left the cage unlocked, and when we looked closely—"

"Excuse me. Sorry." Emma, tearful, stood and left the room.

Noah sighed. "The cats hadn't killed them. The wounds were too precise. Someone had sliced open their bellies."

"I'm sorry," Jake eyed Lillian, who'd turned pale. "Did you call the police?"

"Of course. They came to look, but, no offense, dear"—he nodded toward Lillian—"but the police were useless, and they wouldn't believe this was deliberate."

"You can rest assured I knew nothing of it, sir," Lillian said. "I wouldn't have ignored you."

Noah nodded. "Thank you."

Jake finished his tea and set it on the coffee table. "I'm sorry this happened to you, sir."

"The harassment continued, son. Two days later, I opened the shed in my garden and hundreds of rats ran out, then the day after that, the bastards came back *again* with another offer."

"Was Samantha Kelly there?"

"Not this time. They stayed on my doorstep, mind you. There was no way these bloodsuckers were coming into my home again. I told them to get lost, stopping short of using a broom like Evan. Eventually, they left." Noah looked down and sighed. "That night, Emma looked out our window and saw our garden bench on fire. It was terrifying. We had to call the fire department."

"Surely, the firemen would have known this was a deliberate act?" Jake said.

Noah shook his head. "No. They blamed it on a plug-in patio heating lantern we had beside the bench. We'd apparently made the mistake of leaving it on, and then it had malfunctioned, burnt itself out and ignited the bench. Except, here's the thing, we'd not used that lantern in weeks! Fell on deaf ears, of course."

Jake rubbed his stubbly cheek, shaking his head. The corruption in this area was out of control.

"So, it was us versus them," Noah said and smiled. "And we were the underdogs, wouldn't you say? Next day, along comes Samantha Kelly. She sat opposite me, like you are now, looked me in the eyes and told me I had no choice. That if I didn't sell now, then next time, someone would be sitting on the other bench in the garden when they lit it. Openly admitted to it! The balls on her!"

Jake noticed Emma at the door she'd left through, looking in, clearly summoning the courage to return.

"Did you go the police again?" Jake said.

"No," Emma said. "That's when we said enough is enough."

Jake watched Noah look down, ashamed. Jake assumed it'd been Emma's decision to put this to bed. "I'm sorry it didn't work out."

"Why are you asking us about this now?" Noah looked up, his eyes widening. "Is someone finally going to be held to account for all of this?"

"We will try."

Noah sighed. "You can never win, son. They can never be beaten."

Jake recalled his recent experiences in Wiltshire. *Sounds familiar.*

The next couple of visits to ex-residents of Soft Rain Bay were uneventful. Finally, they drove to see Evan Bell, the ex-resident who was supposedly quite handy with the broom, living in a caravan on the edge of Sharon's Edge.

Despite it being quite cold, Evan was content to sit outside his vehicle on a deckchair. He wore a woolly hat while reading *Zen and the Art of Motorcycle Maintenance* by Robert M. Pirsig.

"How can I help you?" he asked without looking up from his book.

"Morning, sir," Lillian said, "I'm from the Blue Falls Police Department—"

He slammed his book shut and tugged on his long white beard. "Whatever you're selling, I'm not interested."

"We aren't selling anything, sir," Jake said. "This is about what happened with Samantha Kelly and your old property. We're on your side."

"What do you want to know? I told you people everything, and you weren't interested then. Why the sudden change of heart?"

"If you hear us out—"

"They ran my dog over, son. Toby was ten years old, and they drove an SUV over him. Unless you tell me they're finally off to jail, we've nothing to talk about. Mind you, if you're here to talk about the physical damage we can inflict on Samantha Kelly and her henchmen, I'm all ears too."

Jake and Lillian exchanged a look.

"We just want the truth," Jake said.

Evan stood, pointed at them and sneered. "If you're with the police, you're with Gabriel Jewell. You *already* know the truth."

"Yes, I work for Gabriel Jewell," Lillian said, "but I'm not the same as him, and I'm not privy to the truth. Let's just say we have different philosophies."

"Different philosophies, eh?" Evan laughed. "That's good for you, because the last time I was with that man and his *philosophy*, it took three of your officers to pry me off him. He underestimated how much life was left in these old bones."

"I hear you, sir," Jake said. "I've encountered that philosophy too. Apathy, they call it."

Evan nodded. "Yes, exactly right. You tell a man someone murdered your dog, you get out of your chair."

"You also get out of a chair if someone tells you a little girl is missing," Jake said.

"Of course." Evan sat back down and sighed. "You may want to ignore my bravado. You know, going for that smug jerkoff was the worst decision I ever made. They had me. They could have taken me to court and put me away for a long time."

"Let me guess," Jake said. "Unless you sold up?"

Evan nodded. "Toyed with the idea of not doing, fighting them to the bitter end from my jailcell, but, you know, I saw the kind of threats coming the way of the Watsons, and I have family too—a daughter and some grandchildren in Bangor. I couldn't protect them from a jailcell. The game was up."

"They still paid you well?"

"Yes, they gave me a ridiculous amount of money."

Jake nodded at the caravan. "No disrespect, but why here then?"

Evan laughed. "I couldn't stomach using their money, not after what they'd done to Toby. I've got a small pension. It's enough. Sometimes I go and stay with family, and they take care of me. I'm fine."

"What did you do with the money?" Lillian said.

"I gave it all to my daughter. That house would have been her inheritance after all. They live well now, and, like I said, they take good care of me when I see them."

"That's good of you, sir."

Evan laughed. "*Good?* Well, if I'm good, take a long look at me, son. You won't find much more of it around the Skweda. Jewell, Kelly, MacLeoid, Stone—the great and the good, eh? My ass. In the end, you can't beat them. God bless the capitalist machine. It rolled into our towns and turned them to shit." He pointed down at his book, *Zen and the Art of Motorcycle Maintenance.* "Poor guy in that book gave in to overthinking things, and he went mad. They gave him electroconvulsive therapy, changed his personality. Me, I'm trying something different. I've gone back to basics and moved myself away from those vampires." He gestured around himself. "Here is good. Here, I don't overthink. And it's only when people like yourselves walk back in, no offense intended, do I remember, and I get all heated."

"I'm sorry, sir."

"Not at all, young man. I hope you find that little girl, and I'm sorry I couldn't have been more use to you."

"On the contrary, sir, you've been very useful indeed."

───────

SWEATING, Gabriel emerged from the basement. He would have peeled off his dirty vest if not for his guest. He stooped at the living room door and peeked at Kayla watching *American Idol.*

Drowning in one of his T-shirts and a pair of his sweatpants, she looked cute as hell. However, now that she was here on a permanent basis, he would have to invest in some clothing for her. Online, of course. He wasn't about to reveal her location by shopping in town. He was protecting her, offering her something her pig of a father could never do—safety.

He eyed the photograph of Collette on the mantlepiece

and noted the similarity between her and Kayla. *I won't fail this time.*

"Who's going to win?" Gabriel asked, nodding at the television.

"I daren't say. The one I always say is going to win, loses. Ayden always says my endorsement is the kiss of death."

Gabriel laughed.

"What're you doing down in the cellar?"

"Tidying. I've left it too long. There's some old furniture I'm refurbishing too."

"Can I look?"

"When I've finished. By the way, I just got off the phone. We'll be taking your father into custody this evening," Gabriel lied. "Sorry to bring that up now, but I thought you'd want to know."

"Yes, that's good news."

"It'll all be over by tomorrow."

"And then I can go home, back to Ayden?"

"I'll drop you off myself."

"Who is the picture of on the mantlepiece?"

Gabriel took a deep breath. "My sister."

"Where is she?"

"Gone ... I'm afraid."

"Where?"

"I lost her."

"I'm sorry. I didn't mean to pry."

"No, it's okay. I learned from it. I won't ever let it happen again—"

A knock sounded at the front door. He bolted upright, and his head caught the low doorframe. "Shit." He rubbed his head. "Upstairs, *now.*"

Kayla jumped up. "Who is it?"

"I don't know, but go to your room and stay in there. Whatever you do, don't come out."

She slipped past him.

Gabriel went to the bottom of the stairs, his heart thrashing in his chest.

She looked back at him from the third step and whispered, "I'm scared."

"It'll be fine. Don't make any noise. After tonight, you will be safe ... forever. No one will ever hurt you again."

Kayla ran.

After he heard her door close, he turned to the front door and peeked through the keyhole. "You've got be fucking kidding me." He threw a sideways glance at his Remington 700 propped against the wall underneath his jackets.

He opened the door to Jake Pettman.

JAKE HAD ASKED Lillian to drive away.

She'd protested. "He'll know I told you where he lives anyway."

"That may be the case, but you want no part of the conversation I'm about to have."

"Would I sound crazy if I said I did?"

"Yes."

"It's only a job. I can live without it."

It could cost you more than your job. "We are dealing with dangerous people here, Lillian. I'll call you later."

She finally relented and drove away.

Gabriel scrutinized Jake from the front door. "How can I help you, Mr. Pettman?"

"You weren't at your office."

"I'm off duty."

"Is the chief of police ever off duty?"

Gabriel's eyes twitched. "For the second time, how can I help you?"

"I think we are better having this conversation inside."

"What you think doesn't matter too much to me, Mr. Pettman. I don't particularly want you in my home. I know who you're descended from, after all."

"Do you want me to discuss Samantha Kelly and her company on your doorstep?"

Gabriel's eyes twitched again.

"How about the Watsons' burning bench? Or, Evan Bell's dead dog?"

Gabriel stepped aside.

As Jake passed him, Gabriel hissed his ear, "You really should have listened to my warning, Mr. Pettman." He slammed the door.

KAYLA HAD KEPT the bedroom door ajar. She listened to them go into the living room, waited for the door to close then stepped onto the landing. The floorboards creaked. She stopped. Her blood ran cold, and she wished for her father.

Yes, her daddy was a very bad man. The things she'd seen at the pit several nights back had devastated her. But right now, she'd be lying if she said she didn't crave his protection.

When it was clear they hadn't heard her, she crept down the stairs as light-footed as possible, slipping her damp palm down the bannister.

Chief Jewell had really worried her before in the living

room. It had started with that photograph of his sister. When she'd queried it, a strange look had crossed his face. *"I lost her,"* he'd said. *"I learned from it. I won't ever let it happen again—"*

What had happened to her? Her stomach was doing somersaults. She reached the bottom of the stairs and noticed the rifle propped against the wall. It resembled the one her father and her brother carried.

Again, she wished for her father. What had she been thinking? He'd never hurt her. He adored her. In fact, if he loved Ayden even half as much as he loved her, there may have been hope for them as a family. Poor Ayden ... he despised him. He was caring and sensitive, which was the problem. These traits in a son were disappointing to a man like her father.

She approached the living room door.

She couldn't do anything about her father now anyway. He would be taken into custody tonight. Chief Jewell had said as much. She was probably just being paranoid. Chief Jewell was a policeman, after all. But her father had once said that a healthy dose of suspicion would keep you alive. She hadn't quite understood what he'd meant until now.

She put her ear to the door to discover what the two men were discussing.

JAKE MAINTAINED HIS DISTANCE. He'd met many people like Gabriel in his time. Individuals so weighed down by secrets tended to become unpredictable when cornered. Jake hadn't gotten this far in his life by dropping his guard in these situations. He told Gabriel straight what he'd learned today with Lillian. He left her name out of it, but the chief would figure it out. Altruism was at a premium in that police station. There wouldn't be many suspects.

Gabriel paced for a moment then sat on the sofa. He stared at the floor, clearly deep in thought.

Jake was just about to tell him what he wanted in return for his silence on the Kelly Properties shakedowns when Gabriel looked up and said, "You really are holier than fucking thou, aren't you?"

"Let's not drag this out—"

"Do you know what your ancestors, the Bickfords, did, Mr. Pettman?"

"Is it relevant?"

"Maybe. You told me before you've heard different rumors."

Jake shrugged.

"Did you hear the one about the eldest son having an affair with one of the selectman's teenage daughters?"

Jake nodded.

"Not true. How about the rumor that Frank Bickford aspired to be a selectman? And that some of the existing selectmen disappeared under mysterious circumstances?"

"Get to the point, Chief."

"Not true either, but a crowd pleaser for the tourists. Do you want the real truth?"

"Not especially, but I expect it's coming."

Gabriel nodded. "Yes. And it's not pleasant. I'd sit if I were you."

"I'll stand, thank you."

"Very well. The Bickfords ran the Blue Falls Taps as a brothel, Mr. Pettman."

Jake felt his stomach turn. "Not great, but common enough back then, I'm sure."

"So, would it bother you to learn they employed women from local, more impoverished towns?"

Yes, it does, but ... "As I said, it's a long time ago, and times were different."

"And that they took girls, some as young as ten, from these towns?"

Jake flinched.

"And they didn't just take them, Mr. Pettman, but rather, *stole* them."

Jake's stomach turned harder this time. "You're making it up. I'd *know*."

"But how would you know about our town's dirty little secret? Those before us worked hard to cover it up. Pedophilia is not quite as good for tourism as dodgy dealings and assassination, is it?"

Jake took a deep breath, determined not to lose it in front of this prick. "Why would you be telling me then?"

"What do I have to fear? You'll hardly expose the truth about your own people."

"It's bollocks."

"If you want, I can take you to the station and show you the records. After the Bickfords were run out of town, we exhumed the bodies of five girls. Seems your kin could be quite aggressive when trying to tame their prisoners. The youngest one had had her entire skull caved—"

"That's *enough*" Jake stepped forward. The blood was rushing around his body.

Gabriel smiled. "Interesting. Up until now, I did have you pegged as unshakeable."

Jake clenched his fists.

"Will you fall at the first hurdle in your search for the girl, Mr. Pettman?"

Jake took a deep breath and closed his eyes. "True or not true, none of this is relevant."

"I say it is. I say there is deep irony in the fact that such concern for a young girl could come from the direct descendent of child killers."

Jake took another deep breath and took two steps back before opening his eyes. "You want me to swing for you. I get it. It's the way you all work around here. I've come here for a productive outcome. I've come to *tell* you, Gabriel, you will help me, or I'll hang you out."

"Hang me out?" Gabriel took several large steps forward until they were barely a foot apart. "You come into my house, a man descended from savages, and address me, the chief of police, by my first name? How do you intend to *hang me out* exactly, Mr. Pettman?"

"I'll start by going to the press and creating a scene over the property scam."

"You think they'll be interested?"

"Everyone is always interested in an ecosystem, as you called it. The whole town working together to threaten the elderly out of their homes—I'll sell the story; don't you worry about that."

Gabriel sneered. "So what if you do? I've survived worse. Our whole town has survived worse. We survived your family, for a start."

"Your town may survive this scandal, but I'll tell you this—and I speak heavily from experience here—*Gabriel*, your town will not survive a man like Jotham MacLeoid. Not for long. That much evil and corruption in such a small place? It will only be a matter of time before your whole town is rotten."

Gabriel's and Jake's eyes locked.

"You stand there," Jake said, "claiming to love your town, yet you are letting it fall."

"You don't understand."

"I understand that deep down you don't want Jotham's empire at the heart of this beautiful place."

"What I want and what can happen are two vastly different things."

"Why? Forget the threat, Chief. See me as an opportunity."

Gabriel chortled and turned. "This is nonsense."

"Let me do what you cannot do. Use me, an outsider. I'm happy to take out the cancer."

Gabriel stepped backward and sighed. He glimpsed a photograph of a young girl on the mantlepiece. "This place wasn't always like this."

"I believe you."

Gabriel stared at the photograph a moment longer, sighed again and focused on Jake. "I'll tell you one thing, and then you're on your own."

AFTER JAKE HAD LEFT, Gabriel stood alone in his living room, holding the photograph of Collette. *It's for the best, Collette.* He wanted to talk out loud to her, as he'd so often done in the past, but was aware of Kayla's presence upstairs. He returned the photograph, smiled at his beautiful, lost, sister and turned.

When Gabriel's father had been police chief, he'd had to deal with Jotham's father, Boyd. But he was an easier man to deal with—a *simpler* man, a man who could enjoy power and privilege while understanding his place. Gabriel envied his dead father. He'd never had to struggle with a megalomaniac.

Jotham refused to understand the pecking order. One just had to trace his rise to power to see that. As an organizer of dog fights from an early age, Jotham had collected valuable and notorious contacts from around the state. Due to his efficient yet often heavy-handed nature, he'd been entrusted as a drugs mule in the more populous and profitable cities: Portland, Lewiston, and Bangor. His strategic marriage to Amber Colson at thirty, daughter of the wealthiest man and chief selectman in town, was another masterstroke. Henry Colson may not have been pleased with his daughter hooking up with a dog breeder who was assisting the rising tide of drug use in Maine, but he quickly saw the business potential. Colson funded Jotham's rise to the top while providing him the necessary immunity from the town's law enforcement. It allowed Colson's own popularity as chief selectman to grow when Jotham employed the residents of Blue Falls.

And the ecosystem was born.

Even the tragic death of Amber Colson and their three daughters didn't derail Jotham's growing empire. If anything, it strengthened it. The fear and mystery surrounding the kingdom's black, beating heart grew and grew. Then rumors of a killing pit emerged. Anyone who betrayed Jotham, betrayed the town, would disappear into the depths of the earth never to be seen again. The more rational people in the town, Gabriel included, had always considered it nonsense.

After hearing Kayla's story though, Gabriel had to concede that, at times, the most illogical explanations were often the most accurate. Controlling Jotham was now an impossibility and, for that reason, Gabriel despised him. *It's for the best*, he thought again.

The information he'd given Jake Pettman would lead him straight into the black, beating heart of Blue Falls, and who knows, maybe the insistent, big bastard would rattle Jotham to the extent that cracks would appear. Bigger empires had probably fallen on less. Whatever happened, there would be fallout, and, for that reason, he had to be careful to cover his tracks.

He phoned Lillian. "Sorry to disturb you, Lillian."

"No problems, Chief. I—"

"Good. I just wanted to give you some food for thought this evening."

"Okay ..."

"If you spend any more time with Jake Pettman, I will see to it that you will never work as a police officer again.

"Chief—"

"Not here, not anywhere. Do you understand?"

"But, Chief—"

"Do you understand?"

"Yes. But, Chief—"

"Goodnight, Lillian." He hung up on her and reached for the living room door.

Kayla. His heart beat faster.

Kayla. You're safe with me. His breathing quickened. He opened the door.

You'll always be safe with me. He stepped into the hallway and glanced up the stairs, feeling his erection pressing against his trouser legs.

You'll never have to return to that man. I will spare you that fate. He walked down the hallway. At the foot of the stairs, he stopped. His blood froze.

His rifle wasn't against the wall.

10

eter Sheenan had spared him several cracked ribs, so Jake was pleased to see him. It was nice to know someone had his back in this poky little town.

Peter, on the other hand, couldn't look any more annoyed. Predictable. Dogman, as dubbed by Justin Stone and his friends, adored canines. It was the reason Jake had contacted him and why Peter had a face like thunder. Dogfighting was abhorrent to most people, but to a dog lover like Peter, it must have been completely soul-destroying.

Peter climbed into Jake's car.

"Did you know about this?" Jake asked.

Peter shook his head. "You hear a lot of rumors in Blue Falls. Sometimes it's just easier to believe that's all they are."

"Can you direct me to Sharon's Edge?"

Peter nodded, gave his first direction and stared out the window. "I warn you, Jake, if it's true, I may not be able to go in with you. I don't know if I'd be able to control myself."

"I understand. What can you tell me about dogfighting?"

Peter instructed him to turn off Main Street and head

toward the bridge over the River Skweda. "We could begin with the obvious. It's brutal. You'd have to be a sadistic barbarian to be mixed up in it. It makes you wonder who the animals are—the creatures inside or outside the ring?"

The streetlights disappeared behind them, and an eerie darkness settled on them and their journey.

"I'm not clued up on it," Jake said. "Owning dogs for fighting is illegal back home."

"It is illegal to train dogs to fight and allow them to participate, but due to some fucked-up loophole, it's not illegal to own them. I knew Jotham bred fighting dogs. Everyone does. And I also knew he was involved in fighting when he was younger, but I hoped it wasn't still happening. Shit. Maybe I've just turned a blind eye. I thought he loved his dogs."

"Maybe he does. I've encountered men like this before back home. Their version of love and adoration can be significantly different from ours. I don't know much about Jotham, but he seems to be a fighter who enjoys his power. Maybe he's trying to offer this same experience to the dogs he adores?"

"If this is all true, I'll have no choice but to try to stop it."

"As I told you on the phone, that is not why we're going tonight. A little girl is missing, and this is our inroad. After this is done, I'll help you any way I can, but tonight is not about stopping it." Jake drove over the bridge and stared at the Skweda—a dark vein twisting and turning into the black heart of the former Rosstown Plantation.

"Fire in Bone," Peter said.

"Sorry?"

"Skweda is Abenaki for *Fire in Bone.*"

"I see."

"The fire is inside all of us, Jake. We *all* have the choice of how we use it."

"Free will?"

"My ancestors believed that bathing in the Skweda would give you direction and help you choose how best to wield your fire."

Jake nodded. "There's a few people in this town who could do with a wash then."

"Agreed." Peter gave Jake some more directions.

"How do they train American pit bulls?"

"Pump them to the eyeballs with steroids, give them a fitness regime like a boxer, stick them on treadmills, prepare poles with animal hides on them for them to chase. Nothing is as barbaric as the bait dog though. Often older, retired fighters. The other dogs *practice* on them."

"Jesus. Awful. No wonder dogs like this sometimes turn on us. They do say it's the owner and not the dog."

"Couldn't agree more."

The road led them into the center of Sharon's Edge, and the car bumped and rattled over the potholes. It was far more rundown than Blue Falls. Most of the stores were boarded up, and several disheveled individuals congregated in shadows, swilling from bottles in brown paper bags. Some of them stopped to stare at the car as they passed, as if contemplating how best to carjack the vehicle. Such was the air of desperation here, Jake wouldn't be surprised if one decided to throw themselves in front of them to force them to brake. He kept himself alert.

He recalled Gabriel's words earlier: *"So, it doesn't bother you that they employed women from local, more impoverished towns? And that they took girls, some as young as ten?"* Was this one of the towns?

The poverty intensified as Peter directed Jake down

several side streets. He gulped when he remembered Gabriel's reference to the five recovered bodies. Was this where his child-killing ancestors had poached some of their wares? He gulped.

The potholes worsened, and Jake was forced to slow. There was a lack of streetlighting, and most of the residential houses were dark and potentially unoccupied. Jake glanced at the automatic locking button. It glowed a friendly orange. "Are we safe here?"

Peter smiled for the first time since they'd left Blue Falls.

"Don't answer," Jake said.

They hit a stretch of road with no housing. Jake had tried to be conspicuous in his approach, but the lack of light was forcing his hand now. He hit the high beam. "Don't worry, I'm used to the middle of nowhere where I come from. Wiltshire is full of it."

"This isn't the middle of nowhere, Jake. This is a hive of activity. Just because you can't see it, doesn't mean it's not there. Turn left into this industrial estate."

Jake kept his high beam on. None of the properties on this estate seemed open, and so there was no friendly light to guide them in. Jake listened to the tires crunch over litter and waste, wondering if he was likely to get any of his rental deposit back. They rounded a block of derelict garages.

"Here," Peter said.

Jake saw a large open space heavily populated with parked cars and vans. A short walk ahead, through this makeshift lot, was a small building holding its own in this dark world, with a dim red glow. "Well, it seems to be the only place open around here."

"Uh-huh," Peter said. "I really don't want to see what's

going on in there, but neither do I want to stay in this dark parking lot alone."

"Come on then. I'll buy you a drink."

"I won't be wanting anything they're selling, Jake. You can be sure of that."

WITH HIS HEART BEATING FAST, Gabriel knocked on Kayla's door. "Would you like some supper before bed?"

No answer.

Shit! He should have known better. Leaving an armed weapon within touching distance of a MacLeoid—what the fuck was he thinking? He knocked again. "Kayla? Hot milk?"

No answer.

Fuck it. He opened the door. The sweat turned ice cold on his brow; she wasn't in there. He stepped backward, closed the door and saw Kayla halfway up the stairs, pointing his rifle at him. "What are you doing?"

She took another step. Her eyes were red and blotchy.

He watched the end of the rifle bob up and down as she trembled. "Be careful with that. It may go—"

"You're a *liar*!"

He turned so he faced down the stairs, putting her six steps from him. "Why'd you say that?"

"I heard! I *listened*!"

"To what?"

"To you and that man talking down there." She gestured toward the lounge with a quick nod.

"Ahh ... I see. What did you hear, exactly?"

"Everything you said."

He shuffled forward. "Please tell."

"Take another step, and I'll use this. I know how. My daddy taught me. I've shot rabbits."

"I'm not a rabbit, Kayla. I'm the chief of police."

"Yes, and you told me they were arresting Daddy tonight, and yet, you just told that man a whole lot of different things."

"Because he's not a policeman. Hell, he's not even from here. He doesn't get to know what's about to happen."

"So, why did you tell him about the dogfighting? Why did you send him after Daddy? If you were really going to deal it with yourself, why do that?"

"I was getting rid of him. Sending him on a wild goose chase. So, he sees a dog fight, so what? Who around here hasn't seen a dog fight before?" He chanced a step.

She waved the gun. "I'll fucking shoot you."

He showed the palm of his hands. "Okay, easy."

"What happened to your sister?"

"My sister? Why do you ask?"

"Before, downstairs, you told me you *lost* her."

"Figure of speech."

"Where is she?" Kayla took another step.

"We argued. She left Blue Falls. We haven't spoken in years." Gabriel assessed the distance between them again. He could pounce four steps, but it was dangerous. Even if he missed the gunshot, they would tumble. He was a heavy man, which could cause significant damage to both of them.

"I want to go home now."

"I understand. Put down the gun, and I'll take you."

"I don't want you to take me. I just want you to unlock the front door."

"So, you already tried to leave?"

"Yes."

Gabriel wasn't angry, just disappointed. He'd known

their relationship was in its infancy, but he'd not expected her to cut and run at the first opportunity. Gabriel moved down a step. "Okay, I'll unlock the door for you."

Kayla backed down the stairs as Gabriel descended. "Slowly ..."

"Of course." He took two more steps, *slowly*.

"I never should have come here."

"And why's that? Do you prefer it at home with your daddy? Have you forgotten what you saw the other night?"

She stepped off the final step and stood beside the hanging jackets. "At least I know he would never hurt me."

"Maybe not you, Kayla, but he hurts others. A hell of a lot of others."

She flinched. "You had your chance to get him. I told you what he did. You're playing games. You *all* play games." She moved around the end of the staircase into the hallway, allowing Gabriel to complete his descent and approach the front door. "Now unlock it."

Gabriel put his hand in his pocket for the key then paused.

"*Now.*"

He removed his hand, empty. "No."

"I'll shoot you."

"Then you'll have to shoot me."

"I *fucking* mean it."

Gabriel turned. "I know you do. You're a MacLeoid, after all. But, no, I'm sorry. I cannot let you go back to him. I couldn't live with myself."

"Please ..." Her eyes filled with tears. "I made a mistake. My father has always been kind to me."

Gabriel inched toward her. "It's a lie. He lies. Eventually, you'll become expendable. Everyone always does to him. Look how he treats his son, your brother."

"Because it sends a message."

"You really think Jotham is bothered about who comes in? What are they going to do? Contact the police? They're in his goddamned pocket! They won't come and break this up. Do you think the old bastard will care about your statement of intent?"

"I hope so"—Jake opened the reception door for Peter—"because, in order to deliver it, I think we're about to see something rather grim."

Dim red strip lights lit the large room. The view was obscured, because about two dozen men congregated around the ring. With no heating in the disused property, most wore heavy clothing.

Peter and Jake shuffled into the baying crowd.

The dogfighting pit was about fifteen-feet square and walled off with two-foot-high plywood and bales of hay. A bloodstained carpet covered the pit floor. Jake assumed this was so the dogs could get traction when in combat. Two men stood on either side of the pit, holding tickets in the air and calling out for bets. It seemed most of this crowd had already been served.

Jake approached the man on the left side and placed a fifty-dollar bet on Whiplash. He didn't bother checking the odds. Even if he won, he wouldn't claim it. He rejoined Peter, who was staring at his feet. Jake felt guilty. He was exposing this decent man to his worst nightmare. He placed a hand on Peter's shoulder and whispered into his ear, "I appreciate this. You helping me understand this and understanding Jotham will help us find Maddie."

Peter looked up. "Here they come. See the diagonal scratch marks on each corner of the pit? The dogs are set down behind them and released."

A man introduced the two male catchweight dogs,

Nickel and Whiplash, whose owners brought them in on leashes.

"Catchweight means heavyweight," Peter said. "Over fifty-two pounds."

Everyone cheered loudest for Whiplash, who was introduced as a champion.

"Grand champion soon enough!" a man in the crowd shouted.

"They need to win five consecutive matches to be grand champion," Peter said.

The crowd whooped and hollered again as the owners leaned over the plywood and placed their two barking dogs behind the diagonal scratch marks.

Whiplash, on the right, did look the more aggressive of the two. He strained against his owner's hands, who was struggling to keep hold of the canine. "Easy boy!"

The crowd laughed.

Jake eyed Peter, who had curled his lip in disgust.

The dogs were released. They met head on and rolled, desperately trying to lock their teeth onto each other. Most of the crowd shouted for Whiplash, so when he eventually took control of the fight and managed to savage one of Nickel's front legs, the place went wild.

Jake felt Peter's tight grip on his arm and looked at the older man. He'd lowered his head but still occasionally looked up, probably hoping the fight would end before any more damage was caused.

Nickel was on his back while Whiplash chewed his leg. There was a snapping sound.

"*Down dog! Down dog!*" the crowd chanted.

Peter's grip on Jake's arm tightened.

"*Down dog! Down dog!*"

Jake watched Whiplash tear a big chunk of skin from Nickel's head.

"*Down dog! Down dog!*"

It was enough. He patted Peter's hand. "Come on."

As they neared the door into the reception area, they heard someone in the crowd shout, "Fanged!"

"Monsters," Peter said, looking like he was about to burst into tears. "Fucking *monsters.*"

When they entered the reception area, Jake stopped and turned to Peter. "What does fanged mean?"

"When a dog accidentally pierces its lip with its canine tooth."

"Christ."

A lanky, young man with short blond hair came through the corrugated metal door.

Jake pulled the disorientated Peter to one side to allow the customer past.

He didn't accept the offer and stood where he was, surveying them both.

"Can I help you?" Jake said.

"I'm Ayden MacLeoid."

Jake regarded Peter for confirmation, which came in the form of a swift nod. It'd worked; Jake had Jotham's attention —quicker than he'd expected too.

"I'm here to ask if I can help you," Ayden said.

"Just here to place a few bets," Jake said.

"And you're leaving already?"

"It wasn't really to our taste," Peter said. His eyes were wide, and spit bubbled at one side of his mouth.

Jake felt his heart up tempo. His companion was on the edge. Swinging for anyone in this location was a one-way ticket to the hospital, or worse.

"I'm sorry to hear—"

"You're animals." Peter pointed at Ayden. "You, your father, anyone here. *Fucking* animals."

Ayden edged backward toward the door.

Jake gripped Peter's arm in much the same way Peter had gripped his arm in the arena. He searched for Peter's eyes until he was staring back at him. "Not now," he said softly. "Not now."

Peter closed his eyes, took a deep breath, sighed then nodded.

A loud cheer rose from inside. The fight was over.

Jake moved toward Ayden. He noticed the young man looked quite edgy. He certainly cut a very different demeanor to his father—the king sitting on his castle walls. "Did your father send you?"

"Yes. He wants to know what you want."

"I think he knows that already."

"He didn't indicate that to me."

"Maddie Thompson?"

Ayden's edginess quickly became nervousness. His eyes darted left and right, and he grew pale.

"You know something?" Jake asked.

"No."

"Could have fooled me! It looks as if someone has just walked over your grave."

"I don't know what you're talking about."

"You know anyone who helps out now is likely to come out of this whole sorry situation in a more positive—"

The corrugated door opened again. The tall doorman entered. "Is everything all right, sir? Are they staying or going?"

Jake kept his eyes fixed on Ayden's until he looked away.

"Going," Ayden said.

"Okay, come on then," the doorman said.

With Peter alongside him, Jake approached the exit. There, he stopped and glared at Ayden again. "Remember what I said. It can all end okay for you. You can also tell your father it can end well for him too. He can keep his dogfighting ring. I'm just interested in getting Maddie Thompson back. Nothing else."

Ayden didn't respond.

Jake looked at the doorman and raised an eyebrow then pushed the ticket indicating the bet he'd placed on Whiplash in the doorman's pocket. "It's a winner."

The doorman stepped aside and made way for the two intruders.

11

"I DON'T WANT to hurt you, Kayla. I just want to keep you safe. Do you understand?"

"Yes." Her reply was muffled, but he released her from the neck hold. She gasped for air and steadied herself against the wall.

"Now, let's take a look at your new room." He directed her toward the cellar.

She watched as he thrust aside the heavy bolts and opened the door. The cold air rushed out and over her, and she couldn't stop the tears from returning. She felt him lean over her to grab the light cord and shuddered. Her neck still burned from where he'd gripped her so strongly.

Dust swam in the bulb's glow.

"Down please, Kayla."

Her footsteps echoed as she descended. She sensed his looming presence behind her and wiped tears from her cheeks with the back of her hand. At the bottom of the stairs, she turned. "Please."

"Continue. There's no need to worry, Kayla."

She brushed past an old mop and bucket and smelled

the disinfectant. It reminded her of the dog cages back home that she had to sterilize regularly. *Daddy, what a silly girl I have been ...*

They reached another door. Gabriel leaned over her to some broken shelves, rustled around in an old vase and pressed something into her hand. "For the padlock."

She pushed the key into the padlock and tried to turn it. "It's stuck."

"Try harder."

It wouldn't budge. "I really can't."

"Harder."

She turned with all her might, and it clicked open. She looked inside; it was much smaller than the room upstairs.

"I'm sorry, Kayla. You didn't give me enough time to get it as comfortable as I would have liked."

The room had no windows, and she felt a cold stone of dread in her stomach. "Please don't put me in there."

"Do not make this harder than it has to be. I like you. A lot. More than you could ever know."

At his words, the dread in her stomach swelled and invaded her chest. She walked inside. The floor was concrete but looked as if it'd been swept clean. Spiderwebs filled every corner of the room. She gulped.

"Sit on the bed."

She sat on the edge of a low bed outfitted with a bedsheet of Disney princesses. It completely contrasted with the damp, grey cell around her. She noticed the bedside table with a small wireless dome light—it must have been battery operated—a bottle of water, and a small pile of books.

"Look at me, Kayla."

She looked up at Gabriel. He was massive and blocked the entire doorway. *I should have shot you upstairs.*

"There's water and some books. *The Famous Five*. Have you read them?"

She shook her head.

"They're good."

She swallowed. Her throat was dry.

His left hand lingered around his groin next to an uneven lump in his trousers.

She tasted bile in her throat and looked away.

"I'll get you more books. You'll probably get through them in no time."

"How long do I have to stay here?"

"This is your home now."

She noticed him rub that lump through his trousers. "Please ... no." She looked away. The tears came harder now.

"I understand you feel like that now, but it will change. You're safe here with me. A girl of your age needs to be protected. That's what I'm offering."

She buried her head in her hands. She didn't want to acknowledge his presence anymore, acknowledge what he may or may not be doing, wanting only to be lost in her tears. She slumped back on the bed and turned away from her kidnapper, listening to his quick movements and disgusting moaning. *Please*—she stared at the concrete wall —*someone please help me ...*

Eventually, it fell silent, and Kayla hoped he'd left. She considered turning but was glad she had waited when he spoke again. "Behind the bedside table is a bucket. If you put it by the door at the end of every day, I will come and empty it while you sleep. Now, I must go. If you're a good girl, I'll see about getting you a television."

She listened to the door close and curled into a ball. Once she calmed, she considered using the toilet, but after reaching down on the bed and feeling the damp sheets, she realized it was too late.

———

ON THE JOURNEY back to Blue Falls, Peter welled up. "I'm sorry."

"You've nothing to apologize for. I'm anything but a dog lover, but what I saw back there will haunt me for the rest of my days." Jake held back on the conversation, and when they reached the bridge, he chanced a look at the war vet.

He was gazing across the River Skweda, probably seeking guidance like many of his ancestors had done before him.

Jake pulled up to where he had picked up Peter, and Peter turned to him. "You don't have to be a dog lover. Not at all." He put a hand on Jake's shoulder. "You just got to be human." Peter left the car, merely grunting when Jake expressed gratitude.

Eager to talk to Piper, Jake tried her phone while driving to the motel. He connected to her voicemail and asked her to call him back. As he locked the rental car's door, he ran his finger down the scratch mark then glanced over his shoulder just in case Justin Stone and his cronies were lying in wait.

Unfortunately, not, he thought with a smile.

A Honda SUV parked several spaces down from him suggested a new neighbor. He tried to work out which room the new guest had been placed in, but all the windows were dark. They'd probably journeyed into town to visit the Taps. There wasn't really much else to do around here.

He entered his motel room, closed the door behind him and switched on the light—

Jotham was sitting on the stool opposite his bed with a rifle across his lap.

Jake almost jumped out of his skin. "Jesus."

"Not the first time I've been called that."

"How *did* you get in my room?"

"Leland, the owner, was good enough to let me in."

"Did you threaten him with that?" Jake pointed at Jotham's rifle.

Jotham laughed. "Don't be silly. Me and him go way back."

"Obviously far enough for him to risk his reputation and business."

"Such attitude. You all like this back where you come from? Truth be told, if that's the case, I'd like to visit one day."

"Why're you in my room?"

"Same reason you were probably at my pit, son. Curiosity. It gets the better of all of us." He lifted a hand in the air and waved his fingers. "The secrets in the dark."

"I've seen what you hide in the dark at Sharon's Edge. There's no mystery there. You're just a sadist."

"There's no cruelty in what I do. I prepare all my bitches well; I've never lost a single one."

"Do you not care about the dogs that do die? Biting through their own lips? It's a fucking disgrace."

"If the owner is weak, the animal is weak. The animal does not suffer because of me."

"Sounds spineless to me."

"Would a spineless person be sitting here? An open book for you to read? Although, I'm sure you've gone to great pains to find out everything about me already."

"I never found out what gives you the right to come into my room and threaten me."

"Threaten you? Come on!" Jotham held up the rifle. "*This?*"

Jake lifted his eyebrows.

He leaned over and placed the rifle on the floor at his feet. "I'm a reasonable man. Ask everyone in this town, and the next for that matter. You'll find it to be the consensus."

"They will be speaking from fear, not honesty."

"You hear about my legacy, and like any other outsider, you just assume the worst. Yet, you avoid the only fact that really matters. That Blue Falls likely wouldn't exist anymore if not for the choices and sacrifices I have made. Many people in this town now have food on their table where none was before. While large parts of America wallow in unemployment, most people in this town have security."

"The drug trade offers no security."

"Things work differently here, son, than what you're used to. For as long as people can remember, there's been contentment. And it's in no one's interest for it to change."

Jake rolled his eyes.

"No one's. Including yours, son."

Jake smirked. "I thought you weren't here to threaten me?"

"Just a statement of fact."

Jake's phone rang.

"Would that be the beautiful Piper Goodwin?"

Jake narrowed his eyes. "It's best if you leave now."

"Answer your cell, son. She could be on her way over here."

Jake's hand lingered near his jacket pocket, but he didn't reach for his cell.

"She could be pulling up in the parking lot." Jotham

pointed at the door. "In less than a minute, she could be standing right there." He reached for his rifle.

Jake answered the call, maintaining eye contact with Jotham. "Hi, Piper. Where're you?"

"Home. Doris has come down with a fever, so I'm taking her shift at the Taps."

"Okay," Jake said, noticing Jotham had yet to blink. "I'll be in touch later."

"Yeah ... fine. You okay, Jake?"

"Yes, it's just something has come up. I'll call later."

Jotham smiled, and Jake hung up.

"I want you out of here," Jake said.

"It was you who wanted me here."

"Preying on me in the dark? Why would I want that? Why would *anyone* want that?"

"You came to me, son. Bold as you like, big dick swinging, into *my* world."

"I just wanted you to know."

"Know what, son?"

"That I'm not going away until you tell me where Maddie Thompson is."

"I guess you'll need to visit the estate agents come tomorrow then, because I cannot tell you what I don't know."

"A fifteen-year-old girl is missing, and her family remain silent and terrified. Who else would they fear in this town?"

"Oh, you'd be surprised. There's a lot of bottom-feeders desperate to rise to the surface."

"She's a child. Is there no part of you that cares?"

"You have me all wrong, son."

"Where's your humanity? You had three children!"

Jotham took a sharp breath through his nose. He leaned back on the stool and regarded Jake.

"You, of all people, know exactly what it feels like to lose so much."

Jotham didn't respond. He continued to stare at Jake.

"Can you only imagine what it's doing to the Thompson family. If you could've helped your children, wouldn't—"

"Enough." Jotham raised a finger in the air.

"You've a choice here—"

"Enough!" With his finger still raised, he reached for his rifle with his other hand. "If you mention my three children again, I'll kill you where you stand."

Jake took a deep breath and suppressed a reply.

Jotham stood. "Now, I'll leave you to think on this meeting."

"I don't want to go to war with you. I understand how powerful you are. But no matter how many times you or anyone else tell me it's suicide, it won't make any difference. I won't be letting this go."

"I understand."

Jake could hear his heart thudding; he hoped Jotham couldn't hear it too.

"And I kind of admire you for it, son. Tenacity is rarer than many believe. You're just like me. But you were right before." He approached Jake at the door. "You can't possibly win."

Jake opened the door.

As Jotham stepped outside, he looked up at Jake. "We're both tenacious, and we're both fair, Jake. But neither of us are patient." Hunched over slightly, Jotham staggered from the motel—was he carrying an injury?—and turned. "You may think what you're doing is right, Jake, but you might want to consider whether you can best serve the world by remaining in it." He limped toward his Honda SUV, holding the rifle with one hand.

Jake closed the door, stumbled to the bed, sat on the edge, took several deep breaths and lay back to stare at the ceiling.

———

PETER STUDIED the photograph of Prince and ran his fingers over the lab retriever's face. Then he threw it on the passenger seat, took another slug of Old Crow from a bottle and started his pickup's engine. "You're a fucking madman, Sheenan," he said and drove back toward Sharon's Edge.

Along the way, he avoided glimpsing the River Skweda. His ancestors wouldn't agree with his chosen path, and he had no time to deal with the shame.

When he arrived at the makeshift parking lot in the industrial estate, he saw it had emptied. He wondered, briefly, if a full house would have stopped him.

He doubted it.

From the back of his pickup, he took a can of gasoline and his rifle. He approached the building, which no longer glowed and was eerily silent following the whooping and cheering that had sickened him to the stomach earlier. After all that Old Crow, Peter knew he should have been staggering, but a combination of adrenaline and determination coursed through his veins and straightened his gait.

As a Vietnam soldier, he'd never needed to put himself in this kind of danger. His canine companion could always go on ahead and identify the risks. But that was another time. Those companions were long gone, following the ultimate betrayal by his own country.

Seeing these beautiful animals suffer again at the hands of Americans was unbearable. He was under no illusions. The consequences of his actions tonight would be swift and brutal, but he was an old man nearing the end of his days anyway, and, if he could just deliver one final blow in the name of this tortured species that had saved his life on so many occasions, then so be it.

Following his assumption that everyone had left, he was surprised and anxious to find the corrugated metal door unchained. Also, a dim light surrounded the edge of the door, suggesting someone was in the old waiting room. He set the can at his feet, readied his rifle and opened the door.

In the center of the room, Ayden MacLeoid was lying naked on the floor. He sat upright. "What the hell? We're closed!"

Peter lifted the rifle, closed one eye and attempted to take aim.

Ayden held out his palms. "Shit ... What do you want?"

Peter tried to steady his aim, but whereas the adrenaline had helped keep him surefooted outside, it was a hindrance now. He couldn't keep the gun level.

"Money? I can get it from the back for—"

"Stop fucking pleading with me, you spineless shit. You're monsters, all of you. I'm here to burn down this place, and you can go with it—" He felt a crushing blow to the back of his head. Everything flashed. He managed to fire his rifle as he went to his knees. The second blow was to the center of his back, and this sent him face first onto the solid ground. He'd be surprised if it hadn't cost him some teeth. He looked up and saw, predictably, that his bullet had missed Ayden.

The young man was now on his feet, wrapping the rug around himself.

At least you're putting your balls away, Peter thought as he spat blood on the floor.

Someone tugged the rifle from his hands. The beanie-wearing doorman from earlier joined Ayden's side. He didn't bother to cover himself.

Peter snorted then spat some more blood so he could speak. "Jesus, Ayden, what'll Daddy think about this?"

Ayden's eyes widened.

The doorman smiled and raised the rifle. "How's he going to find out?"

Peter laughed. "Fair point. Go ahead then, boy. Do what you got to do. There's no integrity in leaving an old man lying on the floor in his own blood. Especially one who fought for your country." Peter closed his eyes and waited. When the end didn't come, he opened them.

Ayden had pushed down the end of the rifle, and the doorman was looking at his lover. "Even though he knows about us?"

"Yes," Ayden said. "Even though."

"Still," the doorman said, raising the rifle again, "I'd like to keep my job."

Ayden pushed down the rifle again. "You will. He won't tell my father." He nodded down at Peter. "We have shown integrity, just as you asked, you will do the same, won't you, Peter?"

"If you don't kill me, you know I'll burn this zoo to the ground."

"I'm not sure I care very much," Ayden said.

"So, let me get the gas from outside then."

Ayden took the rifle from his doorman lover. "Not tonight, Peter." He turned the rifle around and stepped forward. "Tonight, I'm saving your life."

Peter saw the butt stock coming. Blackness came before the pain.

Blake Thompson had lost his appetite the night his daughter went into the pit. At the kitchen table, he struggled to eat the clam chowder his wife had made.

Marissa sat at the other side of the table and watched him eat. The pan of chowder was on a heatproof mat in front of her. She held the serving spoon and stirred the soup as if it was still cooking.

It hurt to smile, but Blake offered his wife one anyway.

She didn't smile back. "I called my sister. Maddie didn't make it there."

Blake almost choked on the soup in his mouth.

"I'm worried about her. Do you think she's on her way back?"

Blake dropped his spoon in the bowl. He watched it sink and disappear into the soup. "We've been through this so many times, my love. She's with Jotham. Staying with your sister in Vermont was just a lie."

"Jotham MacLeoid! That old rogue! You never said anything about that, Blake, dear."

But I did, my love, so many, many times. Yet how could he blame her confusion? Her daughter was missing, and she was beside herself. The lie they'd given the police must have been so attractive to her—a wonderful safety net for her deteriorating mind.

"I hope he's treating her well. Why is she there?" She lifted the serving spoon from the pan and tipped the soup into the bowl.

Blake told her again about their sons' betrayal and Jotham's revenge. He retained the lie to keep her sanity from crumbling completely. "Maddie will be returned when Jotham thinks we have been punished enough." Which made him wonder something that caused his empty stomach to turn. *Would he one day return her body to us, or do we not even get to properly bury her?* He put his hand to his mouth in case he failed to keep down the three mouthfuls of soup he'd managed.

"Those *fucking* boys," Marissa said.

They were stuck in a loop. They would be having this same conversation for days to come, because she simply would not, *could not*, retain this story he told her. But truth was truth, and one day, she would be forced to face it, *all* of it, and it would destroy her.

"You need to go and get her back, Blake," Marissa said.

"When it settles down, in a few days. I assure you she's safe."

Devin stepped up alongside Marissa and put a hand on his mother's shoulder. "Would you like some hot milk, Mom? Maybe an early night?"

Marissa stood, forcing Devin's hand to fall away, and locked eyes with Blake while one hand remained on the soup spoon. "You condescending little shit."

Her despair was too much for Blake, and he vomited into his half-empty bowl.

"Dad, are you—" Devin then cried out.

Blake looked up from the bowl to see his wife hitting their son over the head with the spoon. "Marissa!" Blake wiped sick from his chin and rose. "Stop that at once!"

Devin raised his hands over his face, but it offered little protection as she struck him.

Devin's pain reminded Blake of his daughter's final moments, and he worried he might throw up again. He circled the table, grabbed his wife's wrist to stop the attack and embraced her as hard as he could.

She collapsed against him. "I'm going to the police," Marissa said between mouthfuls of tears. "If you two won't get her back, I'll find someone who will."

If you do that, he'll feed our other children to that Hellhole, Marissa. "This is on me. I'll get our daughter back."

She pulled away from him. "By tomorrow, Blake, or I'll get her myself." She ran from the room.

Blake turned to his son, who was hunched over, rubbing his head. "Jesus, that hurts."

Blake looked at the serving spoon on the floor then at the boy who'd cost his innocent daughter her life. He kicked away the weapon before he lost control and picked up where his wife had left off.

PETER FELT as if he was waking to a massive hangover. His head throbbed, and the nausea was overwhelming. It took him a short time to orientate himself and to recall what had happened. He was in his pickup's passenger seat, parked outside his own home. *One of them must have driven me back.*

He touched the front of his head and looked at the blood on his fingers. He reached for the bottle of Old Crow on the floorboard and took a massive gulp. That would help with the hangover and the pain from the blow to the head. Then he reached underneath his backside for the photograph he'd left on the passenger seat.

Staring at the picture of Prince, he sighed. "This isn't over yet."

12

WITHOUT OPENING HIS EYES, Jake reached for the other side of his bed. Empty. Then he remembered that following Jotham's impulsive visit the previous evening, he'd asked Piper to stay away. He sighed. It was the right decision, but it didn't make him feel any less disappointed by her absence.

He sat upright in bed, reached for his phone and read a flirtatious message from Piper about how he was only allowed one night off and she'd be round after work this evening.

He texted back, *Fair enough* Xx. Then he phoned Lillian to tell her about the repulsive trip to the dog fight and the equally repulsive visit from Jotham.

Lillian sighed. "I never should have let you get this deep."

"This is a habit of mine. I wouldn't go blaming yourself."

"You need to stop now. Enough is enough."

"Unfortunately, that's my other bad habit: I don't know how to stop."

"You don't have any choice. You're going to get yourself killed. Jotham won't give you any more warnings."

"Yes, he implied as much."

"Do you even know that he's responsible for this missing girl?"

"I've no doubts."

"The chief called me last night *after* you visited him."

"Well, we knew that'd happen. He told you to stand down?"

"Yes."

"Well, you need to do what he says."

Lillian laughed. "You're unbelievable. You've just snubbed the same advice from me!"

"You've got a job to hold onto!"

"I'm not sure I want to hold onto it."

"I'm going to the station to see Jewell this morning. You need to steer clear of me. I've taken you far enough. I don't want to be responsible for what may come next."

"I'm a big girl."

"I know, Lillian, so you know I'm right. Goodbye, and thank you."

WHILE HE WAITED for this morning's heavy dose of painkillers to kick in, Jotham sat on a stool and watched Ayden train Bo. Ayden had offered to fetch a deckchair, but any pressure, even from the thinnest of materials, on his mangled back right now was an unbearable prospect. He took a mouthful of strong coffee from a tin cup. It did little to shake the fatigue. Last night had been the worst sleep of his life. If it hadn't been the pain in his back waking him up, it'd been the dreams of his lost daughter.

Usually, Bo spent every morning on a heavy chain to build her upper body strength, but because she was fighting this evening, she'd been attached to the lighter chain so she could preserve her energy. The focus today was only on building Bo's aggression so she could win with ease this evening and take the accolade of grand champion. Then she would be well taken care of in her retirement. He didn't believe in using his retired dogs as bait dogs; there was no integrity in that. He trained them to be the strongest and to survive, not to be sacrificed when they had reached those levels.

Ayden had tied five rabbits to pegs that circled Bo. Bo's chain would only allow her to travel within several inches of these animals. There, she would bark furiously and try desperately to wrap her jaws around the bait. Throughout the day, Ayden would slacken the rabbits' ropes one by one so they could be mauled. The aim was to make the rabbits achievable for Bo, to keep her enthused; leave it too long and she might succumb to failure, and her aggression would wane.

While Bo darted back and forth between the unreachable rabbits, Ayden walked over and stood close to his father so he could hear over the barking. "I can go tonight, Dad, if you're not feeling the best."

"And miss Bo's defining moment? She's been on a fine journey, and I want to finish it with her. Besides, I need the distraction."

Ayden took several steps backward.

Jotham assumed he was about to say something that could potentially irritate him. He didn't need to worry. He was too stiff and uncomfortable to risk beating the little shit this morning.

"Do you think it's time for us to speak to Chief Jewell?"

Jotham stared up at his son. "You want me to dignify that with a response?"

"We can't find her, Dad. We've *tried*."

"That sounds like defeat to me."

"Your reward is generous, Dad. Your people have knocked on nearly every door in Blue Falls. There isn't a sign of Kayla nor a single clue as to where she might have gone."

"Then knock on every door in Sharon's Edge, and then every door in New Lincoln. If she isn't on this property, she's somewhere."

"She could have left the state, for all we know."

Jotham closed his eyes. He took a deep breath. "I asked you to help set up the training, Ayden, not make me feel any worse than I already—"

"Jewell has resources, Dad. We could be wasting time. She could be in trouble—"

Jotham's eyes snapped open. "That man is a pedophile. What could he possibly know about caring for a child? He will approach the hunt for Kayla in the same way he has approached everything in his twisted little life—with perversion. No. We keep this among ourselves."

Ayden sighed.

"And do you have a problem with that, son?"

"No, Dad."

He nodded towards Bo and the rabbits. "Good, now release one."

Ayden slackened the rope on the smallest rabbit.

Jotham leaned forward on his stool and watched Bo tear the young animal to pieces.

"WELL, here we are again, Mr. Pettman," Gabriel said from behind his desk, ignoring Jake's opening question. "Must be the commitment to our shared profession that keeps drawing us to one another?"

Jake leaned forward in his chair. "Where I come from, the police try to put things right."

Gabriel grinned. "Is that what you tried to do back in Wiltshire?"

"Meaning?"

"I did a little research on you."

Jake tried to maintain a calm demeanor even though his chest suddenly felt full of lead. "A young girl is missing, and you spend your time investigating me?"

"Did you really go AWOL?"

Jake narrowed his eyes.

"Shit ... you did, didn't you?" Gabriel leaned back in his chair. He looked as if he were about to cheer. "Spoke to a few friends of mine over in the UK. It seems you never actually quit. You just upped and left one day. Why would anyone in their right mind do that?"

"It's none of your business."

"Well, maybe I should make it my business." He nodded. "After all, you seem unable to stop taking my business into your own hands."

Jake leaned forward and pointed at the desk. "I came here, *first*, with a problem you haven't attempted to solve."

"I spoke to the family on your request."

"They lied to you."

"And that may be so, but, as I told you before, Mr. Pettman, a necessity for patience exists in Blue Falls. Everyone, me and you included, must tread cautiously."

"Tread cautiously? Where I come from I've watched colleagues sacrifice themselves to put things right!"

"Yes, I've heard. Actually, I've heard all sorts about you, Mr. Pettman." Gabriel paused for a mouthful of coffee from yellowed cup with *Best Police Officer Ever* written in fading red letters. "I believe you've got blood on your hands."

Jake considered ramming the cup down smug bastard's throat. "Everything I did was in the line of duty."

"Killing is killing." Gabriel put down the cup. "To be expected, I guess." He smiled, displaying teeth as yellow as the old cup. "Considering."

"What do you mean?"

"Bad stock ... child-killing stock."

Jake stood and gripped the edges of the desk, desperate to stop himself swinging for the prick.

"Sit down, Mr. Pettman. Admittedly, getting thrown in jail will keep you out of trouble, but it will also create paperwork. You can relax. I was discreet in my inquiries."

Jake struggled to take the advice. His breathing was quick.

"Those you've run from don't know your whereabouts."

Yet, Jake thought and took a deep breath to try to control the surging adrenaline. "I don't owe you anything, Jewell, so let's steer clear of that assumption."

Gabriel shrugged.

"Do you really think I'd be worth chasing all the way here?"

"Maybe. You've certainly made a real impression around here, and you've only just arrived. I imagine you've a lot of enemies. Sit down, Mr. Pettman."

"I'll stay standing. How about getting around to the answering the question I asked you when I got here? How can you stomach dogfighting on your patch?"

Gabriel took another mouthful of coffee.

"Not going to dodge it again are—"

"It's a sport," Gabriel said, avoiding eye contact.

"A blood sport. An illegal sport."

"I agree, but this isn't Midsomer; this is Blue Falls."

"Midsomer isn't a real town."

"You get my point." He made eye contact with Jake again. "There will always be evil in a place like Blue Falls. It comes with the territory. Many would argue that the fucking place was born from it. If you take on the evil, it gets far worse. Allowing some evil, a necessary evil, can keep everything under control."

"Jesus, here we go again. Your balance. The ecosystem. Excuses. All of them! You're just a weak man, Jewell."

Gabriel slammed a palm on the table. "You confront Jotham and see what happens."

"Oh, I intend to." Jake leaned in nearer to Gabriel and curled his lip. "After you admit you *want* me to."

"I don't know what you—"

"Cut the bullshit, Jewell! You pointed me in the direction of the dogfighting!"

"Maybe I thought you'd just go and get yourself killed!"

"But, if you really wanted me gone, why didn't you reveal my whereabouts when you made inquiries about me?"

Gabriel sat back in his chair.

"Listen. I know your hands are tied. To some extent, I *understand* your situation. You want Jotham as badly as I do. Give me something."

"I've given you all I can."

"Exactly what I thought." Jake sneered and turned for the door.

His hand was on the handle when Gabriel said, "You need to stop sniffing around people who have everything to lose. That's not how you get answers. Not round here."

Jake turned. "Who am I looking for then?"

Gabriel cracked the knuckles on his left hand. "Those who have already lost to Jotham MacLeoid."

Jake laughed. "That must be a long list."

"Yes, it's long, but most people on that list are dead, so that should speed things up for you."

JAKE SAW LILLIAN as he exited the department. Not only was she avoiding eye contact with him, but she had gritted teeth and a furrowed brow.

Outside, he leaned against the wall where he'd first met Lillian, leaned over and took big gulps of air.

Shit. The bastard, Gabriel, was on to him.

He stood up straight and slapped the wall behind himself several times, desperate to relieve the frustration. How much had Gabriel revealed in his sinister phone calls to the police in the UK?

It wasn't the police Jake was worried about, it was Article SE—an organized crime outfit that had wound its tendrils around law enforcement in Wiltshire. He too had been gripped by a tendril. And there were others—his boss, Chief Superintendent Joan Madden, included. If she got wind of where he was, she would alert those in Article SE. And they would come for him. Of that, there was no doubt.

He had to find this missing girl and move on before it was too late. He pulled his phone from his Barbour jacket and sighed. He had no choice. Without help, he could get nowhere.

"Lillian, I'm outside."

"What happened to steering clear of you?"

"I noticed you didn't look best pleased about that. Look. I was wrong. I'm sorry. I need you."

"Go on."

"We need to get a list together of *those who have already lost.*"

"As usual, you're making little sense."

"Come and smoke one of your cigarettes, and I'll explain."

13

BLAKE THOMPSON LOOKED into the eyes of the man who'd murdered his daughter and pleaded for the body. Behind him, a dog was barking and yanking on a chain, desperate to reach some tied-up rabbits.

Jotham broke eye contact and looked off into the distance.

Blake knew it wasn't shame that made this bastard avoid eye contact. No. A man like this possessed no such emotion. He did it because Blake was an inconvenience—an unwelcomed distraction.

Eventually, Jotham regarded Blake again with his hunter's eyes. He opened his mouth to speak but waited for one of the rabbits to stop squealing. "What purpose will it serve you to crawl into my pit for your daughter's body?"

Blake forced back the tears. He wanted to remain dignified. "Allow us closure. She should be buried."

Jotham snorted and looked away. "For your God?"

"For us, Jo." Blake kept his hands behind his back, fearful he might impulsively close them around the killer's neck.

"Do you think I owe you something, Blake?"

"No." Blake rubbed a tear from the corner of his eye before it had chance to run down his face. "It's her mother. She's innocent in all of this. Please place my daughter somewhere so she may be found and laid to rest."

"So, you don't just want her body, you would like to put on some kind of show? Stage the manner of her death?"

"Yes ... for her mother."

"Marissa doesn't know?"

"The *truth* would kill her."

"Oh." Jotham nodded and looked across his land again. "So, lay her under a cliff, that sort of thing?"

"Whatever works."

"Whatever works in order to lie to your wife?"

"Yes, Jo." Blake tackled another tear while Jotham focused elsewhere.

Jotham rubbed his long beard deep in thought. *A show. It was always a fucking show with this man.* "No, I don't think so."

Blake gulped. "But ..."

"No."

"Why?" His body quivered.

"I don't have to give you an answer. Go home and tell your wife the truth. Move on with your life. I'm offering a good future to your family."

"But you don't understand. She won't accept it. Her mind, her reasoning, she isn't the person she once was. She won't be able to lie. She'll expose the truth."

Jotham looked back up at Blake. He smiled, and his tongue darted over his top front teeth. "Then silence her, Blake."

"What?"

"Silence her. After all, isn't it the job of every man to purge the weak? Human nature."

"I can't do that." He made no effort to stop the tears streaking his face now.

"Yet, if the truth comes out, one of your other children will go into the pit. Did I not make that clear the other night?"

Blake felt his insides melting. He so wanted to tear this psychopath apart with his bare hands. "Jo, I'm pleading with you—"

"Enough!" Jotham summoned Ayden with a wave. "See our guest off the property."

Blake looked at Ayden then back at Jotham, who was no longer acknowledging him. "Please, Jo."

Ayden took his arm. "Come on, Mr. Thompson."

Blake snatched away his arm. "Get your fucking hands off me. Don't you touch me. It cannot be this way. This isn't right. None of this is right."

"Ayden," Jotham said, "let Bo off her chain."

"Dad? Are you sure—"

"*Now.*"

Ayden wandered toward Bo.

Jotham studied Blake and raised an eyebrow. "Your call, Blake."

Blake heard the chain rattle behind him as Ayden undid it.

"Okay, Jo. I'm going."

Jotham nodded.

"I'll see myself out." He staggered off.

"You tried, Blake!" Jotham called after him. "It was all you could do. Now you must tell your wife."

Blake considered turning back, shouting abuse and daring them to set their wild animal on him. Being savaged to death was preferable to telling his wife the cold truth—that his daughter had been thrown into a pit and killed by *something* down there.

But suicide was not an option. Leaving his wife alone and without the truth was abhorrent. No, the truth she would have. And afterward, when she said she couldn't live with it, he would offer her silence. And after she'd accepted, he would share in it too.

———

It took Lillian a few hours to compile a list of all the people Jotham had treated badly in the past. The surviving members of that exclusive club of "those who had already lost" was far longer than Gabriel had suggested. Fortunately, Lillian had already formed some reasonable conclusions.

Jake smiled. Lillian was both competent and good-hearted. His experience of Blue Falls so far suggested these traits were in short supply.

Lillian had whittled down the list to ex-employees. All had been residents of Blue Falls at the time of working, and all of them had been female. She'd also bulleted ahead and contacted some of them.

"They *really* didn't want to talk to me," she said.

"In fear of their lives, no doubt."

"No, not so much that. It was as if they were grateful to him."

"For being sacked?"

"They accepted their fate. They thought they deserved it. One admitted to stealing some of the product for personal use. Another said she was late all the time."

"And how did he treat them?"

"Two of the three I spoke to actually used the word *gentleman*."

"I don't believe it."

Lillian had yet to talk to other ex-employers on the list. She showed it to Jake then pointed to a name she'd circled. "Marion Springs. She actually made a report to the police."

Jake's eyes widened. "Go on."

"Someone had deleted the files in the folder."

"Shit." Jake considered this. "And yet left the folder there? Sloppy. Let me guess who authored the folder. Chief Jewell by chance?"

Lillian nodded.

"Imbecile. Well, I'm not heading back to try to get more blood from that stone. Let's go straight to the source."

MARION SPRINGS ENTERTAINED Jake and Lillian on the porch while smoking like a chimney. She was a well-built middle-aged woman who looked strong and healthy despite her filthy habit and the lines of experience etched into her face. "My boy has only just turned twelve. I don't want him breathing in this crap."

Jake smiled. "If only all parents were as conscientious."

"Yes, well," Marion said through a plume of smoke, "some are and some aren't. I know a whole load of both."

"So, you said you were happy to talk to us about Jotham?"

"Happy is not the right word. Willing, yes."

"You don't sound like his biggest fan," Lillian said. "Other ex-employees have referred to him as a gentleman."

Marion snorted so hard that she coughed on her latest lungful of smoke. "Have you met him?"

"Yes," Jake said. "And my reaction on first hearing him referred to in that way was similar to yours."

Marion fired up a third cigarette. "But then you can see their point. He offered them work where none existed and paid them very well. Yes, it was outside the law, but who cares about that when you're practically living on fresh air? I know I certainly didn't at the time."

"So, what's so different about you then?" Jake said. "Why aren't you singing his praises like his other ex-employers?"

"Because I tell it how it is. The other girls had a different view of what is acceptable. Or, to put it another way, that old brute really isn't my type, and I wasn't inclined to do what was required of me."

"I don't follow," Jake said.

"At any time, Jotham would have a favorite." She paused to take a long inhalation from her cigarette then stared off into the distance and seemed to lose her train of thought.

Jake and Lillian exchanged glances.

"Mrs. Springs, you were saying something about favorites?" Jake said.

"Oh, yes. Sorry. He only ever had one favorite at a time. And it seems he didn't get bored too easily. I worked there for four years, and in that time, he only had four favorites."

"What happens if you're the favorite?" Lillian said.

"I was hoping you could use your imagination on that one, dear, but being police, I guess you want all the grisly details. It basically meant he'd come into the laboratory on most days, take you to his room and, you know, fuck you."

Lillian cursed under her breath.

"I know." Marion blew out a cloud of smoke. "The perfect gentleman."

"Is that why you went to the police?" Lillian asked.

"Haven't you read the report?"

Jake and Lillian exchanged glances again.

"The file was corrupted," Lillian said.

Marion snorted again. "Ha! I knew on the day I made my report that nothing would happen. But then, what did I expect? I assume you know who Jotham MacLeoid is or you wouldn't be standing here on my doorstep!"

"What happened, Ms. Springs?"

Marion threw her cigarette butt on the floor and stamped on it. "Well, fourth year lucky for me, he selected me to be his favorite!"

"I'm sorry," Lillian said, not looking up.

She shrugged. "Only myself to blame. You put yourself in those situations, you can't go off crying when it backfires."

"No, Marion, you were desperate. This type of man preys on that."

"I was, yes," Marion said, looking up, "but not that desperate. As I told you before, he wasn't my knight in shining armor! In fact, he wasn't anyone's, the old bastard. The others were just scared. Poor girls. But I'm different than them. Most of those girls had been bullied, whether by an abusive father or a trash-talking husband. I was lucky. My daddy wanted me to be a fighter, and he raised me to stand my ground. So I told Jotham I wasn't interested."

"Good for you, Marion," Lillian said.

The color drained from her face. "He sacked me."

"No loss. You were the winner in this. There is no doubt about—"

"No, I wasn't, ma'am." She rolled up her blouse sleeve. "He raped me." She showed Lillian and Jake the white scar on her arm. "Branded me with his zippo. He then gave me my final pay packet, and his son drove me home."

"Jesus," Lillian said.

"I'm sorry that happened to you," Jake said.

Marion nodded. "That's exactly what your colleague, Gabriel Jewell, said. He promised to get justice, and I know for a fact he went to see Jotham, because the other girls saw him on the property and told me. But all he was doing was tidying up the mess. Several days later, Jotham sent one of his men with a bundle of cash—a generous severance package! How nice of Mr. Jewell to negotiate that for me, eh? This man also warned me that the matter was closed and if I continued to make trouble for Mr. MacLeoid, they would cut off my son's balls."

Jake shook his head.

"My son was four at the time, so yes, I took the money, and I let that matter drop. Never spent that money though. Burnt every last dollar. Fuck him. Me and my boy even went hungry that Thanksgiving, but I'm proud I never spent a single penny. If I'd taken that money, I'd have turned it into a transaction rather than what it was—rape."

"Thank you for being so open and honest with us, Ms. Springs," Jake said. "But why talk to us now? Are you no longer worried?"

"When you darkened my doorstep today, I just assumed you already knew. Like I said, I gave a report. Besides, telling you the truth about that twisted beast won't make a blind bit of difference. It's my word against his now, and its water long under the bridge. He won't be losing any sleep over me."

"You can always go to the Maine State Police with the truth," Lillian said.

"No. The only thing that matters to me now is my boy, and I won't be putting him in any danger."

Lillian embraced Marion. "You're so brave."

"Nonsense, dear. There're many out there with far deeper wounds than me."

Lillian pulled back and held her at arm's length.

Tears streaked the abused woman's face. "I'm not the only life he's destroyed, and I'm sure he'll get his just desserts one day. It's how you keep yourself going on the worst days, you know?"

Jake and Lillian both nodded.

Marion looked back and forth between her two visitors. "So, is this it then? Will he finally get what's coming to him?"

"It's a work in progress," Jake said. "But I'm steadily growing in confidence."

JAKE AND LILLIAN interviewed more ex-employees but did not find another story as soul-wrenching as Marion Spring's. It was getting late, so Lillian suggested a drink in the Blue Falls Taps.

"And be seen with me? Despite your boss's warning?" Jake said.

"You said it yourself, he despises Jotham. It's all bluster. As long as we don't go into him gung-ho, I think he'll turn a blind eye for the time being."

It was surprisingly quiet in the Taps, but then again, it was still quite early. Jake was pleased to see the barrels around the place were overflowing with peanuts so their shells weren't yet a health and safety hazard. Jake pointed out the table in the far corner under the watchful eye of Captain William Ross. "Out of harm's way." The oil painting had captured a rather stern impression of the man, and Jake wondered if this had been his usual demeanor when he'd been alive.

"Out of harm's way," Lillian said with a smile. "Doesn't seem like your style."

"Believe me, that's the style I strive for, but it continually evades me. Pint of Stinson?"

"Of course."

"It's crap, but that's the best they've got."

"Don't say that too loud; you'll cause a riot."

Jake surveyed the clientele. It was early, and most were in their seventies. He raised an eyebrow at her.

"Don't be fooled. You criticize the beer they grew up on, you'll awaken something in them."

Jake smiled. "One day I'll bring over a barrel of Wiltshire's finest, and that'll awaken something in them alright."

She nodded and went to the corner table.

Jake offered Piper a smile at the bar.

She returned it, but it was half-hearted.

Jake had spent many years in a failing marriage, so he knew immediately he'd pissed her off. He also knew it was better to deal immediately with the issue rather than let it fester. "We're working."

"I didn't say anything."

"Look. Lillian is a police officer, Piper. Her resources have gotten us this far. If I don't work with her, I'll be charging around like a bull in a china shop."

"Instead, you're drinking in a bar?"

"We're taking a short break to discuss our next move. We've heard some harrowing stuff today."

"So, this will help you think?" She hand pulled a Stinson.

Shit. She really reminded him of Sheila. He could never

win an argument, even if he really believed himself in the right.

"Why don't I bring over a pitcher then? Are you even any closer to finding Maddie?"

"To be honest, I don't know. But I'm getting closer to *him*. And we both know the answer is there."

"I just feel you'd be making better ground with me there."

"Two of us walking around, raising hell in a town with closed ranks, is bad enough. Three of us would be ridiculous."

Piper nodded toward Lillian. "So, you choose her?"

"You know why. And she's good, Piper, not like the rest of that sorry department. We'll get to the bottom of this soon enough. You'll have to trust me."

She poured the second drink. "Well, I'm coming over tonight."

"I expect nothing less." He smiled, and she smiled back.

"So you can fill me in. Not for anything else."

Jake handed her a five and took both drinks. "Thanks for the swamp juice."

"Have you not acquired the taste yet?"

"There's taste?" he asked with a smile.

14

B LAKE THOMPSON COULDN'T see clearly from the blood in his eyes. Through the red fog, he glimpsed the outline of his kitchen table, so this was the way he crawled. The pain in his head was worse than the other night beside the pit, but at least it reassured him that he was still alive.

Close to the table, his hand fell on the iron that she'd used to knock him unconscious ... or kill him. *Had that been her intention?* Not his beloved Marissa. Surely not. His whole existence had been about loving her, protecting her. Let her have her moment of despair, but please God, don't let her have murderous intentions. *Please don't sully her with those.*

He gripped the table edge with one hand and, with the other, lifted his T-shirt to wipe the blood from his eyes. It helped, but it was temporary. The blood was coming thick and fast. Using the table, he managed to ease himself to his feet and saw Sean at the kitchen door.

"Dad, are you all right?"

"Yes ... yes ... I'll be fine."

Sean ran around to him and put an arm around his shoulder to keep him steady.

Devin, his other son, was now at the kitchen door. "What happened?"

"She doesn't know what she's doing."

Devin's eyes widened. "Did Mom do this?"

"Yes, but—"

"Where is she?"

"I don't know. I've been unconscious." Blake's legs buckled in a wave of dizziness, but Sean took his weight and kept him upright.

Devin ran from the room.

Blake heard him bounding around the house, calling for his mother.

Sean helped him into a chair and handed him a towel to hold to his leaking head.

Devin burst back into the kitchen. "She's gone."

Blake stared at the table.

"Dad! She's gone! What happened?"

"Your mother doesn't know what she's doing."

Devin walked to the other side of the table. "What did you tell her?"

Blake didn't reply.

"Dad, *what did you tell her?*"

"Everything."

Devin slammed his fist on the table. "*What?*"

"She's Maddie's mother. She has a right to know."

"Dad, what have you done? She's probably completely lost it! Why would you tell her that?"

Blake dropped the towel and slammed down his hand, although not as hard. He pointed at Devin. "You watch your mouth, son. That's your mother you're talking about."

"She'll get us all killed."

"No, Devin." Blake tried to get to his feet. He heard Sean pleading with him to stay sitting but ignored him. "You'll get us killed. Just like you got your sister killed."

"How do you even know it was me? It could have been Sean."

"Sean hasn't got a bad bone in his body. He wouldn't betray anyone, not even that monster." Blake pointed at Devin. "No, it's you who has always been the spiteful little shit."

"Fuck you, Dad." He turned. "You two sit here, talking trash about me, while I try to sort this mess."

"I don't think you understand, son. We're past that stage."

"You're weak, Dad. That's the problem here—old and weak."

"I agree. I was weak when I made the decision not to pick you, son. It was you who should have gone into that pit, not your sister."

Devin stormed from the room.

"I THINK we've come as far as we can," Jake said and took a mouthful of Stinson IPA. "I'm going in to threaten Jotham with the Maine State Police unless he hands over Maddie."

"If he even has her," Lillian said and finished her drink.

"Fast drinker?"

"It's been an emotional day."

"Why've you changed your mind? You were as convinced as I was that he had Maddie."

"Yes, and I still am. But I'm not sure you confronting Jotham is the way to go. I think it'll land you in an early grave. There's got to be another way to get at the truth."

"How?" Jake shrugged. "Gabriel Jewell is too spineless to help us properly, and, as we've seen today, anyone who has history with Jotham won't challenge this man. We'll never get leverage over him. I've no choice but—"

"This place needs livening up!"

Jake rolled his eyes when Justin Stone and his entourage of three men—one of who was Ayden MacLeoid—entered.

Justin gave Jake a little wave.

Jake ignored him. "That's all we need—the first selectman's arrogant son and the local mobster's boy. A marriage made in heaven."

"The other two, Cole and Isaac, are equally bad news. They work for Jotham. My colleagues have turned a blind eye to a few of their activities, one of which was a car wreck that put a boy in intensive care. They were both joyriding, drunk."

Jake turned around again and watched them approach Piper at the bar. There was no music, and it was quiet, so Jake could eavesdrop on Justin's usual and futile attempt to seduce Piper.

"I'll pour you a drink, Justin, but if you suggest anything about our relationship progressing beyond a polite salutation again, I'll tip it over you," she said.

Cole and Isaac burst into laughter.

Justin elbowed one of them. "Fuck you two. Or you can buy your own."

"Piper is great. So feisty!" Lillian said.

Jake nodded but didn't reply. Something had his attention. Ayden MacLeoid wasn't laughing. In fact, he looked like he wanted to be as far away from this place as he possibly could. Jake recalled his initial impression of him last night in Sharon's Edge at the dogfighting ring. He'd been nervous and completely out of sorts as the *hardman*

167

sent to scare away Jake. He faced Lillian. "Tell me about Ayden MacLeoid."

"I thought I told you already?"

"Not much."

"Okay, well, there's an apple that *did* fall far from the tree. Unfortunately for him, that doesn't stop him from being a MacLeoid, and he has responsibilities—responsibilities, the rumours go, he struggles to fulfil."

"How so?"

"Well, I've not had much dealings with him, but I've heard several of my colleagues say he is the only MacLeoid with a heart."

"I see."

"The problem is that fetches him a few beatings. You often see him battered and bruised."

"Could Ayden be our way to Jotham?"

"I don't know. All said and done, Jake, he's still a MacLeoid. The things he's seen, the things he must have done —it really wouldn't be in his best interest to betray his father."

Ayden MacLeoid gave his apologies to Justin and, with his head lowered, skulked toward the exit.

Cole called after him, but Ayden ignored him.

"That man there is definitely on the losing side," Jake said.

"You think this was who the chief was referring to?"

"I don't know, but I'll try to find out. I'll call you later, Lillian. Stick around and keep an eye on these three for me, would you?"

"Yes, boss," she said with a smile.

"Well, you wanted real police work, Lillian, so right here, watching Justin, is the right place for it." Jake stood and went after Ayden.

KAYLA DESPERATELY WANTED Morris. She wanted to rub his soft head, kiss the little eye that hung down to his chest by a thread, and hold him tight. She was more than aware that, at thirteen, she was far too old to seek solace and safety in a toy monkey, but it was the sentimental value she craved right now; Morris had been a gift from her mother before she died. Despite only being four at the time, Kayla remembered her vividly. It was impossible to forget someone who'd loved her so passionately.

She heard Gabriel panting at her door. This had been the third time he'd returned since he'd locked her away. The first time, she'd turned to look at his eyes through the door slot and begged for her freedom. He'd not responded but simply stood there, making those horrible noises. She knew what he was doing. She'd often heard the boys at school joking about their "habits" and what they did behind closed doors at night.

But now this, Gabriel's third visit, she was at a loss as to why it was so frequent. Was that normal? Did boys really do this again and again without much of a break?

As his breathing quickened and he moaned, she looked around the grey, windowless room. She wanted to cry, but she'd spent most of the day in tears and felt burnt out. Instead, she sat upright on her damp bed, hugged her knees against her chest and rocked.

Gabriel grunted and sighed. After he caught his breath, he said, "I'm sorry."

She didn't respond. She didn't want to listen to this. She closed her eyes and thought about Morris.

"It's better this way."

She felt the urge to scream, so she murmured to herself, "Morris ... Morris ... Morris."

"You're safe here."

"Morris ... Morris ..."

"I won't touch you."

Leave me alone! Leave me alone! Help me! Dad, Morris, anyone, HELP ME!

"This might seem disgusting to you, but this will keep me in control. It will keep you safe."

She put her hands over her ears to shut him out, but there was no need, he was already leaving.

PIPER COULDN'T BELIEVE her eyes. She threw the dishcloth on the bar. "Marissa!"

Maddie's mother didn't acknowledge her call. It was unlikely she could hear over the wolf-whistling from Justin, Cole, and Isaac.

Marissa was barely recognizable from the woman Piper had visited yesterday. She wore high heels, fishnet stockings, a low-cut top, and an above-the-knee skirt. Her hair was pinned back, and her lips were painted red. She'd also taken pains to hide her deathly pallor with some dark rouge. She was dressed to kill.

"Mrs. T!" Justin, on his feet already, pounded the table like a wild chimp in a zoo. "Mrs. T!"

These animals were loud at the best of times, but several drinks had sent them off the scale. When Cole and Isaac swapped their whistles for howls, Piper decided enough was enough and strode to the end of the bar while keeping an eye on the event unfolding.

Marissa walked toward the three young men, smiling.

Piper thought she looked rather menacing, but she suspected her true intention was to look seductive. Why she would want to seduce these three knuckleheads was anybody's guess, especially when they were more or less the same age as her own children. Piper reached the end of the bar, lifted the bar hatch and slipped through.

Marissa stopped at the table and placed her hand on Cole's shoulder.

He stopped howling. He'd clearly not been expecting *this*.

Justin laughed and slammed the table again. "Mrs. T, what're you drinking?"

"Same as you." Marissa ran her fingers across Cole's face then through his hair.

His face glowed.

"Not like you to be shy, Cole," Justin said.

"Why don't you sit down, Justin?" Piper said, coming alongside Marissa.

Justin held up the palms of his hands. "Wow. Is everyone seeing this? Piper is actually talking to me away from the bar."

She sneered at him then touched Marissa's arm. "Mrs. Thompson, can I have a word please?"

"Of course, dear."

They stepped to one side. Piper glanced back to see the three young men eagerly watching them.

Justin, in particular, was making a real show of this. He sat down, propped his head on his elbows and stared, wide-eyed and grinning.

She turned her back to them so she didn't have to see their inane faces any longer. "Mrs. Thompson, what are you doing?"

"I'm out for a drink, my dear." Marissa stroked Piper's

face. "Such a good girl. I can see why my Maddie liked you so."

Liked? Why the past tense? "Do you know who these men are?"

"Of course. Cole and Isaac are friends with my boys. They work for Jotham MacLeoid."

"Yes. So, I think it's best if you stay—"

"And the other one, the showman, he's the son of the chief selectman—the man who has helped turn this town into what it is today—Charles Stone. Although the rumor is that it's his bitch wife, Priscilla, who really runs the place."

"Again, another reason I think you should go home."

"Such a good girl, dear. My Maddie loved you so. I'm old and wise enough to take care of myself though." She kissed Piper's forehead. "Sorry, honey, you may want to wipe that off." She pointed at her lipstick.

"Are you thinking clearly, Mrs. Thompson?"

"This is the clearest I've felt in days, dear." She walked past Piper.

Piper turned and watched Marissa sit on Cole's lap and throw her arms around him.

The whooping and hollering started again.

"Is everything all right?" Lillian asked, coming alongside her.

Piper shook her head. Her blood felt like ice in her veins. "No. She just referred to her daughter in the past tense. *Twice.* I think she knows something terrible, and I think this is about to get very messy."

"I just want to talk to you, Ayden," Jake said, walking quickly to keep up.

They were on Main Street and drawing up alongside Rogers general store.

"I've nothing to say to you. Stay away from me."

It was late, and no one was about. Jake kept pace until they hit a series of busted streetlights then used the sudden patch of darkness to duck and swoop in. His shoulder met Ayden's, and he crashed side-on into the brick wall with a sharp exhalation.

"I asked nicely," Jake said.

"Fuck off—"

Jake delivered a blow to Ayden's abdomen.

He doubled over and went to his knees.

Jake stepped backward and prepared for the young man's rise, but he stayed down.

Ayden looked up and took a few gulps of air before asking, "What do you want?"

"I've made it very clear to you and your father already."

Ayden shook his head. "We cannot give you what we don't have."

"So I keep hearing. Tell me who you really are, Ayden."

"What kind of fucked-up question is that?"

"A serious one." Jake proffered his hand.

Ayden shook his head then reached up to take Jake's hand.

As Jake helped him to his feet, he said, "You're not the same as your father. You're not even the same as the people he employs."

Ayden leaned against the brick wall and shook his head. "You don't know me."

"People speak highly of you, Ayden."

"Who?" he said with a sneer.

"They say you're different to your father."

He chortled. "Don't listen to rumors. I've done awful things. I'm no different."

"Bollocks. If I'd just floored your father, I'd be a dead man walking."

Ayden eyed him. "Who's to say you're not?"

Jake smiled. "No offense, Ayden, but I'm not feeling threatened by you right now."

Ayden snorted. "So, I'm weaker than my father. Any more compliments?"

"You're not weaker. You're different. *Better*, like I said before. You care whether a fifteen-year-old girl lives or dies."

Ayden lowered his head.

Up until now, Jake had been very confident the MacLeoids had taken Maddie; now, after witnessing the young man's sullen reaction, he was completely certain they had. "Your father doesn't love you."

Ayden looked up and glared at him. "How could you possibly know that?"

"Because a man who takes pleasure in beating his own son doesn't have any room left inside himself for love."

"It's not like that."

"What's it like then, Ayden?"

"He ... He ..."

"Go on."

"He's trying."

"To ...?"

"Help me."

"Was he trying to help you when he gave you that black eye and swollen cheek?"

"He just wants me to be stronger, that's all. His father did the same to him."

"He's going to kill you. One day, he'll go too far, and he'll kill you."

"I don't believe that."

"Believe it, Ayden. I'm a police officer. I've seen it time and time again. People who live with this, who accept that this is the order of things, they suffer the consequences and, sometimes, pay the ultimate price."

Ayden shook his head. "What do you think I can do for you?"

"You can do the right thing. You can tell me where Maddie Thompson is, and you can help get her back to her parents."

"Even if I knew where she was and even if I could betray him, I wouldn't."

"Why? Because you're scared of him?"

"No. But it's not just about me."

"I don't follow."

Ayden narrowed his eyes. "If I betray him, what'll happen to my mother?"

———

THE BASSIST of Blues in the Falls was warming up. A steady plucking vibrated the air, but it didn't drown out the sound of Piper's heart thumping the wall of her chest.

Marissa Thompson kissed Cole. Passionately. She gripped the back of his head with her bony hands to keep their lips forced together.

"Go, boy!" Justin shouted, drumming his hands on the table.

"Save some for the rest of us!" Isaac said.

All ten patrons in the Taps watched, but no one was about to get involved.

Piper turned to Lillian, who stood beside her in front of the bar. "We have to stop this."

"No argument from me there, but let me call for backup first."

"Your colleagues would just join in!"

"I wasn't talking about them. I was thinking about our mutual friend."

Piper nodded.

While Lillian used her cell to summon Jake to the bar, Piper approached the stomach-churning show. As she neared, Marissa pulled away from Cole, swung her head toward Isaac and kissed him instead.

The bass player slapped his bass harder.

Piper felt the thumping in her chest intensify. "Stop this!"

The bass player stopped slapping, and Justin stopped drumming. If not for Isaac's groans under the pressure of Marissa's lips, the place would have fallen silent.

"Marissa, stop kissing Isaac!" Piper said.

She ignored the request.

Justin smiled in Piper's direction. "Here comes the fun police."

"Fuck you."

Justin stood. "What gives you the right to talk to me like that?"

Piper ignored him. Lillian came up alongside her and whispered, "Jake's on his way back. Shouldn't be more than a minute or two. He said he was onto something with Ayden."

Marissa broke away from Isaac, leaving his mouth red with her lipstick. The lipstick was worse on Cole; it was spread across his cheeks. Marissa stood, leaned forward and put an arm around each of their shoulders. "So, which of you two lovely young men will tell me where my Maddie is?"

Cole and Isaac stared at one other.

Piper wondered if they were speechless over their sexual experience with Marissa or over the suggestion that they were responsible for Maddie's disappearance. She suspected it was a little bit of both.

"Cole," Marissa said, "for years, you stopped by ours for dinner after school while your mother was working. Do you remember? Could you tell me where my Maddie is?"

"We don't know what you're talking about," Cole said.

Marissa looked at Isaac. "Is that the same for you, Isaac, dear? Isn't your sister good friends with Maddie? Surely, you can find it in your heart to tell me where my daughter's body is."

Piper steadied herself against Lillian. *Body ... no ... no.*

"I'm sorry, Mrs. Thompson," Isaac said. "I don't know—"

Piper stepped forward. "Please, Marissa, come into the back with me." She eyed Justin, expecting another wisecrack, but he looked rather stunned himself. Maybe he knew nothing about Maddie. After all, he didn't work for Jotham MacLeoid. No need to, really, when you were the son of the richest man in town.

Marissa nodded. "Okay, Piper, dear. I'll come. I don't blame these two boys anyway." Rather than turn and walk toward Piper and Lillian, Marissa sidestepped to her right and marched around the far side of the table. "No. The responsibility lies with Blue Falls, with the corruption." She drew alongside Justin. "The cancerous filth."

Justin watched Marissa as she passed him but didn't respond, nor did he turn to follow her.

"Marissa, *please*," Piper said.

"A man like Jotham shouldn't be allowed to do what he does. The problem is bigger than him." Marissa stopped behind Justin, reached behind herself and appeared to be fiddling with the belt on her skirt. There was a glint—

Piper lurched forward. "Marissa!"

Marissa raised a kitchen knife and slammed it into Justin's upper back.

Piper managed to get her arms around Marissa from behind. She offered no resistance, and Piper managed to pull her backward. They were forced to a stop at the next table along.

Justin leaned forward with his hands on the table. The knife was stuck deep between his shoulder blades. He was groaning.

Cole and Isaac were on their feet and coming around either side of the table to assist.

"Jus!" Isaac shouted.

"Jesus," Cole said, taking hold of Justin's arm. He turned to Lillian. "Call an ambulance!"

Lillian was already dialling.

Justin brushed away Cole's hand and stumbled to the side.

"Easy, Jus," Isaac said.

"Get off me," Justin gurgled. "Both of you."

They were seated near the entrance, so Justin staggered forward, clearly intending to leave.

Piper eased Marissa into a chair. Her face was blank, and her eyes stared off into space. "Wait here, Marissa."

Justin was still staggering toward the doors, his friends alongside him.

"You're hurt, Jus. You need to stop," Isaac said.

Cole reached again from the other side, and again, Justin brushed away his hand.

"I'm okay. I just need some fucking air," Justin said with a strained voice.

Piper started after the three men. "Justin, wait."

Justin stopped.

Even in this moment, she held some sway over him.

The door to the Taps swung open. Jake marched in and halted when he realized Justin obscured his path. Jake looked around, clearly trying to comprehend what was happening, before Justin slumped forward into his arms. "What—"

"He's got a knife in his back, Jake," Lillian said. "Be careful how you lay him down."

Justin slipped down Jake's front.

"Bloody hell." Jake lowered him onto his side.

"The ambulance is coming, Jake," Lillian said.

Jake knelt and put his fingers to Justin's neck then shook his head at Lillian and Piper.

15

OUTSIDE THE BUILDING, Jotham waited in the front seat of his pickup. Bo stood on the passenger seat. Many vehicles surrounded him. The nights when a MacLeoid dog fought were always the busiest.

"And rightly so," Jotham said, allowing Bo to nuzzle him and lick his face. "Everyone wants to watch a champion."

At this stage, minutes before the fight, Jotham should be building Bo's aggression, or at least *sustaining* the bloodlust they'd spent the day developing with rabbits. But Jotham trusted his dog. She was a fighter, like her owner, and he had no doubt she would deliver success.

"We do this for Kayla. Then, when she's back, I'll give you to her, Bo. You've been my most loyal dog, and there is no better reward than being taken care of by that precious princess."

He climbed from his pickup and led Bo to her final fight.

WHEN THE DOOR to the Blue Falls Taps opened, Jake looked up, expecting to see a paramedic rather than two barrels of a sawed-off shotgun.

Devin Thompson.

Jake rose from Justin's body and stepped backward.

Devin glanced down at the victim. "What happened here?"

"Your mother happened," Cole said.

"Shit!" The shotgun shook in Devin's hands as he moved it from person to person.

The scattered patrons, including the musician, had their hands in the air.

"Calm down," Jake said.

"Shit ... Shit!" Devin panned the shaking shotgun from target to target.

It was Russian Roulette, and Jake's blood ran cold.

"Mom. Come with me!" Devin's pale face twitched. "Now!"

Jake was not inexperienced with people on the edge before; it was clear to see that Devin was about to fall. Jake couldn't hear movement behind him, so he glanced back.

Marissa remained in the chair, slumped over. Her hair hung limply over her face, framing her empty eyes. She made no effort to move.

Jake turned back to Devin. "How did you know she was here?"

"Dad called me."

"It was me," Piper said. "I contacted Blake Thompson when Marissa first arrived here."

"Mom, you need to come with me now, or we're dead," Devin said.

"You're all dead anyway," Isaac said.

Jake glared at Isaac. *Stupid, stupid boy.*

Devin came quickly and struck Isaac across the face with the butt.

Isaac staggered backward. A table stopped him falling. He stared up at his assailant, clutching his cheek.

Devin stepped forward and put the shotgun barrels against the idiot's forehead. "Well, if that's the case, I'm not going down alone."

"Please ... okay ... sorry ..." Blood dribbled from the corner of Isaac's mouth.

Devin stepped away from Isaac and headed toward Piper, pointing the shotgun at her.

"Devin ..." Jake said.

"Shut the fuck up!" Devin glared at Jake. "You've caused enough trouble."

Jake felt a wave of nausea as Devin neared Piper.

"Go and get my mother, Piper," Devin said.

"Your mother isn't well—"

"Get my mother!"

Jesus, Piper, just do what he says! Jake thought.

"Okay, I'll ask her—"

"Quickly! They'll be here soon. And then I'll start shooting."

Piper darted to Marissa, knelt, took her hands and peered into those sad eyes. "Devin wants you to go with him now."

Marissa didn't respond.

"I don't think he'll harm you. I think he wants to protect you."

Still no response.

"You need to stand—"

"Hurry up!" Devin shouted.

Piper glared at him. "This is your mother, Devin, and she's terrified."

"I'll go." Marissa slipped a hand from Piper's and placed her palm against her daughter's friend's face then smiled. She rose to her feet.

"Come on, come on!" Devin said, tapping his foot.

Marissa approached her son, and when she was close enough, Devin lurched out and grabbed her arm.

He then coaxed her to the front door while keeping the sawed-off shotgun moving from person to person. "Stay back." Devin pushed his mother through the door then followed after her. "Don't come after us."

After the door closed, Isaac said, "We won't have to, dickhead, someone else will."

Jake went to Piper and embraced her. He then looked at Lillian. "Are you okay?"

Lillian nodded.

———

FROM HIS CORNER of the ring, Jotham listened to the crowd chant Bo's name. They weren't doing this out of respect for Jotham, but out of adoration for Bo and her passionate, athletic displays. She'd become known as the "ultimate finisher." In her last fight, she'd torn out Athena's throat even after she'd broken her back and incapacitated her.

Mercy was weakness, and Jotham believed he'd bred it out of all of his dogs, just like Boyd had bred it out of him— just as he'd tried so desperately to breed it out of Ayden ...

Bo and Nyx rolled.

"Bo ... Bo ... Bo!" the crowd chanted.

Earlier, the referee had introduced Nyx to her debut fight as the "Greek goddess of night and possessor of exceptional power." At the time, Jotham had rolled his eyes.

Now, watching the young bitch perform, he had to give credit where credit was due. She was holding her own against Bo and had even taken a small chunk from his bitch's side.

"Bo ... Bo ... Bo ..."

He was yet to hear anybody chant Nyx's name. Hardly surprising. No one had seen Nyx or her breeder before. The fact that Jotham also didn't recognize the breeder was unusual. Didn't matter how far they traveled within Maine, or New England for that matter, Jotham *always* knew them.

Nyx's breeder was young and wiry with a shaved head. He also wore a suit, which was often the case with more affluent breeders. There was a steady supply of wealthy businessmen, for example, who simply did this as a hobby on the weekends while conquering the stock market on weekdays.

Jotham listened to a yelp from Bo and felt a tingle run down his spine. For the first time in the longest time, he felt some concern. Bo looked to be flagging, and Nyx was coming again and again with savage intent. *Lift your head, girl. You've got a lot more to give.*

The chanting intensified and fed the tiring Bo with a burst of energy. She evaded Nyx's jaws with a deft maneuver, and the crowd exploded. "Fanged! Fanged! Fanged!"

Nyx had split her own lip.

In his younger years, Jotham would have expressed delight, but in recent years, he'd adopted decorum. He smiled. *Well, some, anyway.* He spied the well-dressed breeder. The bastard didn't look concerned about his faltering dog. This disappointed Jotham. Maybe he should've cheered after all and antagonized him.

Nyx staggered backward, dripping blood from her

damaged mouth.

No mercy, Bo, no mercy.

His beautiful dog charged.

Nyx swooped, rose up and sank her teeth into the side of the oncoming dog.

Jotham straightened up, feeling the burn of the deep, bandaged wounds on his back. *Impossible! That bitch had been finished!*

The animals rolled again, tearing at one another.

"Bo! Bo! Bo!"

The back and forth continued. Every time one of the dogs seemed to gain the upper hand, it was snatched back with renewed fervor from the other.

Jotham checked his watch. This was the longest fight he'd ever seen. He knew Bo's capabilities like the back of his hand and realized, with gnawing anxiety, she would soon tire.

Bo stumbled. Unless Nyx too reached the end of the line, Bo was done for.

Nyx darted in, bearing bloodstained teeth.

Bo staggered backward, panting.

"Bo," Jotham said.

She regarded her master, her eyes glassy.

"You don't give up, girl. You just don't—"

Nyx was on top of her, seemingly with as much energy as she'd started this fight with.

Impossible. Jotham glared at the breeder again. The bastard looked contented. Jotham nodded at the referee. He wanted the fight stopped.

The referee nodded back then stepped forward—

Bo squealed. Then both she and the crowd fell silent.

Despite Nyx, Jotham jumped in.

Nyx released Bo's throat and barked at Jotham.

He kicked out at the beast. "Get the fuck away from me."

The pit bull paced from side to side, barking and baring its teeth at Jotham.

The other breeder entered the ring and put on her collar.

Jotham didn't bother kneeling to Bo. He looked down at the blood pooling around his shoes and knew already that she was gone. He had eyes only for the sonofabitch breeder right now. Jotham had been involved in this industry his whole life. There was only one way a pit bull could maintain ferocity for such a sustained period of time—chemical assistance.

He narrowed his eyes.

AFTER HEARING about Justin Stone's death, Gabriel did not bother with the Taps. He knew exactly where the trouble was heading. He parked outside the Thompson's Cape Cod-style farmhouse alongside an assortment of vehicles. From his back seat, he grabbed the Remington that Kayla had threatened him with earlier and exited the car. Keeping his rifle in both hands across his chest rather than slung over his shoulder, he mounted the covered front porch and kicked the bottom of the front door twice. Then he stood back against the railing. "Blake? It's Chief Jewell here. You in there?"

The living room window beside the front door opened. "Chief, what can I do for you?"

Gabriel shook his head. "Don't be ridiculous, Blake. Open the fucking door."

"Why?"

"So you can thank me, for a start. It's a godsend I'm standing on your porch, considering what's coming."

"Thank you, but I don't need you to worry about us."

"Don't we both wish that was the truth? Open the door so I can come in and tell you your best route out of this shitstorm."

"Sorry, Chief, I won't open the door."

Gabriel kicked the railing with the back of his foot. *Stubborn old bastard.* "Can you send one of your sons to the window?"

"No need. We're all in agreement."

"They agree with suicide. Hard to believe. Lads like that have a lot of living left to do."

"Thank you for stopping by, Chief."

"Unbelievable! You do realize the next time I come here it'll be a crime scene."

"One you'll have no trouble covering up, no doubt."

Gabriel laughed. "Unfair, Blake. I'm here to stop it getting to that!"

Devin appeared beside his father at the window. "So, what's your suggestion then, Chief?"

"Get back in the kitchen, son!" Blake glared at Devin.

"You let me do this properly, Devin," Gabriel said. "I'll arrest your mother for killing Justin, then she'll be safe. You'll *all* be safe—"

"And watch my wife go to prison for the rest of her life?" Blake asked, raising his voice.

"The alternative does not bear thinking about. You and your family only have one way out of this, I'm afraid."

"It makes sense, Dad."

"No!"

"Be reasonable," Gabriel said.

"She stays with us," Blake said.

"But, Dad—"

"Stay the fuck out of this, son."

Gabriel heard the cars approaching.

Blake's eyes widened. "I didn't expect so many of them."

"Your wife killed Charles's son, Blake. I don't think he'll be cost cutting on this little venture."

"This'll be a massacre," Devin said.

"Shit! Let me think!" Blake said.

Gabriel stepped forward. "My offer still stands."

"To throw my wife in jail?"

The cars screeched to a halt.

"Look again, Blake. And please come to your fucking senses for the sake of your family."

"Why don't you stop them?" Blake pointed at him out the window. "Do your job. Turn around and stop them."

Gabriel heard the car doors opening. "You really think I can do that? How do they look?"

"Determined."

Gabriel nodded.

"They've brought a small army," Devin said.

"You can't talk your way out of this, Blake."

Blake's eyes widened. "Jotham killed Maddie. I watched them throw her into a fucking pit."

Gabriel looked down.

"I listened to my daughter die, Chief."

Gabriel could hear the so-called small army trudge toward the house. "I'm sorry for your loss, Blake. It's not right."

"Not right? It's an abomination!"

Gabriel looked up, nodding. "Jotham will get what's coming, whatever happens. You don't need to worry about that."

"I hope so. Now, you may want to get out of my way." Blake pointed his own rifle out the window.

"Don't, Dad. They'll kill us all."

"Blake, listen, I've got an idea. It's your family's only way out, but you must let me take Marissa. Will you let me protect her?"

Blake looked over Gabriel at the reckoning approaching his house.

"Think about what Marissa would want if she was thinking straight. It wouldn't be to lose her remaining children."

"Dad, listen, he's right."

Blake narrowed his eyes. "Fuck you. Both of you." He sighed, nodded and pulled the rifle back into the house.

Thank Christ. Gabriel stepped to the window, told Blake and Devin his idea and turned to see what he was up against.

Six men dressed in hunting gear had fanned out in front of the house.

Gabriel recognized the weaponry and was surprised to see the one closest to him was holding a B&T APC9—a hardy submachinegun. The next one along held an M4 Carbine. This wasn't just revenge; they were here to enjoy themselves.

Chief Selectman Charles Stone was using a cane and looked weaker than he'd been the last time Gabriel had seen him two months earlier. He'd disappeared from the public eye of late and was rumored to be fighting cancer. His wife, Priscilla, was a tall, dark-haired woman, who looked half his age, despite being older.

Gabriel met them at the bottom step. He acknowledged the weary man with a lowered head. "Mr. Stone, I'm sorry for—"

"You can address me, Gabriel," Priscilla said.

Gabriel regarded Priscilla. "Certainly, Mrs. Stone. I'm sorry for your loss."

Priscilla raised her eyebrows. "Are you?"

Gabriel was lost for words.

"Tell me the truth, Gabriel. Apart from a few of his deadbeat friends, who'll be genuinely sorry over Justin's death?"

Gabriel had expected a mother in anguish; instead, he'd received an ice queen.

"I can't answer that, Mrs. Stone, but I can tell you I'm here to get to the bottom of what happened."

"How so?"

"I'm taking Marissa Thompson into custody."

"Into custody? Why?"

"To interview her then charge her."

Priscilla laughed. Because she was holding her husband's arm, the tremble from her laugh slightly lolled his head and lengthened the drool hanging from his mouth. "I thank you for your diligence, Gabriel, but I'm here to save you a job."

"It's no bother."

She nodded. "I'd like you to leave, Gabriel. I'm in charge of this town."

"It's your husband who's in charge, Mrs. Stone."

"He's too unwell to do his duty. He's here to give me his blessing. Aren't you, Charles?"

Charles managed a nod and a grunt. The line of drool snapped.

"Well, it doesn't work like that, Mrs. Stone. And this matter concerns the law, which, in effect, makes me in charge of this situation."

"You really want to do this? Here? Now?"

"My job? Of course, Mrs. Stone."

Priscilla sneered. "Pause for a moment, Gabriel ... and think."

"I don't follow."

"Think and remember who you really work for."

It's hard to forget, Gabriel thought, *but there are some things I just can't allow.* He moved his gaze from one armed soldier to another. *Some lines that cannot be crossed ...* "I'd like you to leave Mr. and Mrs. Stone so I can take Mrs. Thompson into custody. Again, I'm sorry for your loss."

"No, Gabriel, we're not leaving." She clapped, and her soldiers raised their weapons. Still supporting her withered husband by the arm, she moved backward, leaving Gabriel standing alone at the bottom of the porch steps.

Gabriel climbed the steps.

"You have about ten seconds to decide before we do what we came here to do. On a personal level, Gabriel, I really hope you choose to move. I've always been an admirer of you and your capabilities."

"Ten seconds?"

"Seven now."

Gabriel faced the house and raised his voice. "I am here to arrest Marissa Thompson for the murder of Justin Stone. If she comes out now with her hands up, I will safely take her into custody." He turned back.

"Foolish." She prepared to clap.

Gabriel heard the door open behind him. "I wouldn't do that if I were you." He turned and raised his voice again. "Blake? Is your son still filming on his cell?"

"Yes."

Gabriel turned back to look at Priscilla and smiled. He reached a hand to his side and, over his shoulder, said, "Come to me, Marissa."

Chewing her bottom lip, Priscilla kept her narrowed eyes pinned on Gabriel. Her hands remained ready to clap.

"Listen, Blake," Gabriel said loudly, feeling Marissa's hand envelope his. "I'm going to walk Marissa to my vehicle. If anything happens to us on route, ensure the video is uploaded to a social media site. Is that clear?"

"Yes, Chief." It was Sean Thompson's voice. "I'm ready."

"The whole video, Sean, including the moment your mother came peacefully."

"I will."

"You think you're smart, don't you?" Priscilla said. "How do you think this will end? Ultimately?"

Gabriel smiled. "After we have left, Sean, email the video directly to me. You'll find my contact details on the Blue Falls PD website." Gabriel led Marissa down the steps and glanced at her.

She looked pale and languid and didn't seem too concerned about what was transpiring around her; he was counting on her not panicking.

Around him, the soldiers kept their guns trained on Marissa and him, still awaiting their master's clap.

As he passed Priscilla, he said, "You may not realize this now, Mrs. Stone, but I did this for you and your husband. You would never have gotten away with this."

Priscilla exhaled sharply. "We are capable of making our own decisions, Gabriel. I hope you don't live to regret this."

"I hope not too. If anything happens to that family in that house—or me, for that matter—I will ensure that video Sean is making finds its way to the Maine State Police. Even with your power and influence, Mrs. Stone, I think a visit from them would be one hurdle too many."

"My son died today, Chief. Or have you forgotten?"

"No. And I am truly sorry. Justice will be served, Mrs. Thompson."

"Your justice is not justice enough."

"It is what we have."

"Tread carefully, Gabriel."

"I always do," Gabriel said and walked Marissa to his car.

Priscilla opted to keep the guns on them all the way to the vehicle, and even when they were inside and driving away, but Gabriel was confident no one would fire.

Not yet anyway.

AFTER JOTHAM HAD WRAPPED Bo in several towels to soak up the blood, he slipped her into the trunk of his car. Then he went to the front of his vehicle to retrieve his handgun from the glove compartment. He concealed it in a holster under his jacket.

As he returned to the building, rubbing his bloodied hands on his jeans, he nodded farewells to the last of the exiting spectators.

They nodded back, but every single one tried to avoid eye contact. It was an awkward situation. No one had ever seen Jotham MacLeoid lose. No one had a clue of how to console him, making it safer not to even try.

When he was back inside, he clutched Anthony Rogers' shoulder. "Is he still in there?"

"Yes. I said exactly what you told me to. He was happy Nyx had impressed you and that you didn't feel aggrieved. He also kept pressing me on this lucrative opportunity you're offering, but I deflected most questions."

Jotham nodded. "Good job, Anthony. Are you ready for what comes next?"

Anthony nodded. "Yes, sir."

Jotham squeezed his shoulder. "You're a good boy."

They headed into the fighting arena and found the breeder sitting on a bale of hay.

Nyx paced back and forth at his feet, panting excessively. She growled when Jotham and Anthony approached, so the breeder pulled tight on her chain.

"Sit down, Nyx."

She obeyed.

Jotham smiled. "Your bitch still got energy after that?"

"She's a feisty one." The breeder smiled. "Best I've bred."

"She certainly gave mine a lesson. I thought I had a grand champion on my hands."

"No hard feelings. We've all been there."

"What's your name?"

"Mark Riley."

Jotham raised an eyebrow. "Well, Mark, can I congratulate the victor?" He pointed at Nyx.

"Of course. If she'll let you."

Jotham leaned in and stopped his hand inches from her muscular head. "She does look twitchy."

"Your dog put up a fight," Mark said. "You trained her well."

"Thanks." Jotham surveyed Nyx. "Yes, Bo did take a few chunks from you, dear. And look at that lip." He gently stroked the pit bull's head then knelt and brought his own face closer to hers. "You're a beautiful girl." He looked into her eyes. "It's such a shame you have to lose."

"Sorry? I don't understand. Nyx won. It's over."

Jotham stood and towered over the breeder sitting on

the hay. "She's been disqualified, Mark. You've pumped her full of narcotics. It's against the rules."

Mark shook his head. "It's not true."

Jotham took a deep breath and sighed. "Bo is the winner."

"But your dog is gone. Dead!" Mark said, still shaking his head.

"Yes, Mark, and that's a problem. You've just killed my grand champion."

While they'd been talking, Anthony had edged around to the back of Mark.

The breeder flinched when he felt the gun against the back of his head. He dropped his dog's chain and raised his hands. "This is a mistake. I've not given Nyx any—"

"I've been around dogs a long time, Mark, since before you were born. I can see it in her eyes, the way she moves, the way she fights. I can even smell it in her fucking sweat." Jotham reached into his jacket and unholstered the handgun.

"This is a misunderstanding."

Jotham looked at Anthony. "If he even twitches, you finish it."

"Yes, sir."

Jotham knelt in front of Nyx again and put his forehead against hers. "Sorry, girl. This isn't your fault." He lay a hand on her back but was gentle, knowing she'd be sore. He tilted his head back, stood and placed the handgun against the side of her head.

"No!" Mark said. "No, please—"

"Fuck you for making me do this," Jotham said and pulled the trigger.

16

"SLIP DOWN IN your seat," Jake said.

Jake and Lillian, who had parked beside an old barn and tractor a reasonable distance from the Thompson farmhouse, peered over the dash. Three vehicles passed.

"It's Chief Selectman Charles Stone," Lillian said.

"How do you know? It's too dark to see any of their faces."

"Who else can afford three Porsche SUVs in this town?"

"Fair enough."

They'd already watched Gabriel drive away with Marissa in the back of his car.

"Okay, so we've heard no gunfire, that's good news, right?" Lillian said, wriggling herself back up in her seat.

"Maybe the only good news so far today. Let's check it out."

On this occasion—his second visit to the Thompson farmhouse—Jake didn't hang back against the railing on the porch. In fact, he was the one doing the knocking. Incessantly.

He felt Lillian's hand on his shoulder. "Enough. You'll take the door off its hinges."

"If they don't answer, we'll have to do that anyway, check they're alive."

The door opened. An older man with a bruised face stood there. Having never met him, Jake assumed this was Blake.

"Hello, Mr. Thompson," Lillian said. "Is everything okay in there?"

Blake's top lip quivered. "Anything but."

"Is anyone hurt?"

"Not hurt, young lady, but broken. Everything is in pieces." He turned his glazed eyes to Jake then back to Lillian. "You know what happened earlier tonight, Lil?"

Lillian nodded. "We were there, Mr. Thompson. I'm sorry."

"I've lost her ... my precious Marissa. She's going to jail."

"I'm truly sorry, Blake, but right now, it's definitely the safest place for her."

"My father once told me that a home without a woman is no home at all." Tears formed in the corners of his eyes.

Jake said, "So, Charles Stone was here for the arrest?"

Blake wiped away the tear. "In a fashion. His wife did all the talking." He looked at Lillian. "It seems the rumors about Priscilla are true."

"What rumors?" Jake asked.

"That she runs the town." He called Sean to the door. "Show them the video, son."

"Of course, Dad." He handed the cell to Lillian.

Jake watched over her shoulder and was surprised to see Gabriel defending the principles of law and order. He was also surprised to see confidence and competence in the way the police chief brought about the right outcome. "I didn't know he had it in him," Jake said to Lillian.

The look she returned suggested that she hadn't either. Lillian handed the cell back to Sean. "What're you planning to do with that video?"

Blake shrugged. "Nothing personally. But we've sent it to your department."

So Gabriel can use it as leverage and make himself a more powerful player in Blue Fall politics. "Have you thought about sending that directly to the Maine State Police?" Jake said.

"No. Would that be wise?"

"Well, it might bring a swifter end to the corruption in your town." *But would also lead them to Jotham and the people who work for him.* He eyed Sean. *Before you know it, you could be sitting completely alone in this house.*

"I think I'll leave it to Chief Jewell."

Wise but disappointing. "With everything that's happened, can you give us an update on the whereabouts of your daughter?"

"What do you mean?"

"What happened to Maddie, Mr. Thompson?"

"She's with her relatives, as we've said all along."

"Your wife seems to think your daughter is dead. In fact, she was so convinced she just murdered someone!" He could feel Lillian's eyes boring into him. He ignored her. His patience was wearing thin.

"She wasn't thinking clearly. In fact, she's not been well for a long time. I don't know what else to say, young man."

"The truth?"

Devin appeared beside his father and brother, sporting his usual aggressive stance and scrunched face. "It *is* the truth. Now, we have to contact a lawyer, for Mother. So, if you don't mind ...?"

Jake took a deep breath, trying to prevent a sudden rush of blood. "Well, please get in touch if you can figure out why your mother suddenly thought your sister was dead."

He looked up in time to see Blake's solemn expression before Devin closed the door.

Once they were back in the car, Jake hit the steering wheel with the palm of his hand.

"Well, at least they're alive," Lillian said. "I can only imagine the firepower in those SUVs."

"Yes, great, three selfish bastards survive while an innocent girl is left somewhere to rot. I'm over the fucking moon." He hit the wheel again. This time, he felt the pain in his palm and welcomed it.

Lillian put her hand on his arm. "Jake, listen. You don't know Jotham like we know him. He won't care about politics, the law, or the Maine State Police if Blake betrays him. Jotham will move on his remaining children. Blake's behaviour is not that of a selfish man, it's the behaviour of a terrified one."

Jake ran a hand through his cropped hair. "I know, I get that." He turned to look at Lillian. "You think Gabriel will let you talk to Marissa in custody?"

"Unlikely, but I could try."

Jake nodded and eyed the house. "I wonder how much those selfish idiots told Marissa. I doubt they went as far as saying where she was. Do you think she's really dead?"

Lillian looked away. "I think that's a new level for Jotham MacLeoid. He has a teenage daughter himself."

"So, that's a *no* then?"

Lillian looked at him but didn't answer. She didn't need to; he saw the answer in her eyes.

"You know I'll kill him if he's done the unthinkable?"

Lillian didn't reply.

"How do you feel about that as a police officer?"

Lillian sighed, looked out the window for a moment then faced him again. "You mentioned before that you were getting somewhere with Ayden."

"Yes, he was opening up."

"You think he'll turn on his father?"

"No. Because like everyone else, he's shit-scared."

"It's one brick wall after another."

"Not necessarily. I don't think he's scared for himself. From the way he was talking, I'm not sure he cares whether he lives or dies. Now, his mother on the other hand, he worships the ground she walks on."

"Louise Scott?"

"You know her?"

"Yes. She's an ex-sex worker in Sharon's Edge who now runs a charity called Start Again. They work with prostitutes to get them off the game. We've done some impressive work with them. The idea is that instead of arresting the sex-workers, we help them kick drugs and ditch their pimps."

"Wow! That's quite forward thinking for this place."

"True. Not all of my colleagues are fans, but locking up sex workers is counterproductive. It just drives them deeper into desperation, and it becomes harder to help them long term."

"Makes perfect sense to me. I worked with similar charities back home. So, what is her history with Jotham?"

"Exactly how you would imagine. He paid for her services, except she gave him more than just sex; she gave him a child too."

"I see. But Ayden is only around thirty. I doubt

contraception was a foreign concept around the time of his conception."

"He didn't use contraception when he raped her. She makes no secret of it. She's open and honest about her past."

"But why would he rape her if he was paying for it anyway?"

"For the same reason he raped Marion Springs then sacked her. The man thrives on violence and aggression. I'll never forget her telling me the story. His visits with her started normally enough, if you consider paying for sex normal, but over time, he became rougher and more forceful with her. At first, she consented, but eventually, it became too violent for her. This spurred him on even more. She said he raped her over ten times before he eventually grew bored of her."

"Did she not have a pimp?"

"There is no protection from Jotham MacLeoid. He does what he wants. After she had Ayden, she left the job and set up the charity. She sees it as the good that came from her experience. He took Ayden when he turned eight, probably because he would be less effort at that age."

"Did she try to fight it?"

"No. He offered her visitation rights and money. It was better than the alternative."

"Dumped in the Stinson?"

"Precisely."

"So, Jotham does not mind her shouting about her horrendous experiences with him?"

"It seems not. He's probably happy to wear it, like a badge of honor. Just increases his fear factor."

"You know that's our way in, don't you?"

"Louise? How so?"

"Someone who lost her dignity and her life? What more

has she got left to lose? She'll hold the answer to the end of Jotham MacLeoid."

DRINKING from a fresh bottle of Old Crow, Peter Sheenan waited half a mile from the MacLeoid property. In his rearview mirror, he watched the reflection of the Honda minivan's headlights crest the hill behind him. He took one last swig from the bottle and threw it on the passenger seat next to the photograph of Prince. He reached to his back seat for his rifle and exited the vehicle.

Outside, surrounded by nothingness, a sharp wind bit into him. He was glad of the whiskey in his belly. It kept both his body and soul warm. He also felt no fear regarding what he was about to do; however, that could be due to his experiences in the jungles of Vietnam rather than the alcohol.

The Honda minivan drew to a halt behind his pickup. The driver wasn't visible in the gloom. The headlights went off, and the minivan door opened.

Peter readied his rifle.

Oliver Sholes stepped from the truck and raised his hands.

Peter lowered his rifle.

"No, keep it up," Oliver said. "Someone might drive by and see."

"Good point." Peter reraised it and edged toward Oliver.

Oliver shivered; poor lad didn't have a bellyful of whiskey to keep him warm. "You're going to get me killed, Mr. Sheenan. You know that?"

"No, Oliver. Look." He nodded at the flat tire on his

pickup. "I waved you over for help then ambushed you, exactly how we discussed."

"Maybe ... But maybe Mr. MacLeoid will just torture me for the truth?"

Peter sighed and looked down. Yes, it was a possibility, but it was a risk he had to take. He thought about Prince, and he thought of Nickel's front leg snapping in that fighting ring; he couldn't let this go on anymore. Peter moved closer to Oliver so he could see him more clearly, and his heart sank.

The boy—because that's all he was really, *a boy*—was pale, his eyes were wide, and his pupils were dilated.

"I'm sorry, Oliver, but this has to happen."

Oliver was Jotham's driver. He picked up the women who worked the laboratory every morning and dropped them home every evening. He often drove Jotham out of town on business. Like Peter, Oliver was also part of the Abenaki community. His father had died when he was a child, and his mother, Janet, faced poverty alone and had sought sanctuary in their community. They were offered somewhere to live, financial support, and more importantly, the sustainable option of further education. Eventually, Janet worked her way into a secretarial position and steadied their ship.

Peter sat on a small council the Abenaki community had organized. He'd been a massive influence in ensuring the community supported families, such as Oliver's, in times of crisis. Many, including Janet, revered him, and none of them would dream of refusing him a single request.

Initially, out of blind fear, Oliver had refused Peter. He knew he'd traveled to a new low in threatening to tell Janet that her son had turned his back on their family's savior, but what choice had he been left with? Oliver would never disappoint his mother and so had grudgingly agreed.

"He's out all evening then?" Peter asked.

"Yes, he'll celebrate late into the evening with some of his friends and prostitutes in Sharon's Edge. He's routine with this. He drove himself there, as I had to return the workers, but he'll contact me later, blind drunk, to collect him."

"But at that point, you'll be tied up, *literally*, and unable to answer."

"You'll have to do more than that. You'll have to leave me practically *in pieces* for this to wash."

Peter sighed and nodded. "Don't worry. It'll be convincing, Oliver, and you'll come out of this just fine. I promise you. His son, Ayden?"

"At the Taps, which means he'll be gone most of the evening too."

"Good. Let's get a move on."

Oliver opened the minivan door, and Peter transferred five foldable cages from his pickup then climbed in. He lay on the floor and slid between two sets of seats with the rifle on top of him.

Oliver slid into the front seat and started driving. "All of this for some dogs, Mr. Sheenan?"

"Yes, Oliver. And call me Peter."

"I love dogs too, but this ... it just doesn't seem worth it."

"Have you been to that pit?"

"No, Mr. Sheenan— sorry ... Peter."

"Well, if you had, you might feel differently."

"Maybe, but ultimately they're just animals."

"We're all animals, Oliver. Would it be acceptable to torture us?"

"No ... but I'm worried you won't get them out and all of this will have been for nothing."

"Our plan is solid, Oliver."

"*Really?* No disrespect, Peter, but it feels like *Mission Impossible* to me. Okay, we're at the gates."

"Remember to lure out the security guard. It's the only way we can get a clear run at it."

"I know."

Peter listened to the electric window go down.

"Hi, Brad, just me returning the vehicle."

There was a crackle of static and then, "No problems, Oliver. Just drive it into the lot, and I'll let you out with your vehicle."

Peter heard the hum of the gates opening.

"Thanks, Brad, but I'll be staying on until Mr. MacLeoid needs picking up."

"No need. He's already back."

The alcohol and experience of the jungle did nothing to fight off the sudden wave of fear that engulfed Peter.

"Oliver? You still there?" Brad asked through the speaker.

"Yes ... Just surprised. He usually stays out late on fight nights."

Snap out of it, Oliver! You sound terrified.

"Something came up ... but not over the speaker. Tell you what; park and I'll come out to update you."

"Okay." Oliver started driving again. "Jesus ..."

"Calm down," Peter said, trying to sound reassuring despite feeling nothing of the sort himself. "At least he's coming out, as we planned."

"Calm? How? You do realize we're both dead, don't you?"

"If anyone is dead, it's just me. I've got you at gunpoint,

remember?"

"This is ridiculous. All this for a couple dogs! Couldn't you have just climbed over the fucking fence?"

"We went through this. How would I get them out without your vehicle?"

"You're going to have to kill Brad."

Peter took a deep breath. "That wasn't part of the plan."

"I know, but it gives the whole thing more impact, and incapacitating him is too risky if Jotham is here."

Oliver stopped the minivan. He jumped out, opened the side door and leaned in. "I can see him approaching. I'll chat to him at the front of the vehicle so you can come up behind him."

"We're not killing anyone. I don't want to go to jail."

"What do you think will happen if you leave a witness to your breaking and entering?"

"Nothing. Because once I've got them, I'm leaving town. There won't be a manhunt over a couple of stolen dogs, but if you throw killing into the equation—"

"He's here." Leaving the door open, Oliver walked away.

Their voices were muffled from the front of the vehicle, but Peter could hear most of the conversation.

"Bo's dead," Brad said. "Torn to pieces."

"Shit."

"The dog that did it was narced off its skull. Jotham disqualified it and then put it down."

Listening to the conversation about the two dead dogs, Peter felt himself dying inside. What had gone so wrong in these bastards' lives that they had to treat these incredible creatures in such an inhuman way? Peter slid across the floorboards to the open door, breathing as quietly as he could. He kept the rifle pinned to his chest.

"Shit. We best stay out of the old man's way this evening," Oliver said. "I imagine he's emotional."

"He's emotional alright, *and* it's not over. Him and Anthony brought the dog breeder back with them."

"Why?"

"Why do you think?"

It wasn't good news to hear others were on site, but it was far too late for Peter to go back now, so he gritted his teeth and slid through the open door. His feet touched the concrete.

"At least you don't have to worry about bumping into him," Brad said. "They've headed out in the fields already."

"To the pit?"

"Of course."

Pit, Peter thought, *what pit? Not another dogfighting pit, surely?* Gritting his teeth, he crouched and crawled slowly to the front of the vehicle.

"Will he need me again tonight?" Oliver asked.

"I don't know. He didn't say. If you hang back with me, I've got a six pack in the surveillance room."

"Sounds good."

Peter stood and stepped in front of the vehicle with his rifle ready. Brad, a larger and broader man than Oliver, had his back to Peter and blocked Peter's view of Oliver. He put the tip of his rifle against the back of Brad's shaved head. "Down on your knees."

"Fuck you!"

"Now!"

Brad lowered himself to his knees, revealing a wide-eyed Oliver.

"Hands behind your head."

"What the fuck's going on?"

Peter nodded at Oliver then cocked his head to indicate

that the boy come alongside him.

He obliged.

"You don't need to get hurt–" Peter felt a gun press against the side of his head.

"Really, Peter? Did you really think I'd be this idiotic?" Oliver said.

Shit ... "What're you doing, Oliver?"

"What does it look like I'm doing?" He laughed.

"Think about this."

"I've thought about it since the moment you came to see me. How could this ever have been an option, you stupid old man?"

"You lying little bastard."

"Drop the rifle."

Peter threw it to the ground.

Laughing too, Brad grabbed it and stood. He turned and pointed it at Peter.

"You're Abenaki, Oliver," Peter said. "This isn't right."

"Are you about to tell me about how my ancestors would feel about this? If so, save it."

"No, I was going to ask you about how your mother will feel about it."

"Why? She'll never know."

"She'll know. Mothers know."

"I'll take my chances with my mother rather than with Jotham. It is ironic though, Peter."

"How so?"

"You helped us get ahead in the past, and now you've helped us again. When Jotham realizes what we've done for him—me and Brad—he'll reward us, I'm sure."

"You're delusional. The only reward a man like that gives is his permission to live—"

Brad shot Peter in the stomach.

17

MARK RILEY HAD, yet again, bitten off more than he could chew. It had been a recurring problem for him ever since he was a young man building his own online property business and studying law while playing football semi-professionally. Unbelievably, the house of cards had stayed standing, and although his football career had faded with age and knee injuries, he'd grown rich marketing and had also tinkered in freelance legal work to keep his lawyer mother and father happy.

Developing an interest in breeding and fighting American pit bull terriers though had proved to be one card too many, and while spending the journey from Sharon's Edge to Blue Falls in Jotham's pickup at gunpoint, he'd realized the house he'd kept steady for so long was shaking.

Outside the vehicle, Jotham's soldier had gagged and blindfolded him. It'd been a ray of hope. *Did they intend to let him live?*

The walk to his fate had been long. Several times, he'd slipped over damp mud, and each time, his kidnappers had let him fall and struggle back to his feet on his own—a hard task with tied hands. They'd also stripped him of his windbreaker earlier so the fierce weather could wreak havoc on him.

Now, he felt old wood crack underfoot, and he guessed he was in a forest. He confirmed this with a collision with a tree trunk which winded him. He desperately wanted to scream at his kidnappers to stop treating him like a fucking animal. When his anger subsided, he was grateful for the gag that kept the outbursts contained, because he still believed there was a chance they'd let him live.

Farther into the journey, a fetid stench crawled into his nostrils. He desperately wanted to cover his nose, but his tied hands wouldn't allow it. It was also difficult to breathe through the rag in his mouth, so he had to endure it. The smell intensified as they continued, and on more than one occasion, he forced back vomit, knowing the rag might cause him to choke on it.

"Stop walking," Jotham said.

He obeyed, and someone tore off his blindfold. Disorientated, Mark's heart accelerated. He wanted to ask where he was, but the gag wouldn't let him. As his blurred vision cleared, he realized he stood at the edge of a circular pit, possibly fifteen feet wide. He felt his entire body go numb.

Fingers yanked the rag from his mouth, and he instinctively took a deep, cloying breath of air—laced with death. He retched and looked to his side into the young soldier's face and envied him for having black plugs wedged up his nose. There was a short break in the sound of wind over the fields, and he heard scratching in the pit below. He looked down into the gloom, his vision becoming clearer by the second.

Shapes drew themselves in the darkness. It seemed as

deep as it was wide. Small piles dotted the darkness, with a rectangular shape to the right side, which was possibly a small hut or kennel of some kind.

"What's down there?" he asked.

"Nature. Power. Control. There are many ways of looking at it," Jotham said.

As Mark's eyes adjusted to the darkness, the piles took on greater clarity. He could see clothing ... limbs ... bones ... The impact of sudden fear turned his stomach. "Why? Why have you brought me here?"

"Because this is where I harness ..."

"So many bodies!"

"Nature ..."

"They're all dead!"

"Power ..."

"Did you do this? Did you kill them? *All of them*?"

"Control."

"I have money. A lot of it. More than you could imagine."

"So do I."

Mark turned from the pit and looked into the old breeder's eyes. "I'm sorry. You must believe me. I'm *so* sorry. I made a mistake. I'll pay you back whatever you want."

"You took from me, Mark."

"I'll give you everything I have."

"You cannot recompense me."

"Tell me ... Tell me what I can do to make this right. *Please?* Anything you want."

"You can accept my judgement."

"I don't understand."

"You can go down there yourself."

Mark gulped. "No ..." He tasted stomach acid. "No ... Anything, anything but that. I've seen what's down there."

"Not everything, Mark."

"*Please* ... I'm begging you—"

"It's over. Spare yourself more indignity. Go into the pit. It's natural. And we shouldn't fear nature."

"I can't," Mark said, welling up. "I just can't."

The wind blew Jotham's long hair across his eyes. "Spineless until the end. Your opportunity to go with dignity has passed." He pushed the hair from his eyes and nodded at his soldier. "Look at me, Mark. Look into my eyes and take this moment with you."

The back of his ankle burned. He screamed as his leg buckled, then he fell until the ground smashed the air from him. Pain rushed up and down his spine. He kept his eyes closed and groaned. *If the fall hasn't killed me, at least allow me unconsciousness* ... He sucked some oxygen into his lungs. *No, I won't give in.* He opened his eyes, screaming. The pain in the back of his ankle *seared*. "You cut me, you old bastard! You fucking cut me!"

He dropped his head to the side and stared into the empty eyes of a skull. Gasping, he rolled away. The pain in his back was excruciating, but at least he hadn't been paralyzed. Maybe he could get out of this— He stopped dead at a pile of clothing. Something cold landed on his face. He snapped his head backward and saw a grayish mottled hand emerging from the sleeve of a shirt. "Shit!"

He attempted to scurry backward, but his hands were tied behind his back, and his right foot was practically unusable. Surprisingly, he made it to another pile behind him. Here, the stench was overpowering, and he couldn't bring himself to turn and look at what he was pressed against. "Let me out! Please! Let me out of this fucking pit!"

Movement to his left.

Shit. What the fuck was that?

Someone poked their head from a small doorway in the three-foot-high wooden kennel.

"No. Fuck this!" He tried to roll away, but again, another pile blocked him. This time, a young girl stared at him. She didn't look long dead; her gray face contorted, her teeth bared. "Fuck ... fuck ..." He turned the other way.

The person from the kennel crawled toward him.

He sat upright and, unable to use his hands, leaned into the small pile of bodies, trying to wriggle himself over. The dead girl's cold skin pressed against his face as he managed to crest the pile, fighting the eye-watering pain in his ankle and the incessant burning in his spine. He heard the pit's occupant shuffling closer. With a deep breath, he pushed with all his might. One or possibly two corpses slipped free, and he slid with them. He heard and felt the crunch of decay beneath him. *Disgusting ... so fucking disgusting.* The top of his head touched the pit wall—nowhere left to go.

The shuffling grew louder.

He felt wetness on his face as he cried and warmth in his crotch as he wet himself.

Her face appeared over the mound of bodies and looked down at him. Tangled hair framed a gaunt, sore-ridden face.

"Please," he said, shaking his head. "Please don't hurt me."

She placed a finger to her withered lips and hushed him.

Louise Scott led Jake and Lillian to the rear of the Sharon's Edge Community Center. She unlocked the door adorned with the START AGAIN plaque.

The three of them entered an office that had seen better

days and wasn't heated. Jake expected charity cases were in abundance round this neck of the woods and one that supported sex workers wouldn't be finding itself anyway near the top of the budget priority list.

She switched on a plug-in radiator in the corner. "It'll take until tomorrow to warm this place, so I'd leave on your jackets." She offered the two wooden chairs to Lillian and Jake and perched herself on the edge of the desk.

"No, you take the chair," Jake said.

She winked. "Don't believe in polite men. Show me the man, and I'll show you the crime."

Jake smiled and sat down.

Louise had pinned-back dyed purple hair, a suntan, and an enthusiastic tone of voice. Jake hadn't expected such a colorful character after hearing her harrowing story. He recalled an old proverb his good friend Michael Yorke had told him once: *Plant flowers in others' gardens and your life becomes a bouquet.* Jake wasn't sure he believed in the proverb, but he could vouch for one thing: helping others did at least distract one from the car crash of one's own life. This was precisely why he struggled to keep himself to himself.

"Lillian tells me you're quite vocal when it comes to your experiences with Jotham MacLeoid."

She didn't bat an eyelid. "Of course. Nothing for me to be ashamed of."

"Do you think he's ashamed?"

She laughed. "Of course not! Shame is a foreign concept to Jotham. His daddy beat that out of him from a very early age. God, if he was ashamed, I'd be long gone by now! The only thing his father ever allowed him was pride, and he definitely feels that in abundance."

"I've noticed. Ms. Scott, I—"

"*Louise*. Please."

Jake nodded. "Louise, I'm here because I'm worried about Ayden."

Her eyes dropped, and her airy demeanor fell away. "You've been talking to Ayden?"

"Yes. Have you spoken to him recently?"

"Of course. Every day."

"And how does he seem to you?"

"Same as always. Jotham works him hard but keeps him out of his more illegal activities."

Jake and Lillian exchanged a look.

"Don't worry, I'm not that naïve! Obviously, I don't believe it! He just tells his mother what she wants to hear."

"Because he reveres you," Jake said.

Louise smiled. "He told you that?"

"He didn't have to. I could tell."

"You seem to know more about my son than I do. Anything else you'd like to share?"

Jake sighed. "Just that he's desperately scared, Louise."

She stood from the chair and went to the plug-in radiator. She double checked the plug was switched on. "Shitty thing. My reward for wanting to help people? To freeze to death."

"Sorry, Louise. Did you hear what I said?"

She turned back to him with wide eyes. "Of course. Scared, you say? It's the first I've heard of it!"

"He's trying to protect you."

"All children should share their problems with their parents; it's up to us to protect them." She took a deep breath and sighed. "But that old bastard has even taken that away from me. What's he got my boy mixed up in?"

"Everything. Drugs, dogfighting, and ..." Jake looked at Lillian again. Her eyes were wide. Was he taking it too far?

Was this vulnerable woman really in a fit enough state to hear that her only son was involved in the death of a girl?

"What else?"

"I'll tell you, Louise, but afterward, please reassure yourself that your son still has a way out of this. That's why we've come—"

"Just get on with it!"

"We believe he is involved in the disappearance of a young lady."

"No, I don't believe it."

"There have been suggestions that she's been killed."

She shook her head. "This is a mistake. Ayden is not like that. He's not like his father."

"I agree, Louise. He's doing all these things to protect you. He believes if he doesn't make Jotham happy, he may come for you."

She placed her hand against her chest.

"You aren't alone anymore, Louise. We're here."

Louise smiled. "You don't know how many women I've said the very same thing to."

"We want to help you save your son."

"And how do we do that?"

"You need to tell us what you know about Jotham. His whole persona is built around reputation; we don't understand who he really is."

She smiled. "You want the truth behind Jotham MacLeoid? You want to know who he really is? You know I'm as good as dead when those words leave my lips?"

Jake stood and approached her at the radiator. He put his large hand on her shoulder. "No harm will come to you, Louise. You have my word."

"HUSH, little baby, don't say a word." Despite the gravelly voice, she sang in tune. "Papa's gonna buy you a mockingbird." She crawled over the pile of bodies that sandwiched Mark with the pit wall. "And if that mockingbird don't sing"—she reached to touch his face with long, jagged fingernails—"Papa's gonna buy you a diamond ring."

Mark recoiled, but his head just bounced from the wood that reinforced the walls. "Please ..."

Her skeletal face moved closer, and he smelled her fetid breath.

"Did he throw you in too?"

"And if that diamond ring is brass," she sang, showing her broken teeth, and slipped down from the bodies to maneuver herself into a sitting position behind Mark, "Papa's gonna buy you a looking glass."

"We can help each other!"

A clammy hand pushed his neck upward so she could ease herself underneath him and lower his head onto her lap.

He desperately tried to understand what was happening, but too many questions raced around his mind. How did all these people die? Had they been left here to fester and starve by the old dog breeder? Was this woman the last person to be thrown into the pit? Or—and this question made his heart thump wildly—was she the one doing the killings?

"And if that looking glass gets broke ..."

"My hands are tied, and they tore my ankle to shreds."

"Papa's gonna buy you a Billy goat." She stroked his cropped hair.

"Please ..." Tears welled in his eyes. "I don't deserve this. I don't deserve to be down here."

"*And if that Billy goat don't pull*"—she slipped her hand beneath his chin—"*Papa's gonna buy you a cart and bull.*" Her fingers squeezed his cheeks, forcing his mouth open.

"What're you doing?" The pressure on his face muffled his words.

She thrust something into his mouth then tightly gripped his chin.

He struggled to turn his head from side to side and dislodge the object.

A disgusting taste filled his mouth, and he caught the pungent odor of disinfectant.

"*And if that cart and bull turn over ...*"

He tried to bite down, but his teeth met the lip of some kind of bottle. He gagged as the fluid raced down his throat. Then the burning began.

"*Papa's gonna buy you a dog called Rover.*"

His throat felt as if it were being incinerated. He tried to writhe free of the woman, but she kept the pressure on the top of the bottle and his chin so he couldn't dislodge it. He felt the caustic fluid in the top of his chest burning his esophagus and, potentially, his lungs.

"*And if that dog called Rover don't bark ...*"

Liquid also spilled down the side of his face, and some of it had run upward into his eyes; they felt like they would burst.

"*Papa's gonna buy you a horse and cart.*"

His screams couldn't escape his mouth, so they came from deep inside himself.

Eventually, she let the bottle slip from his mouth and held his head tight against her lap. Even through his immense suffering, he could *still* hear the lullaby. "*And if that horse and cart turn around, you'll still be the sweetest little babe in town.*"

"Amber Colson," Louise said.

"Jotham's late wife," Lillian said. "She suffered postpartum psychosis and killed their three babies by forcing them to drink bleach. Jotham stood by her, but it didn't stop her taking her own life."

Louise sighed. "As is always the case with stories like these, some part truths but mainly a whole lot of lies." She went to the plug-in radiator. "This story will make you feel a lot colder than you already do. Amber Colson did poison her three children, but she's not dead. Far from it."

Silence threatened the room. Jake quickly stepped in. "What happened?"

"In a moment, you're going to judge me; in fact, you'll probably hate me. If I was standing in your shoes, I'd feel the same. All I can say, in my defense, is Jotham gave me no choice. I either remained silent or our son would die. Jotham is very black and white and very reliable with his ultimatums. I've allowed something to come to pass that no humane person has business doing."

"Go on," Jake said.

Louise wiped away a tear. "The first lie is Jotham never stood by Amber. She poisoned his children, so why would he? As I said, Jotham is black and white. He couldn't care less about mental illness. All he cared about was revenge. And his revenge, just like the man himself, was monstrous. It probably would have been better for her if he'd just killed her."

"I don't understand," Lillian said. "There was a body."

"Oh, yes—the suicide. The woman burned beyond all recognition with her teeth obliterated by a shotgun for good measure? That wasn't her."

"Who was it?" Jake said.

"My guess, a sex worker from Sharon's Edge. One of the reasons I set up Start Again was that workers would often go missing, and no one seemed to care less. Now if a worker goes missing, we find them, and, if we don't, we put pressure on the relevant authorities to try. Back then, when that poor young woman died in a so-called suicide, there were missing women left, right, and center, and no one bothered to try to make a link."

"So, where's Amber then?" Jake asked.

"He took her prisoner and tortured her for what she'd done to his children."

"For over twenty years?"

"I don't know. Maybe? I don't know if she's still alive."

Jake shook his head as the full weight of the atrocity sank in.

"Where did he put her?" Lillian said.

"Again, I don't know for sure. I can only tell you what he said to me, that he'd returned her to nature to be cleansed. But nature could be cruel in its duty. She would fester somewhere dark and somewhere cold, but he would do just enough to keep her alive—feed her, waterproof her shelter, and provide her with blankets."

"Jesus," Lillian said.

"But why would he tell you all this?" Jake asked.

"I don't know." Louise ran both hands through her purple hair. "He was drunk and experiencing a rare moment of vulnerability as he talked about the daughters he had lost. He started to rage, and it all slipped out. God, I wish it hadn't. You can't even imagine the burden I've had to bear to know this maniac is torturing someone out there, but what could I do? When he woke the next day, he could hardly believe what he'd confessed. And he was very clear with his threat. If I told anyone before they got to him and Amber, he would take them all out of the equation—our son Ayden included." She put her head in her hands. "Did I do the right thing? Or have I just been selfish?"

Jake sighed. He didn't want to judge her. Jotham proved calculating and evil. Louise was just another victim of his manipulation.

"But there is something that always makes me wonder," Louise said.

"Go on," Jake said.

"The rumor about Jotham's pit."

"I don't follow."

"It's nonsense," Lillian said.

"Yes, I know, but—"

"Can someone fill me in, please?" Jake asked.

"That he has a pit on his land where he throws those who cross him," Lillian said. "It's just another bullshit rumor that Jotham let play out—anything that feeds the image of him as a monster."

"In my experience, rumors often start with some kind of truth," Jake said.

"Yes," Louise said. "That's what bothers me. What if he *did* put Amber into a pit? He told me he gave her back to the earth, somewhere cold and dark. What if he's imprisoned her in this place many now refer to as *the killing pit?*"

Jake considered it. "Well, pit or no pit, I think it's about time this prick's reign came to an end. Louise, please contact Ayden. Bring him to us here. This ends tonight."

Louise nodded. "There's something else, I'm not sure it's relevant ... Maybe it's best—"

"Tell us," Jake said.

"One of the triplets didn't die. She was given up for adoption."

"He gave away his child?" Lillian said. "Doesn't sound like him."

"No, but he was too distracted with building his empire. With no mother to rear his infant, he couldn't afford the distraction. It was the same when I had Ayden. Except, he demanded him back when he was eight." She looked down. "Because he was male and would eventually support the business. I think he looked at this daughter's home, saw that she was content and left her be—potentially, the only unselfish act that man has ever performed."

"Where did she go?" Jake said.

Louise stared at Jake. "She's still here, of course. In Blue Falls. You didn't think he'd allow her to go too far, do you?"

"Who is it?"

"They don't know. It's best *you* don't know."

"No more secrets," Jake said.

She sighed. "Piper Goodwin. Do you know her?"

Jake steadied himself against the desk.

18

PETER SHEENAN THOUGHT of Prince and all the other dogs he'd loved and cared for in what now seemed like a reasonably short lifetime then focused on the bleeding bullet hole in his gut. He was familiar with stomach wounds. In Vietnam, he'd seen friends die from them, and he'd seen friends survive them. Once he'd adjusted to the sudden pain and confusion over having gastric acid and bacteria flood his abdominal cavity, he inspected the bleeding wound.

He couldn't be certain, but the wound's location gave him some hope. There was a good chance the damage was exclusively to his stomach and that other organs and other vital innards had been spared trauma. If he got medical attention, he could survive what was coming—blood loss, fever, paralysis of the intestines, and sepsis. One soldier he'd patrolled with had been found forty hours after his belly wound and had pulled through. So, if it wasn't for Brad, Jotham's security guard, standing over him and pointing his own rifle at him, Peter would have cause for optimism.

At least Oliver had left. If, by some miracle Peter did get out of this, that little shit had better start running.

Peter had been dragged to the dog cages. His head fell to one side, and he looked into the beady eyes of the American pit bulls.

They yapped and growled at him from their cage doors.

He smiled back at them. Beautiful animals. Wasted in this life of misery. *If only Oliver hadn't betrayed me, I would have gotten you out.*

He'd tried talking to Brad on several occasions, but each time, he was rebuffed. Still, he persisted. "You can't just leave me to bleed out on the floor."

"Shut up. You're disturbing the dogs."

Peter had a hunting knife in a sheath on his calf. If only Brad came closer, he could put it to good use.

Jotham stepped from behind the farthest cage. "Good evening."

Brad said, "Mr. MacLeoid, this man—"

"Save it, Brad. I just saw Oliver. You head in now."

Peter watched the bastard who'd shot him walk away. "Me and you aren't done!"

Jotham approached, closely followed by Anthony Rogers.

This was particularly saddening; Peter was good friends with Anthony's father and had only recently helped him renovate the convenience store. "How's your dad, Anthony?"

Anthony avoided eye contact.

"I'm sure he'd be proud of you."

Jotham laughed as he approached. Beside him, his dogs whined and pawed at the cage doors for his attention. "You think you can appeal to Anthony? You tried that with

Oliver, and where did that get you? My men pick the winning side, Peter."

"You're a cancerous worm, Jotham MacLeoid."

"Says the man spilling his entrails all over my path?" Jotham paused a yard from Peter and rubbed his beard. "Maybe you should be asking for help rather than dealing out criticisms."

"I'd rather die. I've been to your dog pit, Jotham."

"I know. I paid a visit to our mutual friend."

Peter widened his eyes.

"Don't fret, Peter, he's fine. Which is more than I can say for you. How bad is the wound?"

"Why don't you come take a look?" *And then I'll slip my knife into your black heart.*

"Best not get too close. I've yet to wash, and you need to avoid infection."

Peter felt a sudden wave of pain and nausea. Avoiding the wound, he felt around his stomach. The walls were tightening to protect his other organs from the growing pressure in his abdominal cavity. "It's an abomination, Jotham. Those poor animals. How can you live with yourself?"

"Live with myself?" Jotham edged nearer. "Why don't we talk about how you live with yourself?"

"I don't follow."

"You led your canines around a burning jungle."

"*We* took care of them."

Jotham laughed. "Were you taking care of them when they were deemed as surplus equipment during US withdrawal? Did you even say goodbye to the poor beasts you left behind?"

"We begged, we tried."

"You could have tried harder. How many made it back? Two hundred? From thousands ..."

Peter remembered saying goodbye to Prince—his best friend, the dog that had saved his life. They'd pressed their foreheads together. Prince had whined. He'd known that was the end of the line. Tears of both pain from his stomach and the anguish over Prince and thousands of other lost dogs streaked Peter's face.

Jotham stood over Peter. "What happened to the dogs you *cared* for Peter? Were they euthanized, abandoned to be slaughtered by the enemy, or given to the South Vietnamese military to live in misery?"

"Robby's Law, you prick. We fought so it would never happen again. Since the year two thousand, not a single dog has been left behind."

"Better late than never, I suppose." Jotham kneeled beside Peter's head.

That's it, you bastard. Come close ... Peter's hand crept from his stomach to his thigh.

"I've a use for you, Peter."

"Is that before or after I get to hospital?" He slowly lifted his knee to draw his knife-armed ankle closer to his hand. Keeping his eyes firmly on Jotham's, he gritted his teeth against the pain, forcing it back inside himself.

"You came here with the intention of helping my bitches, yes?"

"Yes." His hand was now just touching his calf muscle. His jean leg was sliding up, and he felt the coldness of the ankle sheath.

"Do you know what a bait dog is?"

"Yes." His fingers touched the hilt of the hunting knife.

"We don't usually use live bait dogs here. It's not a fair retirement for a fighting dog. I tend to reward mine."

"You saint," Peter said, unclicking the strap.

"Yes, but tonight, I'll make an exception."

Peter's hand closed on the hilt.

"I have three of my most promising bitches in the final cage. If I let them compete over one bait dog, it would really help with their aggression."

He slipped out the blade—slowly. *Here it comes, you vile, murderous, prick.*

Jotham stood up.

Peter quickly released his hand and lowered his leg. Thankfully, his jeans slipped over the sheathed weapon.

"Remember though, a bait dog knows how to bite and tear as well as the game dogs. So, first"—he grabbed his rifle from his shoulder—"we have to ensure that doesn't happen."

Peter saw the butt of the rifle coming but had no time to move. He felt the pressure on his mouth, everything turned white, and then came the splintering pain. He opened his eyes. Stars rained through his vision. The butt hovered, ready to come again. He tasted blood.

"We do this by taking its teeth."

"No—"

Two more blows in quick succession. His mouth felt full of stones. He dropped his head to the side, dribbling out teeth and pieces of his lips. He tried to open his mouth to beg for mercy but felt only excruciating pain. His jaw was surely broken. Unbelievably, in this spinning world where the pain and nausea threatened to overwhelm his senses, he remained aware of what was happening.

"Hold him, Anthony," Jotham said.

Hands slipped under his armpits and lifted him into a sitting position.

"No, no ... stop." He wasn't sure if the words found their

way from his broken mouth. While they dragged him, he tried to wriggle free, but this only intensified the pain in his stomach, and his flayed mouth burned under a sudden burst of vomit and intestinal juices.

"Got you a treat here, ladies." Jotham opened the cage door. "Play nice." With a stick, he waved the snarling pit bulls to the back of the cage.

"Stop ... stop!" Peter said, kicking out with his legs.

They rolled him in and slammed the cage shut behind him.

"Forgive us for not staying," Jotham said. "I don't like to watch my bitches squabbling over bait."

"You can't—"

Teeth sank into his right wrist. He stared into the glassy eyes of a pit bull.

"Jesus, Minx," Jotham said, laughing. "Anyone would think we hadn't fed you in a week."

Minx shook her head from side to side, growling.

Peter felt his skin rip.

"Farewell, Peter," Jotham said.

Snarling, two other pit bulls closed in on Peter while Minx savaged his arm. Their top lips curled, and their canine teeth shone.

Less than a minute, Peter realized, was how long he had left on this planet. *Unless ...*

The voices of Jotham and Anthony quietened. They were some distance away now.

There was an option. An awful option ...

Minx tore a chunk from Peter's arm.

He issued a loud, guttural scream, and his eyes rolled back in his head. *Fuck you for making me do this, Jotham.*

Jaws closed on his right leg.

Practically blinded by concussion, pain, and blood loss,

Peter reached with his left hand, yanked the hunting knife from its sheath and slammed it down where he felt the burn. He heard the dog whimper. And it broke his heart. He drove the knife home again, and the pressure on his leg ceased. He felt more teeth in his right shoulder.

With no time to despair over what he'd just done, he turned the knife on the other innocent animals too.

———

Kayla faced away from Gabriel.

"Please," Gabriel said, looking through the slot in the door. "Let me see you." No reply. He wondered if she was asleep. "I know it's not what you had in mind when you came to me, but you're safe now."

"I'm locked in your basement."

"Where your father can't get to you. Where he can't hurt you anymore."

"He never hurt *me*."

He rested his forehead on the door and sighed. "Please turn around."

"So you can do those things to yourself again?"

"No. I just want to talk."

"I *hate* you."

"I understand that's how you feel now. I did a good thing today, you know. I saved some people."

"I don't care."

"I'm saving you."

"Let me *out*."

"I can't do that now."

"When?"

"When you realize this is where you belong, then I'll be

able to trust you. One day that will happen, I'm sure of it. You're not like the other MacLeoids—"

The doorbell rang.

Kayla flipped over. Her eyes were wide. "*HELP ME! HELP ME!*"

He slammed the slot closed. With his heart thrashing his chest, he sprang up the stairs. He'd soundproofed the basement a long time ago, but the door at the top of the stairs was wide open.

"*HELP ME! I'M IN THE—*"

He slammed the basement door closed and bolted it. The doorbell chimed again, and he glared at his front door. *Shit! Shit! Did whoever it is hear?* After using his sleeve to wipe the perspiration from his brow, he sprinted to the front door and looked through the peephole. He felt like throwing up.

Jake, Lillian, and Ayden—two police officers and the brother of the girl in his basement. Could there have been a worst combination?

The doorbell rang a third time. He latched the security chain. If they'd heard Kayla, they'd come in quickly. The chain might give him enough of a delay to grab his rifle, which was in reach beneath the coats.

He opened the door.

"BICKFORD? What the hell are you doing here?" Gabriel asked.

Jake was in no mood for any of his bullshit, not since the truth about Piper. "We know."

Gabriel's eyes widened. "Know what?"

"Everything."

Gabriel darted to the side.

Jake was quicker. He propelled himself forward, looped an arm around the chief's waist and slammed him into the banister at the bottom of his staircase. Having winded his opponent, Jake had a second to adjust his position, so when Gabriel lifted his head, gulping for air, he drove a fist into his face.

Gabriel crashed into the wall. "I'm the chief of police—"

Jake delivered two body blows and an uppercut.

Gabriel slid down the wall, and Jake stepped backward, shaking his hand. "I've said it before, Jewell, you're a weak man."

Gabriel smiled up at Jake. "I'm going to fucking kill you."

Jake stepped forward.

Lillian's arm shot across his chest. "No more, Jake."

Jake looked at her; she was right. He sneered at Gabriel. "A fifteen-year-old girl is dead, Jewell. Where's your integrity?"

"Get out of my *fucking* house!" Gabriel drew his sleeve across his broken lip. "I'm not talking to you."

"Then talk to me, Chief," Lillian said. "Maddie Thompson is dead."

"How would you even know that?"

She eyed Ayden hovering in the doorway with his head lowered. "Ayden was there."

"Did you know?" Jake asked.

"Of course not!"

"You don't look too surprised."

"How long have you been in Blue Falls, *Bickford*? Nothing surprises you here."

"Call me Bickford again, Jewell, and I'll break you in half."

"Bring it on."

Lillian glared at Jake. "This is getting us nowhere."

Jake nodded and refocused on Gabriel. "Okay, Jewell, so now you know; what's your plan?"

Gabriel shook his head. "You're a stubborn bastard. You really aren't getting it. Even if he did kill her, you'll never pin it on him. He's too connected. I may be the chief of police, but I'd be dead five minutes after calling in a search team."

"If you can't handle the risk, you shouldn't be doing the job."

Gabriel grunted. "Has it not sunk into your thick skull yet? I hate him as much as the next man. I've been helping you as much as I can without jumping into the crosshairs."

"Those shitty little hints?"

"Well, they must have had some impact. You seem to have turned up here well-informed." He raised an eyebrow at Jake. "Care to share?"

"His wife, Amber Colson, is alive."

Gabriel shook his head.

"It's true," Lillian said.

"She blew her head—"

"It's *true*," Ayden said, stepping forward to join Jake and Lillian. "She's alive ... if you could call it that. He keeps her in his pit."

"The famous pit!" Gabriel looked between the faces of his three intruders. "An imaginative rumor."

"No, Chief. You may not have seen it, but you've shared enough time with my father to know it exists," Ayden said.

Gabriel sighed. "Maybe ... but keeping someone in it? How could they possibly survive?"

Tears welled in Ayden's eyes. "He shelters her in a little wooden kennel. He feeds her dog food and keeps her warm with old shit-stained blankets. He *does* keep her in that pit, Chief—a pit reinforced with wood so it doesn't fall in on itself."

"You just told us nothing surprises you, Jewell," Jake said. "You *know* what that man is capable of. And for years, on your watch, you've allowed this to continue."

"Fuck you. If I'd known about *that*, I'd have gotten her out."

"You wouldn't have," Ayden said, "because anyone who goes into the pit doesn't come out. He incapacitates them when he sends them in. Then, when they are down there, she mothers them, reliving those last few moments of her own children's lives. My father provides her with industrial-strength bleach to force into them."

"Sick bastard," Gabriel said. "And you were there, Ayden, when he did that to a child?"

Tears streaked Ayden's face. "He made us do it. You don't understand. If we don't—if we say *no*—then ..." He put his hand on his head. "Jesus ... what have I done?"

"Not now," Jake said. "You must *pay* for this, Ayden. But first, you can atone. You do the right thing."

Ayden nodded.

"Why? What do you intend to do?" Gabriel said.

"You mean, what do *we* intend to do," Jake said. "There's a plan."

"We're police. There's procedure—"

"Really? Don't make me laugh! Fuck your procedure. Tonight, all four of us standing here are just going to do the right thing."

19

JAKE'S CELL PHONE was on silent. After it'd vibrated for the third time in his pocket, he removed it and saw he had several missed calls and text messages from Piper. He stared at the screen, and as they neared Stinson Lake, the reception bars dwindled. He toyed with the idea of phoning her before he was out of range, telling her he was fine, asking how she was coping after her experience in the Taps earlier, but he couldn't bring himself to do it.

Just like Sheila had on so many occasions in their marriage, Piper would immediately see through Jake's pathetic attempts to conceal his anxiety. She would immediately know something was very wrong, and no one deserved to discover such an awful truth alone. He needed to be with her.

Even if he could lock away the truth forever, he wouldn't. She deserved to know that members of her biological family were alive and close by. Roles reversed, he'd expect the same courtesy.

After Ayden and Gabriel had parked their cars, the four

of them walked silently down a long muddy track. Ayden led the way with a headtorch, but they all had Maglites. Nobody spoke—not because they valued a stealthy approach, but rather because Jake didn't really want to share words with Ayden or Gabriel. Truth be known, he was disgusted by their existences and saw them only as a means to stop a more malevolent force.

Eventually, they broke from a small, wooded patch and reached the water's edge.

Gabriel slipped, but Lillian reached out to steady him in time.

Jake felt some disappointment. Yes, it may have compromised their approach, but to see the impotent chief of police floundering in the lake would have been some consolation.

Ayden pushed a small, wooden boat from behind a tree to the water's edge. Everyone, apart from him, climbed in.

"Remember, you must row directly across," Ayden said. "The opening in the wall is only ten feet wide. Remember to moor it tightly to the post or you may have to swim back. Do you have the compass?"

Jake patted his pocket and nodded.

"Remember, it is almost a mile and a half from the house to the pit. It stinks like you wouldn't believe, but you have to stay there. Be patient."

"We will. You're doing the right thing," Jake said as Ayden pushed them into the water.

"I know. I just wish I'd done it a long time ago."

"No one more so than Maddie's family," Lillian said.

The boat drifted out. "Good luck," Ayden said and turned to head to his vehicle.

As Jake rowed across the Stinson, he scanned the lake flecked with the white light of the moon. In the distance, he saw the watchtower where Jotham had sat several days back when Lillian had first told him about the MacLeoid family.

He took a deep breath and rowed hard.

AYDEN STEPPED onto the back porch.

"You took your time, son," Jotham said, leaning forward in his chair. Reclining was not an option with his diced back.

"You told me you had it under control."

Jotham drank from a hipflask. "We did, but there's always room for an extra pair of hands."

"Even when you have Anthony helping?"

"Ah ..." Jotham smiled. "I see."

"See what?"

"Anthony. He bothers you."

"Not at—"

"Surrounded by the flames of jealousy, the jealous one winds up, like a scorpion, turning the poisoned sting against himself."

"I don't understand."

"Nietzsche."

"I don't know it."

Wincing, Jotham rose slowly from his seat. He groaned and took a deep breath when he'd made it to full stretch. "Should I be worried about your poisoned sting, Ayden? Have you turned it against yourself?"

"Sorry, Dad, I'm completely lost. If you're worried about me being jealous of Anthony, you really oughtn't to be. I'm not."

Jotham shuffled toward his son. "Listen, my little scorpion. Anthony is a good soldier." He put a hand on

Ayden's shoulder. "But that's all he is. A soldier. You're my son."

His father's eyes held a gentleness Ayden had never seen before. He felt a numbing sensation in the pit of his stomach. Not knowing how to respond, he simply nodded.

Jotham put his hand to Ayden's cheek. "Everything I do, I do from love. You know that, don't you, son?"

No ... no, I don't.

"Boyd did the same for me. It felt unfair at the time. Actually, that's an understatement! It felt fucking merciless, but not a day goes by now that I don't thank him for it. Because of him, I have all this. And one day, it will be yours. Not Anthony's, little scorpion, *yours—*"

A flare burst open in the sky.

Jotham dropped his hand from Ayden's face and turned to look out.

Another flare ruptured. His land glowed red.

"What's happening?"

"Flares," Ayden said.

"I know that, son. I'm not a fucking idiot. But who the hell is setting them off? And more importantly, who the hell is on my land?"

A third flare rose.

"Anthony!" Jotham shouted. "*Anthony!*"

Anthony came running onto the back porch. "Yes, sir?"

Jotham reached for his rifle by the chair he had been sitting in. "Anthony, get your rifle. Someone's on my land."

"Shit! Yes ... two seconds." He ran back in.

He turned back to Ayden. The gentleness in his eyes from before was gone. "You stay back and call for backup." He raised his chin to focus on the red sky.

So predictable! You don't want me by your side; you never have, and you never will.

Anthony returned onto the porch with his rifle.

"When the cavalry arrives," Jotham said to Ayden, "you march out to join us."

Ayden nodded. *Goodbye, Father.*

Jotham and his good soldier headed to locate the source of the flares.

GABRIEL, the first to crumble, had vomited into the pit.

Jake had gone down to his knees to fight a wave of nausea. He'd seen his fair share of atrocity in his time and had a strong constitution, but this was another level.

What had been most disturbing when they shone that torch into the pit wasn't the sheer number of bodies—some skeletal, some still rotting, some still fresh—nor was it the contorted expressions that spoke of agonizing death; neither was it the emaciated Amber Colson sitting by the wooden kennel, playing with her tangled hair and humming to herself; but rather, it was the sight of that young girl, Maddie Thompson, identified by Lillian. Her young, pale face forever frozen in anguish.

Lillian had taken it better than both Jake and Gabriel. She'd unzipped Jake's backpack while he knelt over the black, twisted, and *still* beating heart of Jotham's monstrous world and removed the flare gun.

Her three flares lit the sky.

"Come and get us, fucker," she said while Gabriel vomited into the pit again, and Jake balled his fists so hard that his nails dug into his palms.

IT SOON BECAME obvious to Jotham that they were heading toward the pit.

"Sir," Anthony said, "this feels wrong. We should wait for Cole and everyone else."

"That would probably be the safest option," Jotham said, keeping a steady pace, "but no, we continue."

"I don't understand how anyone could have found the pit."

"Never underestimate those around you, Anthony. Plenty of resourceful people are out there, and no fortress is impenetrable, even this one."

"But this one is so strong."

"Yes, it is. But a true fortress is built around fear, Anthony. And there are those who have chosen not to fear."

"They must be fucking crazy."

Jotham halted.

Anthony stopped and turned to his master. "Are you okay, sir?"

"Have I been wrong about you, Anthony?"

"Sorry, sir? I-I don't understand what I—"

"You called our enemies crazy."

"But they are, aren't they? Surely you see that."

"I see anything but, Anthony. Bring forth my resourceful and fearless enemies, and, in the words of Roosevelt, 'I ask you to judge me by the enemies I have made.'"

Anthony nodded. "Yes, sir. I apologize. They're not crazy."

Jotham smiled. "I accept your apology, Anthony. Now, shall we go kill them?"

"Yes, sir."

Jotham marched toward the pit, clutching his rifle strap to stop it bouncing off his sore back.

———

JAKE HAD BEEN STANDING with his back to the pit for some time now, listening to Amber Colson's gentle humming and staring at a glorious full moon. He thought of Paul Conway, the young boy in Wiltshire who'd been caught by the debris from a car bomb that fateful evening. He remembered holding the boy's broken body. All his fault. Was Gabriel right? Was he just another Bickford? Another product of a diseased line responsible for the most tragic of deaths? His thoughts turned to his own boy Frank and wondered what he was doing right now.

Jotham and a young man he didn't recognize stepped from the woodland.

The young man had his rifle at the ready, whereas Jotham didn't. Despite this, Jake kept his eyes trained on the old bastard. He had no real interest in his soldier or in any of the drug lord's puppets. *Cut off the head of the snake, and the body will die.*

"Well, you're right where we need you to be, Mr Bickford," Jotham said.

"Pettman," Jake said.

"Pettman, Bickford. Do you think the pit cares?"

"I care."

"And that's your problem really, isn't it? Caring."

"It's your problem now."

"How so?"

"Come closer and find out."

Jotham laughed and looked at his young soldier, who smiled but struggled to force out a laugh.

Jake took a deep breath. Nerves in the enemy were not a good thing when they were pointing a loaded weapon right at you.

Jotham looked around. "Do you expect me to believe you came alone?"

Jake shrugged.

"You know, son, in a way, I like you. A lot. I've seen many things in my time but never anything like this. Look at you! Look at where you stand! You're the enemy I never had, the enemy I doubted the existence of. I'm in awe of you."

"I'm disgusted by you."

"Why? Think about it, son. I'm a driven man; you're a driven man. Enemies can be so much more powerful together. I could use you. Hell, you could use me, for all I care. No one has to lose here. *You* don't have to lose here."

"You killed a child. That was the moment you lost, when your empire fell. Every second since then has been borrowed."

"Child? Come on, man! She was fifteen!"

"A *child*."

"That may be the case where you come from, son, but here, fifteen doesn't make you a child. I certainly was no child at fifteen. I could take you to Sharon's Edge one night. There are fifteen-year-old girls there who don't behave like children."

Jake eyed the young soldier. "You've the chance to walk away now. I'm not here for you. You may not believe this is over, but it is. You're best trusting me on that."

The soldier looked at Jotham then back at Jake. He shook his head.

"Don't follow him," Jake said. "You don't want to go where this man is going."

"Really?" Jotham said. "Unless you have an army with you, where do you think you're sending me?"

Jake smiled. "Do you need me to answer that? You know exactly where you're going, Jotham MacLeoid."

Jotham shrugged. "Kill him, Anthony."

"Before you do that, Anthony, let your master see what's behind him."

Jotham turned and gasped.

"Your fall," Jake said, smiling over the burning glow in the distance.

"No! No! My son? *Ayden!*"

"Who do you think lit the fire, Jotham?"

Jotham turned, eyes wide and teeth bared. "You're a fucking *liar!*"

Jake shook his head.

"He wouldn't. He's a MacLeoid!"

"He's just another of your victims."

"I won't believe it!"

"Who do you think showed us the way in?"

"Kill him, Anthony! Kill him, *now!*"

His young soldier aimed—

Anthony's head snapped sideways in a cloud of blood, his eyes rolled up, and he slumped to the ground.

Jotham rubbed at the blood in his eyes, and Jake charged. Jotham raised his own rifle, but Jake knocked it aside and drove his fist into the bastard's throat. The child killer stumbled backward, clutching his neck.

Jake swooped in, disarmed him of the rifle and kicked his legs out from beneath him.

Jotham folded up on the ground.

Jake backpedaled and pointed the rifle at the choking, old man. It was possible he'd gone in hard enough to crush his windpipe.

Gabriel, who had ended Anthony, came up on one side

of Jake and Lillian on the other. Together they watched Jotham struggle.

Eventually, the killer controlled his breathing and glared at them, his beard dripping with Anthony's blood. "Three cops? You serious?"

"We're here as concerned citizens," Lillian said.

"So, now what?" Jotham said, sneering.

"We watch your empire burn," Gabriel said.

"I thought you'd have more sense, Chief Jewell! I always knew you were a slave to your impulses, but to actually go ahead and make a move on me?"

Gabriel struck Jotham across the mouth with his rifle. "Shut up, Jo."

Jotham spat blood then eyed Jake. "Has the good chief not told you about his impulses?"

Gabriel pulled back his rifle to swing again, but Jake put his arm in front of him. "No more, Jewell."

"Yes, Chief, you like them young, don't you?"

"Shut the fuck up!" Gabriel strained against Jake's arm.

"Remember those fifteen-year-old girls at Sharon's Edge?"

"You're a fucking liar!" Gabriel broke through Jake's resistance, but Jake was quick enough to seize his shoulders before he swung for Jotham again.

"Enough, Jewell!"

Gabriel grunted.

Jake lifted a hand from Gabriel's shoulder and pointed into the distance. "Look. It's done."

"Your empire is gone," Gabriel said, seemingly calming.

The old drug lord turned toward the inferno destroying his world. "Those you answer to will be crawling all over this place soon."

"They'll find the pit and put an end to your soulless

creation," Jake said. "They'll return the bodies to the families, and Amber, your wife? Hopefully, they will try to give her some kind of peace."

"She deserves no peace."

"That was never your call to make."

"Fuck you. I made it."

"Yes, you did."

"You know what she was responsible for?"

"I do, but one of your children survived. Maybe you should have turned your attention to her instead of building this abomination."

"Ah, so you know everything, do you?"

"Unfortunately."

"She's my seed, son." He laughed. "Are you ready for a MacLeoid in your life?"

"No more," Jake said. "It's time, Jewell."

Gabriel walked around the back of Jotham.

The old man tracked him with his eyes. "No cage can hold me, Chief."

"We know that," Jake said. "That's why it ends tonight."

Jotham laughed. "Three officers? Two of whom are supposed to be upstanding citizens of Blue Falls. Execution? I don't buy it!"

Gabriel knelt behind him and forced a gag into his mouth.

"Silence," Jake said. "You don't deserve any last words."

Gabriel tightened it sharply.

Jotham winced.

As the police chief tied it off, he leaned in and whispered something into Jotham's ear.

Jotham's eyes widened. He tried to climb to his feet, but Gabriel stood and kicked him onto his side. The monster tried to shout through his gag.

Jake shot him in the forehead. He lowered Jotham's rifle and let it fall to the ground. "Roll Jotham and Anthony into the pit and set off another flare. And throw all the rifles into the Stinson. I'll see you at the boat." As Jake trudged away, his thoughts turned to his ancestors, the Bickfords, and the dead children they had discovered after they left.

Then, far in the distance, he heard emergency vehicle sirens. When they arrived at the killing pit, they would find tragedy. But, with the death of Jotham MacLeoid, hopefully, they may find some kind of hope.

20

SEVERAL MILES OUT, Ayden sat and watched the home where he'd spent more than twenty unhappy years burn. Then, smiling and feeling somewhat cleansed, he headed into town. He'd already decided to spend the night at a Blue Falls motel. Going to his mother, putting her in any danger, was not an option. He passed the Taps, which was closed following the death of Justin Stone, and continued onward to the motel.

With the MacLeoid empire in tatters, he'd be best taking a sharp exit from Blue Falls. There'd be plenty of people with grudges against his family in this town, and it was a perfect time for them to crawl out of the woodwork. The Thompson brothers, Devin especially, would be rabid for vengeance. And rightly so.

However, leaving Blue Falls without his sister Kayla wasn't an option. She was still alive. He just knew it. She'd run for a reason, and there was no need to be afraid any longer. The laboratory, the dogs, and the killing pit were gone. Their cruel father was no more.

Kayla *would* come back to him. She had to ...

But then a thought occurred to him in the motel parking lot; now with his father gone, who would be looking for her? The men he had hired to actively search for her would no longer have a monetary incentive. And the police? Well, the police didn't even know about it!

He reversed out the parking lot and drove to Gabriel's house. He suspected the chief would not be back yet, and the absence of his car confirmed that. He grabbed an energy drink from the dash and exited the car to sit on the hood. It was cold and windy, but if there was anything positive to take from that lifetime on the MacLeoid property, it was the love he'd developed for the outdoors and the fresh air.

After finishing the drink, he headed to Gabriel's trashcan. He lifted the lid, and his breath caught in his throat. The lid fell from his hand and clattered on the ground. He grabbed his old Converse sneakers from the can. Kayla had found them stuffed in the corner of his room among a pile of other discarded footwear. She'd begged him for them. He remembered his words to her. *"Well, they must be two sizes too big for you, but what the hell? Go ahead!"* She'd kissed him on his cheek ...

He touched his cheek. "Kayla." He looked up at the house. "Kayla!"

With adrenaline whipping his insides, he slammed the Converse into the can. He surveyed the house and noticed the wooden gate that led to the path down the side of the house. After reaching over it, he patted the wood. "Come on ... Come on ..." His hand settled on a bolt. "Gotcha." He slid it with a clunk and opened the gate. He slipped through and closed it behind him.

He ambled down the narrow path lodged between a fence and the stone wall toward a single-paned window. He removed a boot and smashed the glass. What did he care if someone heard? Let a neighbor call the police. Then they could ask their chief, in front of the world, why Kayla's Converse sneakers were in his trashcan.

He worked his boot around the frame, knocking in the protruding shards. Then, after sliding on his boot, he hoisted himself through onto a work surface. He felt the window glass crunch under his jeans, so he was careful not to slide and risk cutting himself through the fabric. He also tried to keep his bare hands off the surface as best he could, but he could already feel his palms burning, so he must have picked up some debris.

He landed on the floor with another crunch, reached into his jacket pocket for the headtorch he'd been using earlier in the woods, slipped it over his head and fired it up. He scanned the kitchen. "Kayla?" He left the kitchen for the hallway. "Kayla!"

He paused to listen. He *could* hear something. "Kayla!" He waited.

Yes … someone was definitely replying.

He darted into the living room. When he found nothing, he tried the adjacent office. Again, nothing. "*Kayla?*" He paused to listen.

A muffled voice! He couldn't be sure, but it sounded like someone calling for help but from far away—deep underground perhaps?

He ran out of the office and saw the door beneath the stairs. "*Kayla!*" He pressed his ear to the basement door.

"Help me!" Still muffled but definite now.

He tried to slide the old bolts, but they were stiff, and his bloodied hand slipped off. "Fuck!" He dried his palms on his jeans, ignoring the pain, and tried again—two-handed this time. He thrust both bolts back with a heavy clunk. He opened the door and felt the cold air rush over him. "Kayla! Are you in there?"

"Help me! Ayden. It's me!"

His heart felt like it was going to explode. "I'm coming, Kayla! *I'm coming!*"

The overhead light shone on the worn-out and unstable-looking wooden steps. *Fuck it*. He charged down, his footfalls echoing. "Hold on!"

"Ayden, please, get me out of here!"

At the bottom of the steps, he tripped over a mop and bucket and landed on his knees.

"Ayden, are you okay?"

"Yes," Ayden said, wincing. "I'm fine." He rose to stand at the door that separated him from his sister. He lifted a flap and looked through a slot. He welled up.

Kayla. On her feet. Inches from the door. Staring at him. Pale, exhausted, her eyes swollen from crying, but it was her ... *God, it was her!*

Alive!

He tried to push the door. A padlock rattled. *Jesus, fuck no!* "Stand back, Kayla. It's locked. I'm going to kick it in."

"No! He leaves the key out there in one of the pots."

Ayden spotted a set of decaying shelves littered with old ornaments and vases. He started to shake them out.

GABRIEL SPENT most of the journey home smiling. This night had been so full of glorious moments! Moments he'd be joyfully reliving until his final day. The moment when he'd whispered the truth to Jotham; the moment when despair had exploded on that psychopath's face; the moment when the bastard had writhed on the ground, trying to shout through his gag—so many of them. If only Jake hadn't ended the bastard so quickly! He'd love to have seen Jotham melting just a few minutes longer with the knowledge that he now owned Jotham's daughter.

As he turned into his driveway and parked alongside Ayden's vehicle, he sighed. What did this pest want? Irritation quickly became dread. The car was unoccupied. He surveyed his house, and his eyes widened. He reached into the glovebox for his holstered hunting knife, clipped it to his belt then grabbed his handgun. He disabled the dome light so it wouldn't reveal his presence when he opened the car door. He slipped quietly outside and darted past the front entrance toward the back gate.

He noticed the trashcan lid on the ground and the Converse sneakers resting on top of the garbage. Every nerve in his body felt like it was on fire.

Ayden knew.

He went to the wooden gate and noticed it was slightly ajar. He raised the handgun and prodded it open with his foot and slipped in to see the smashed window. He moved quickly and quietly down the side of his home. He looked through the smashed window but could see very little; nonetheless, he knew the layout, so inside, of course, he would have the advantage. He took his keys from his pocket and went to the back door. Despite the cold, sweat pooled in the center of his back. He unlocked the back door as quietly as he could and entered with his gun ready.

He saw light from the basement creeping under the hallway door.

The basement door must be open.

Ayden had found his sister.

Kayla tried to control her breathing. She'd suffered many panic attacks over the past couple days, but these had been mainly from sheer hopelessness. Now, she was within touching distance of freedom, and the anxiety over potentially having it suddenly torn away was debilitating.

"That's it!" Ayden said.

She placed her hand to her chest. *The key ... he has the key!* She was moments from embracing the person she cared most about in the world. "Please, Ayden, hurry!" She heard him wrestling with the padlock.

"Come on, come on ... Fucking thing ..."

"Keep trying, *please*. It'll work."

"Yes!" A thud sounded as the padlock hit the floor. The door opened. Her older brother was there, rubbing away tears with bloodied hands. He came to her quickly, knelt and embraced her.

She let her cheek settle on his shoulder and closed her eyes.

"I'm sorry. I'm so sorry, Kayla."

She rubbed her face against his shoulder. It felt so good. "It's not your fault."

"Has he hurt you?"

"No ... not yet, but he will, eventually. We have to go."

"I let you down. I should have protected you from *him*."

"You've saved me." With her eyes still closed, she kissed his cheek. "But we must leave now."

"I'm going to kill him."

"Ayden, please."

"Okay—" Ayden shrieked, his shoulder disappeared, and her head lolled forward. "Get off me!"

While being dragged backward by his hair, Ayden managed to claw at Gabriel's hand, but the police chief showed his determination with wild eyes and bared teeth. She imagined the grip to be fierce.

"Let go of him!"

"*Stay back, Kayla,*" Ayden managed to say while trying to wriggle free.

Gabriel showed Kayla the hunting knife in his other hand.

"Please ..." she said.

"He shouldn't have come here," Gabriel said, yanking on Ayden's hair.

Ayden wailed as Gabriel dragged him backward toward the door.

"Please," Kayla said, feeling her mouth fill with tears. "I'll do anything."

Gabriel's tongue darted out and touched his top lip. "Anything?"

"Yes."

Ayden writhed. "No, Kayla. I'm going to kill you, Jewell."

Gabriel drew the knife across Ayden's throat.

Kayla screamed.

Ayden's eyes widened. One hand flew to his neck while the other darted in her direction.

Gabriel released her brother's hair, and he fell forward onto his front, gagging.

"Ayden!" She scurried toward him. "*Ayden!*"

He gurgled.

She reached underneath him, lifting and pushing with all her might, until he rolled over.

His face was pale and blood-streaked. The wide gash on his neck bubbled. He attempted to speak but managed only gasps.

"Ayden? Please ... Ayden?"

He stared at her as he lifted a hand to her face.

"You came for me. I knew you would."

His hand dropped. The gagging slowed and then stopped.

She maintained eye contact with him but knew he'd gone.

"You're safe now, Kayla," Gabriel said.

Crying too hard to respond clearly, she screamed at her captor instead.

"Finished?" he said.

"MONSTER!"

"The MacLeoids are no more."

"I'm a MacLeoid!" She pounded her chest with her fist.

He shook his head. "No. Not anymore. You belong to me now."

She gritted her teeth and pounced.

He slammed the door closed before she reached him.

She pounded at the door until exhaustion set in, then she sank to the floor.

"I'll give you time to say goodbye to him," Gabriel said. "Then I'll come back to clean up."

She crawled to her brother, dropped her arm across his still chest and lay beside him in a pool of blood.

AFTER ...

THE BANDAGE AROUND Peter's mouth inhibited the conversation. Fortunately, the arm of the hand he used to write had been spared injury, so he scribbled into a notebook: *I hate hospitals.*

"Well, at least you're in one," Jake said, "and not lying burnt to a cinder."

Peter winced. He'd obviously tried to smile.

"Sorry," Jake said.

Jake had been sitting beside the hospital bed for the best part of an hour while Peter drifted in and out of sleep.

Earlier, Peter had scribbled: *Glad of the company. Don't rush off.*

"I won't," Jake said, who then sat and read from an Elmore Leonard paperback he'd grabbed from the hospital waiting room earlier.

The emergency services had found Peter in the field a short distance from the burning farmhouse. They were still none the wiser to how he'd got there.

"What happened, Peter?"

Managed to kick open the cage door and crawl away after.

"After what?"

Sadness invaded Peter's eyes. *We'll talk another time. Just read to me.*

Jake read a few paragraphs from the Elmore Leonard book out loud while Peter stared off into space. Jake had been vague on the details as to what had happened at the killing pit. Walls have ears, after all.

Peter waited until Jake finished the chapter and wrote: *Jotham's definitely gone?*

Jake nodded. "I spoke to Jewell this morning. They pulled him and Anthony out of the pit."

Peter wrote: *Anthony's dad will be broken.*

Jake sighed. He'd given Anthony the opportunity to walk away. It was his decision. "They also found upward of twenty other bodies."

Fuck.

"That's one word for it. At least a lot of families will now get closure."

Ayden and his sister will be in danger.

Jake nodded again. "They've skipped town already."

Good.

Jake checked his watch. "Well, old soldier, your time is almost up. Any last requests before I kiss you goodbye?"

Make me handsome again.

Jake laughed. "I'm not a genie."

On my pension, I'll be able to afford a new false tooth a year.

"I'm afraid not, Peter. You'll have to spend your money on holidays. Your medical costs, including full dental reconstruction, will be covered."

Don't be ridiculous. I can't let you.

Jake squeezed his arm. "It's done."

WHILE HOLDING HER HAND, Piper surveyed Amber Colson's wasted arm, her skeletal body, and then let her eyes settle on her emaciated face. *What did that man do to you?* Piper glanced at the hospital room door to check that the armed guard had not strayed inside to listen to what came next. She lifted her natural mother's rough, weathered hand and kissed it. "I forgive you for what you did. You were sick, and I was lucky. My life has been good. I'm so sorry for what *he* did to you."

Amber didn't stir. If it wasn't for the machines beeping alongside her, you could be forgiven for thinking she'd died.

Piper felt a tear in her eye. Amber now had a chance at peace.

She met Jake in the waiting room.

He enveloped her in his large arms and held her tight, like he'd done throughout the entire night after telling her the truth.

She cried gently against him. "Thank you."

"Please don't keep thanking me."

She pulled back so she could look up at him. "You told me the truth."

"Others would've done the same. You'd a right to know."

But many others wouldn't have told me. It took courage to tell someone they were the daughter to a monster. Many would've taken the easy way out, reassured themselves that the person was better off not knowing, that they were doing them some kind of favor ... "What will happen to her?"

"I don't know. I honestly don't."

"Well, whatever happens, she doesn't have to do it alone."

Jake nodded.

"Do they know who killed Jotham yet?"

Jake shook his head.

"Is it wrong that I'm glad he's dead?"

"A lot of people probably feel the same."

"I'm glad I never had to look him in the eyes and acknowledge him as my father."

Jake put his hand to her damp cheek.

"I think he would have enjoyed that too much."

He kissed her forehead. "Let's get some lunch."

"I have a brother and a sister." She smiled. "That's the first time I've ever been able to say that."

Jake smiled back.

"Ayden and Kayla." She took a deep breath. "I hope they're all right."

"They will be. They got away."

"Good. I hope they're happy. After everything they went through with that man, they deserve to be."

It took Gabriel several cups of coffee to get himself going; he'd spent the entire night disposing of the body. Down in the basement, he saw that Kayla was exhausted too; she lay curled up, sobbing on her bed. He'd brought a chair with him and, after unlocking the door and slipping quietly into her room, he positioned it beside her bed.

She kept her back to him.

He leaned over and touched her shoulder.

She pulled away.

"It's okay. I understand. It takes time." He reached for

one of the books on her bedside table—*Five on a Treasure Island* by Enid Blyton. "How wonderful. This was one of Collette's. Her most treasured book." Gabriel started to read, "'*Mother, have you heard about our summer holidays yet?' said Julian at the breakfast table ...*"

He read for a long time and, over the course of the day, she sobbed less and less until, eventually, she rolled onto her back and stared at the ceiling. She listened until day turned to night and even managed a wry smile over one of the lines: *It wasn't a bit of good fighting grownups. They could do exactly as they liked.*

BLUE FALLS TAPS was due to reopen in the evening, so Piper had headed in to help steady the ship.

Jake sat alone on the edge of his bed, staring at his photographs of Frank. He really should be moving on from Blue Falls now, but the idea of drifting into another town, one without Piper, suddenly didn't appeal to him. And for now, anyway, he was out of danger due to that final conversation between Jotham and Gabriel. *"Remember those fifteen-year-old girls at Sharon's Edge?"*

Jake had confronted Gabriel on the return journey from Stinson Lake. *"Is it true, Jewell?"*

"Is what true?"

"About the girls?

"No ... don't be ridiculous. He was lying. He'd have said anything to discredit me."

"I hope so, Jewell, I really do. But maybe you should know I'm not taking your advice. That I'm thinking I might stick around Blue Falls."

"When did that become an option—"

"Just now."

"I—"

"Think very carefully about your next words, Jewell. If information about where I am finds its way back to England, I'll find out everything about you, and if it confirms Jotham's accusations, I'll come for you next."

They'd not spoken for the rest of the journey, and Jake had taken his silence as an agreement.

Now, alone in his motel room, miserable without anyone else's problems to distract him from his own, Jake sighed. Gabriel's agreement was merely a stay of execution —a little more time with Piper, nothing more. Sooner or later, Gabriel would make that phone call to the people Jake had run from. Why wouldn't he? Jake would always be the chief's shadow while he remained in Blue Falls, second guessing his every move regarding matters of the law. Yes, his time here was very limited indeed.

He dialed his ex-wife's number. "Hey, it's me. Are you okay?"

"Fine," Sheila said. "He's not here."

He looked down at the photograph of his boy. "Ah, okay. Where is he?"

"With Mum."

"I see—"

"And, where are you?"

Jake sighed. "Will he be back later?"

"After bedtime, I'm afraid. She'll bring him in asleep though."

"Okay. I'll try tomorrow."

"Great, but I won't be promising him. He waited all day yesterday for your call, Jake. He wanted to tell you about his football game."

Jake rubbed his forehead. "Something came up."

"Nothing changes, does it?"

Jake sighed again. "You're probably right, Sheila."

"Where're you, Jake?"

"At least tell him I'm sorry and that I tried today."

"You enjoying the self-pity?"

If only that was all it was. If only ... "Goodbye," Jake said, but Sheila had already gone.

FREE AND EXCLUSIVE READ

Delve deeper into the world of Wes Markin with the **FREE** and **EXCLUSIVE** read, *A Lesson in Crime*

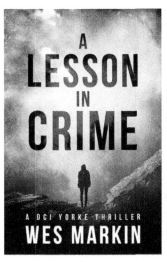

Scan the QR to READ NOW!

A chief of police out of control. A suspected child killer from a bygone era. And a schoolgirl washed up on the banks of the River Skweda.

A storm is coming to Blue Falls, Maine.

An unprecedented storm.

And in the eye of the storm stands ex-detective Jake Pettman. A man desperate for sanctuary and desperate for the truth.

But in a place of undying and heinous secrets, such desperations become dangerous.

Both to yourself, and the people that you love.

Fire in Bone is an adrenaline-pumping crime thriller novel from the Amazon best-selling author of One Last Prayer for the Rays and the DCI Yorke series. Perfect for fans of Chris Carter, James Patterson, Chris Brookmyre, and Stuart Macbride.

Read what everyone is saying about Fire in Bone:

'In this book Wes Markin has really **ramped up the tension and suspense**, the story **grabbed me by the throat** and **shook me like a rag doll**. I literally have **no nails left. A twist I never saw coming** this is a **heart stopping, gut wrenching five star read** and **I did not want it to end. LOVED IT!!!!!!**'

Peggy Beaver, ★★★★★

'**Whoa, what a ride!** I mean this just **fies along, bam bam bam, shock after shock. No holds barred, no slow build up with the action. Bam, done, off again,**'

Donna Morfett, ★★★★★

'The second installment of the Jake Pettman series kept me **fearfully gripped. Blue Falls, Maine is the crime thriller equivalent of Stephen King's Castle Rock - full of interesting characters** and **gothic undercurrents,**'

Bill Forrest, ★★★★★

Fire in Bone is a heart-pounding crime novel with a devastating twist.

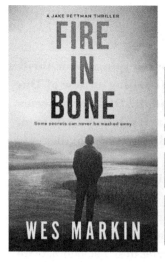

Scan the QR to
READ NOW!

"An explosive and visceral debut with the most terrifying of killers. Wes Markin is a new name to watch out for in crime fiction, and I can't wait to see more of Detective Yorke." – *Bestselling Crime Author Stephen Booth*

The disappearance of a young boy. An investigation paved with depravity and death. Can DCI Michael Yorke survive with his body and soul intact?

With Yorke's small town in the grip of a destructive snowstorm, the relentless detective uncovers a missing boy's connection to a deranged family whose history is steeped in violence. But when all seems lost, Yorke refuses to give in, and journeys deep into the heart of this sinister family for the truth.

And what he discovers there will tear his world apart.

The Rays are here. It's time to start praying.

The shocking and exhilarating new crime thriller will have you turning the pages late into the night.

"A pool of blood, an abduction, swirling blizzards, a haunting mystery, yes, Wes Markin's One Last Prayer for the Rays has all the makings of an absorbing thriller. I recommend that you give it a go." — *Alan Gibbons, Bestselling Author*

One Last Prayer is a shocking and compulsive crime thriller.

Scan the QR to
READ NOW!

JOIN DCI EMMA GARDNER AS SHE RELOCATES TO KNARESBOROUGH, HARROGATE IN THE NORTH YORKSHIRE MURDERS ...

Still grieving from the tragic death of her colleague, DCI Emma Gardner continues to blame herself and is struggling to focus. So, when she is seconded to the wilds of Yorkshire, Emma hopes she'll be able to get her mind back on the job, doing what she does best - putting killers behind bars.

But when she is immediately thrown into another violent murder, Emma has no time to rest. Desperate to get answers and find the killer, Emma needs all the help she can. But her new partner, DI Paul Riddick, has demons and issues of his own.

And when this new murder reveals links to an old case Riddick was involved with, Emma fears that history might be about to repeat itself...

Don't miss the brand-new gripping crime series by bestselling British crime author Wes Markin!

What people are saying about Wes Markin...

'Cracking start to an exciting new series. Twist and turns, thrills and kills. I loved it.'

Bestselling author **Ross Greenwood**

'Markin stuns with his latest offering... Mind-bendingly dark and deep, you know it's not for the faint hearted from page one. Intricate plotting, devious twists and excellent characterisation take this tale to a whole new level. Any serious crime fan will love it!'

Bestselling author **Owen Mullen**

Scan the QR to
READ NOW!

ACKNOWLEDGMENTS

I have to admit to being quite nervous about starting a new series even though I cheated a little and used an existing character! However, Jake was good to me, and *The Killing Pit* seemed to occur naturally despite the radical change of scenery. I hope you enjoyed it as much as I loved writing it, and it is important to thank the many people who made this possible. It certainly wasn't a solo affair.

Firstly, my family, Jo, Janet, Peter, Douglas, Ian and Eileen for being *solid* rocks of support during those long hours I have to spend behind my computer. And my two children, Hugo and Beatrice, who are becoming more colourful by the day – how is that even possible?

Thanks, as always, to Jake, who helped me start this adventure. Huge appreciation to Cherie Foxley who nailed the pit perfectly!

Thank you to Jo Fletcher, Kath Middleton, Karen Ashman and Jenny Cook for getting their teeth into those earlier drafts. Thank you to all my Beta Readers who took the time to help shape my new episode in this journey – Keith, Dee. Carly, Cathy, Donna, Yvonne, Holly and Alex. Thank you to the bloggers who remain behind me – Shell, Susan, Caroline and Jason.

I hope you all join me in June for the sequel when something unexpected washes up on the banks of the River Skweda ...

STAY IN TOUCH

To keep up to date with new publications, tours, and promotions, or if you would like the opportunity to view pre-release novels, please contact me:

Website: www.wesmarkinauthor.com

facebook.com/WesMarkinAuthor

instagram.com/wesmarkinauthor

twitter.com/markinwes

amazon.com/Wes-Markin/e/B07MJP4FXP

REVIEW

If you enjoyed reading **_The Killing Pit_**, please take a few moments to leave a review on Amazon, Goodreads or BookBub .

Printed in Great Britain
by Amazon